MW00774968

DARIA STONE
MIA DUNN

THE ERA OF THE ROSE

This book is dedicated to the people in our lives that said, yes.

The people in our lives that told us to push further, to try harder and most importantly.

To never give up.

And while no one will truly understand why, we also dedicate this book to Stan Lee.

Without him, this would never have come to be.

Warning

Some of the subject matter in this book can be considered triggering. We want you to enjoy what is to come in these pages, but if you are sensitive to certain topics, then this story may not be for you. You will find the list of topics in the back of this book.

This is not for the faint of heart. Many did not heed our warning and what happened in these pages disturbed them deeply.

However, if you are an innocent soul that wishes to be corrupted by darkness, then we welcome you into our world of magic and roses.

Long Live The King

Contents

The Era of the Rose

When the Stone turns,
And the Rose grows,
She will come to unite the world.
So it was seen, so it will come to pass.

In the grand hall, gilded with golden archways and marble columns, stood King Farandorn Rose. For decades he had tried to ease the suffering of his people. Touring the lands, meeting the citizens of the cities that spread across his realm. For days he would see them in, one by one and listen to their pains and troubles, helping where he could and simply understanding where he couldn't. The main focus of his work was uniting the humans and the elves. No small feat as both sides considered it impossible. But the job was his, the birth right that was passed to him from his father. Until his reign ended, the King of Novastraad would never stop trying to bring peace to his lands.

All of this, his travels and his work had earned Farandorn the title of The Gentle King.

The throne had been in human hands since the first royals came to be. King Edgar Brass built the throne on which he sat and named the first Era. He held the title for three decades before he died. His daughter had married Lucian Stone, and with that, the Era of Brass had ended, and the Era of Stone began. Four thousand years passed under the Stone regime, and close to the end of that time, the elves had arrived on human shores seeking asylum from what they called 'Ilvanya Vo'. Loosely translated, it meant 'The Certain Death'. The King at the time, Ignatius Stone, had agreed to their request under duress from his wife. But he made it clear to those first settlers that this land was human, and they could never claim their own part of it.

It took a hundred years of oppression before the great war began, ripping through the country of Novastraad as the King watched from his throne. The elves had risen up, tired of their roles as second-hand citizens to humans, unable to own lands or titles of their own. The children of the first settlers had watched their parents be treated as dirt under the shoe of the lords and ladies. Even the human peasants looked down on those with pointed ears. They were considered as low as the cattle themselves, forced into servitude just to ensure they didn't starve on cobbled streets.

The war spanned twenty-seven years and was fought with sword and shield. Many thousands of lives were lost, and it was considered the greatest tragedy to ever befall Novastraad. In the end, a man named Elador Rose had risen to his feet and impaled King Lucian Stone the third as he sat in his great hall upon his throne. In those days, the rules were clear. If a King was slaughtered in fair combat, then his title changed hands to the victor, and in the time of war, all combat was considered fair. Elador Rose went from farmhand to King in the span of twelve minutes, and so the Era of the Rose began.

The new King's sympathies for the elves led him to change the laws of the land once and for all. They were citizens of the king and had equal footing with the humans of Novastraad. An uneasy peace was brought, and for another thousand years, the Rose family kept the Era.

King Farandorn looked down at the baby in the crib that was set before him and smiled warmly as his eyes began to well with tears. This beautiful girl was all he had left of his wife, Alina, who passed quickly in childbirth. With all the healers and magic they had in the court, still, nothing could save her from her fate. It seemed that the Gods still made choices, calling home those who had completed their work. But the gentle king would love his daughter eternally. The red tufts of hair that stuck out of the edges of her bonnet matched her mother's, and her ivory face scrunched as she slept. In time, she would grow up and become the Queen of Novastraad, finding a husband of her own, taking his name, and bringing forth the end of the Era of the Rose.

Before the tiny bundle lay a world of work A lifetime of trying to keep the Elves and Humans united. A task that the king himself had grown weary of in his old age. Discrimination had crept back into the city over recent decades; he saw it on his journeys. The desire the elves had to fight for the throne was an overwhelming one; he knew that. But the Elves knew better than to begin a war again. Millions of lives would be lost on both sides, while the lands would be bathed in blood. A price neither side was willing to pay.

King Farandorn had brought in a Court Mage from the Elves in an effort to offer representation for all. She was his advisor, his friend, and mostly, a woman for his daughter to learn from. A feminine influence in the Princess' life. It was a step in the right direction, as was filling his court with an elven majority. An act many humans saw as treason against the crown itself. But with each offer of equality from the king, it became clearer that nothing but the throne itself would satisfy the elves of the realm.

The king looked down at his daughter as the honoured guests were ushered into the hall. This was her naming day. The moment the kingdom would meet their future queen. They would lay eyes on her for the first time, and she would remain hidden within the palace walls until her twenty-fifth birthday. Only then would the doors of the castle open, and the young woman would be seen once more.

Blinking back the tears, King Farandorn lifted his daughter from her cot and held her in his arms. Cheers erupted from the crowd, and the baby opened her tired eyes. With a smile, Farandorn looked out over the sea of smiling faces. 'People of Novastraad, your future Queen: Scarlett Rose.'

More cheers, more applause. The fact that a baby girl had been born was a cause for great celebration. It seemed that finally, the seer's prophecy was true. The hopes of all the realm rested on Scarlett's shoulders, for she would unite the world.

Elegant Mistress

Scarlett was unchanging. At least that's how it felt to her, as though she were frozen in time. The same red hair, the same green eyes and the same pink lips. If you asked her father, he would say she had grown so much, and so quickly that he was truly not prepared for it, no father ever is. A truth that he repeated to her often enough. Scarlett huffed as she tried to keep the unruly waves of crimson hair away from her face. There were many days that she thought about taking shears to her long red hair and hacking away. Such an act would not be quickly forgiven by her father, especially on her birthday of all days.

On this day the Kings only daughter and heir to the throne was to turn twenty five.

It wasn't as though Scarlett didn't understand her obligations, of course she did. Now she was of age, Scarlett would simply pick a random man from the parade and choose him as her husband for the rest of her life. No romance, no passion, just duty.

It was an obligation the princess didn't want. Didn't want to choose a stranger for a husband, didn't want to unite the kingdoms and certainly didn't want to bring about the end of an era. But that would be her burden to bear. She would marry, take her husband's name, and the era of the rose would come to an abrupt end.

With a yawn and a stretch that felt both glorious and exhausting, Scarlett prepared herself for the long day ahead. She stood in front of the mirror, lifting her long hair and pinning it atop her head. Errant curls tumbled past her soft cheekbones, and she brushed them aside absentmindedly. Scarlett had been blessed with her mother's complexion and required only a pinch of the cheeks to add a dash of colour.

Her bedroom was lined with carved wooden panels covered in thick, woven tapestries telling the tale of the Rose bloodline. It had been added to her room on her eleventh birthday by her father. A gift to remind her of her duties within the family and the passage that she had memorised since she was a child. The stone had turned, and the rose had grown. As the first woman born into the Rose family line since the era began, it was believed by most that the prophesy was for her. That it would be her duty to unite humans and elves for eternity. It was an awful amount of pressure to be placed on a young woman, and as each birthday crept by, she began to fear the worst. Scarlett didn't care much for her obligations; she was more afraid that her soul would be alone forever. Companionship was the thing she truly craved, longed for, even. The princess was a lonely woman.

But in her lowest moments there were still worlds she could escape into. The court mage Alessandra, while stoic and serious, would often bring Scarlett books filled with love and soul mates that the princess would devour in a matter of hours. The idea that out in the Kingdom somewhere existed the soul that would match hers lit her on fire inside. She burned for romance. At night she would lie in bed imagining the tall, strong handsome man that would swoop in and save her from peril. That would watch over her and protect her, that would love her deeply and be loved in return.

That was what Scarlett Rose longed for.

But deep down she knew that fated love was not her destiny. The princess of the realm would choose her husband out of duty. He would honour her, and she would bear his children. But the passion of true love would not burn between them. She blinked back bitter tears as she sucked in a deep breath, reminding herself once more that today was her birthday.

And today, Scarlett would choose a husband.

Moving past the tapestry, she averted her eyes, ignoring the prophesy and concentrating on the wardrobe ahead. Today was a day for celebration and she must be dressed for the occasion. As she pulled the thick red velvet dress from the closet that housed it, a gentle knock echoed through the room.

'Come in.' Scarlett called out and the door creaked open. Mrs. Belmont walked in looking as weary as always.

'Oh, let's get your dressed, love.' The old woman chattered as she took the dress out of Scarlett's arms and helped her into it. As it was her birthday, today would be the parade. Men from all the cities in Novastraad would flock to meet the princess, to hope they were enough to catch her eye and become the future king. Scarlett shivered slightly, wondering if it was the cool air or her nerves that had her shaking. She wished Alessandra were here instead of Mrs. Belmont. The dark elf always knew what to say to calm Scarlett, almost as though she had a unique perspective on the princess' emotions. Alessandra, as intimidating as she was, was also a source of great comfort for Scarlett. The princess had never known her mother and the court mage was the only woman Scarlett could look up to. She was the kind of woman Scarlett wished she could be. Calm, confident and beautiful. Scarlett smiled slightly as she thought about her.

'Happy birthday, pet.' Mrs. Belmont gushed, interrupting Scarlett's mind as she tightened the dress around the princess' waist. 'You've grown into such a woman. Your mother would be so proud of you.'

Scarlett's lips formed into a thin smile. 'Thank you.' She muttered.

'You must be excited. Meeting your husband today. I remember when I first met Mr. Belmont...' The old women's voice trailed off as she meandered her way down memory lane.

If Scarlett was honest with herself, there *was* a big part of her that looked forward to this day. She had waited what felt like an eternity to be loved. But there was a streak of fear that was making her heart pound. What if the men weren't appealing to her? What if she didn't like any of them? The only thing worse that marrying someone that was merely fine, was knowing you'll never truly feel the burning desire she had read about in Alessandra's books.

As Scarlett left her room, she had become nothing more than a bundle of nerves. Walking the long corridors of the palace, she tried to take deep relaxing breaths. Theirs was a vast castle with beautiful roses planted all throughout the stonework. During each Era the castle underwent additions. The Stone's had carved beautiful archways and towers. Her family had covered them with exquisite roses.

As her thoughts dwelled on flowers blooming and eras past, Scarlett felt someone fall into step beside her.

'Hello Princess.' The voice was feminine, rich and deep. Scarlett turned her head to look upon Alessandra the court mage and personal advisor to her father. She was at least a foot taller than Scarlett and a few hundred years her senior. With midnight black skin and silken white hair, she was an incredible example of the dark elves. Her beauty was unparalleled and thanks to the long, warm sun filled days that the city enjoyed, it was a beauty that was a rarity in these parts. The dark elves did not stay long in the sun and Alessandra was given a windowless room to ensure her comfort. Long, elegant ears poked through her perfectly coiffed hair and her black eyes looked over the princess intensely. Scarlett smiled warmly at the mage. 'Good morning.'

'Another year older today, Princess.'

Scarlett nodded once more. 'You know, you don't have to use the official title when we are walking the halls. Please, call me Scarlett.'

For a brief moment, a wicked grin flashed across Alessandra's lips, revealing the dark elf's pointed canines. It was always shocking to see the mage smile. She stepped ahead to block Scarlett's way, turning to face her, 'You wish me to be more familiar...Scarlett?' She whispered the last word and the princess' eyes widened as she took a step backwards. Alessandra matched her pace perfectly, keeping the distance between them the same. There was no menace, just a cool calm demeanour. The mage leaned in and pressed her lips against Scarlett's cheek 'There is a great deal you could learn from me.'

Scarlett bit her lip to maintain silence. She knew Alessandra would never harm her, but it didn't stop the adrenaline rushing through her veins.

'Scarlett...' The mage continued, 'Today you will sit through a parade of fools. men who wished they were good enough for you. But they never could be.' She gently stroked the back of her hand down Scarlett's cheek. 'You're very precious to me, child. I want you to have everything you deserve.'

'What do you mean?' Scarlett asked.

'After the parade I'll find you. There's an artifact in my possession that will show you your true soul mate.' Her black eyes bored holes into Scarlett as she spoke. 'You deserve true love. I won't allow you to settle for anything else.'

The princess' heart pounded at the court mage's words. Was it really possible to find a soul mate using elven magic? Scarlett's lip quivered at the thought and quickly stepped forward, wrapping her arms around Alessandra who stood frozen on the spot. 'Thank you.' Scarlett whispered before letting go and rushing away down the corridor.

Alessandra smiled to herself as she continued back to her chambers. Today was the day that a centuries old plan took its first tentative steps into reality. Once the princess became aware of Cadian it would be fruitless to try and stop her from loving him. The mage arrived back at her room and waltzed inside, placing herself in front of her vanity and adding a layer of deep red to her full lips.

'Well? How did it go?' The voice came from the back wall of the room. Glancing away from her own reflection, she looked through the mirror at the tanned elf strapped to her wall and smiled, 'It went perfectly. She's primed for romance and love.' She rose from the seat and crossed the room, glancing at the growing bulge in his pants. Her face went suddenly stern as she took hold of his manhood, 'It's sick.'

Mateo flinched under the invasive act and his teeth dug into his lower lip, betraying his desire for more. A flicker of annoyance crossed her face as she released her grasp and rolled her eyes. 'You are a stain on our kind, Mateo.' She crossed back to the dresser and slowly opened a drawer, glancing at his reflection to gauge his reaction as she lifted a dagger into view. She watched as he struggled against the bonds holding his arms. 'You've always had a desire for humans that I don't understand. They *despise* us.'

With a cruel smile, she returned to face him and pressed the cool metal of the blade against his bare chest. His breath quickened, 'Please, Alessandra, don't.'

'Remember, this is your punishment. You are not here to enjoy yourself.' She slid the dagger gently lower and growled into his ear 'You are here for *my* entertainment.' With that she eased the blade into the waistband of his boxers, stopping only as the tip reached the base of his member. Mateo grunted slightly as he felt the sharp point against his flesh.

With the dagger firmly in place, Alessandra turned and sauntered to the corner of the room. With surprising ease, she turned a handle, loosening the bonds holding Mateo and allowing his arms fall to his sides. 'Urgh' was the sound that escaped his lips as they fell. The sudden movement pushed the dagger deeper against his tender region and his shoulders ached from the hours he had spent chained in this room at the court mage's behest.

There had always been rumours about Alessandra and her tastes. Mateo was one of the guardsmen of the king and heard it all. That men had fled weeping, battered and bruised yet returning days later for another taste of her darkness. His own kinks had been humiliation. To be degraded was all he wished for. It was why he joined the guards in the first place. Being screamed at during his training. Told he was pathetic, nothing more than a worm. Being beaten down for talking back in front of his peers. Each night he had finished himself off in his bunk at the memory of the humiliation. So, seeking out the attention of Alessandra became his priority, and now he had her. Or more accurately, she had him.

As the court mage turned away from the panel, she unbuckled her velvet overcoat and let it slip off her shoulders. Dropping it on the floor to reveal her firm breasts and a layered underskirt.

'Kneel properly stain.' The dark elf commanded, her words dripping with disdain. She watched his eyes flick between her nipples as he manoeuvred into a kneeling position, his hands firmly clasped behind his back. Her pathetic little submissive elf.

Closing the gap between them, Alessandra lifted her leg, slamming her leather booted foot against the wall beside Mateo's head, the heel barely missing his cheek. His lip quivered in anticipation, he knew what was to come next and like a good little stain, he would succumb to his mistresses desires. Bravely he ventured closer to her warm, shaven mound. He could smell her excitement and felt a twinge in his pants. The sting of the dagger quickly reminded him that this was not for his pleasure.

Gently he explored the familiar landscape of her inner thigh with his soft, moist tongue revelling in the sigh that escaped her lips. Slowly he traced a line up her supple skin and deeply inhaled her intoxicating scent.

Alessandra sighed once more, as she pinched one of her nipples between thumb and forefinger the pain only adding to her enjoyment. She felt herself becoming slick as he slowly worked his way closer. But impatience got the better of her and she pulled back the underskirt that covered Mateo's head, revealing his dark hair. She twisted her fingers in the locks and pulled him into her opening. Gasping as his tongue plunged into her depths. A shiver ran down her spine as she felt him press against her clit.

Gently he swirled patterns against the hard nubbin while the hair on her neck stood on end. A moan escaped her lips, and she pinched harder against her nipple, the pain mixed with the pleasure, and she felt her juices begin to flow. She thrust herself hard against his hot, wet mouth in time with his tongue as it delved deeper into her.

She released his hair and leaned a hand against the wall to steady herself. He may be nothing but a stain to her, but he certainly knew his way around a pussy. Mateo began slowly working his tongue in slow, circular motions around her perfectly sculpted vulva and Alessandra could feel the blood course through her veins, rushing down her entire body, her labia began to swell as she felt his heated breath.

A moan escaped from the lips of the dark mistress and as the wanton pleasure began to escape from her jaws, she felt Mateo pull away, pulling the flesh tenderly between his teeth. Before she could object, she felt a slender finger slip inside and explore her hot, tight tunnel. Another finger joined the first, sliding in and out gently as his lips kissed her aching clit.

The pleasure built quickly in her core and her hips bucked forward as he added a third finger. She felt his free hand around her, cupping her firm cheeks and keeping her pressed firmly against his mouth. She was close now, there was no peace from the ecstasy, no lull in the overwhelming pleasure. Alessandra allowed herself to become lost in it as the fingers pumped into her, harder and harder. His thumb replacing his tongue against her most sensitive area.

She felt the heat of sex spread up her tingling skin, curling her toes in her boots. Her harsh façade dropped as her breathing became heavy and laboured as the wave of pure pleasure crashed over her. Her wetness flowed into Mateo's waiting mouth as she cried out, grinding hard against him while her orgasm rolled over her.

With speed Alessandra composed herself. Dropping her raised leg back to the floor and straightening her skirt. She looked down at Mateo's glistening face and supressed a grin. Kneeling before him she took the dagger out from his boxers. The tip dripped with red blood.

'You are truly pathetic, Stain.'

Suitor Parade

The throne room was a grand affair. Pillars of white marble supported the ceiling above, painted with the house crest of The Rose family. A beautiful rose with sharp thorns adorned with a crown. The thrones sat higher than the rest of the room to allow the royals to see the people beneath them. In the lower space, pews for congregating were currently filled with humans and elves.

Scarlett entered the room beside her father, her arm linked into his, and he led her to her throne. It was smaller than his but more beautiful, with pink silk covering a thick cushion, making it a wonderfully comfortable seat for the Princess. The rest of the throne was platinum, dotted with diamonds. It was extravagant to say the least, but it was hers and she had loved it all her life. Beside her throne sat a glass table, placed there only for this purpose. To hold a single red rose. Gently, Scarlett picked it up, avoiding the sharp sting of thorns and laid it on her lap.

Soon the steady stream of suitors would begin their parade through the palace. Smiling faces moving in a line before Scarlett who, thanks to her royal training, would sit upright with a genuine looking smile on her face. To look upon her you would believe with all your soul that this was the moment she had waited an eternity for. One by one the suitors would smile and bow hoping that she would rush to them and hand them the rose.

If she handed it over then she would marry him that very night. If not, there would be a court feast followed by dancing late into the night to celebrate the twenty fifth birthday of their Princess Scarlett Rose.

Oftentimes Scarlett felt that the old traditions needed to die to allow her to explore the world and the people in it. There was the daydream she often had during lessons of being out of the palace, wandering through small towns, drinking with the locals in their taverns. Perhaps there she would meet a handsome stranger. He would slide onto the seat beside her and they would laugh together. A spark would grow between them, one that felt both comforting and electric. They might fall in love, have children and live happily ever after.

All by chance.

But that was not to be Scarlett's life. There would always be the feeling that she was missing out on so many things, so many new experiences. Underneath it all was the constant hope of meeting her soul mate. Like the books Alessandra brought to the princess. They were tales of fated love and magical connections. In her heart, she knew that not a single person she saw today would be handed the rose in her lap. How could she possibly marry when the promise of her soul mate was sitting with the court mage.

Shortly after Scarlett and her father had taken their seats, the parade officially began. It was intensely difficult for the princess to refrain from rolling her eyes at the men that walked past. Some were old, too old—wrinkled and grey, just hoping on the off chance they might become king.

Unlikely.

Some were young, sent by their parents to make royal connections. Boys of no more than twelve representing the lords houses all across the land, hoping to combine houses and make an eventual move for power. The princess shuddered at the very concept of marrying a child.

At midday King Farandorn stood and opened his arms to the room. 'My people. I thank you for your attendance here and while my daughter has not yet chosen a suitor, I am confident that by the end of the night, she will have found her love.' He smiled warmly at Scarlett, and she returned it, knowing full well that Alessandra was to show her the man of her dreams before the evening was over. Her true love existed, and she had a chance of finding him.

'Please.' The king continued, 'Enjoy the food that is brought here, nourish yourselves and we shall continue the parade after we've filled our bellies!' Farandorn laughed heartily and held his arm out for Scarlett. She took hold and allowed her father to lead her from the throne room.

The difference between the throne room and the private dining room was insurmountable. It was difficult to comprehend that they were even in the same building. This room was much smaller and the walls were stone. Candles flickered, making shadows dance on the rough walls. There was a large mahogany table in the centre of the room that would have looked plain if not for the intricately designed swirl that served as the central table leg, supporting the lunch laid before them. Nothing grand, just a few tasty morsels on a plate, decorated with edible flowers and tiny herbs, accompanied by a glass of Mir'El Fortana—an elven wine, meaning *The drink of Fortune.*

'Happy birthday, darling,' the king wrapped her up in his big arms and squeezed her tightly. He was a plump man who enjoyed his wine a little more than he should and didn't exercise. One day his heart would give out thanks to the life he enjoyed but there was very little Scarlett could do. He was a stubborn old fool at times and Scarlett had long since stopped lecturing him. Instead, she just hugged him back. 'Thanks dad.'

They sat at the table and began the meal together. Scarlett forked a piece of warm, juicy meat into her mouth as her father looked up from his food, stared at her for a moment, then began to speak. 'So, none of this morning's suitors piqued your interest?'

Scarlett stared at her plate. 'I'm sorry, father. I know this is important. It's just...' Her voice trailed off, so the King continued her thought. 'It's just that you're waiting for the overwhelming rush of love when your eyes meet?'

Scarlett almost dropped her fork as her father spoke. It wasn't often that he spoke of love. Chuckling he continued, 'That's what your mother used to say about the day we met.' He drained his glass and continued.

'I was twenty five, like you. It was my birthday and your mother was in the parade. I had spent almost the full day watching so many beautiful women glide past me, but none that were more than superficial.' He smiled at the memory and as Scarlett watched she saw his eyes mist over as he continued. 'Your mother was breath-taking, and I found myself on my feet, standing right in front of her. I took her hand in mine and kissed it.' Scarlett reached out and took his hand in her own as he spoke. She knew how much he missed her mother and when he spoke of her it was like he was losing her all over again.

'There was never a doubt in my mind that she was the woman I was supposed to love for the rest of my days. And I will, Scarlett. I will love her until my final breath.'

Within seconds, Scarlett was on her feet, wrapping her father in a hug. 'I know you will.'

The embrace lasted a few moments before Farandorn composed himself and Scarlett returned to her seat. 'I just want to know you're taken care of, and that you're happy.'

Scarlett smiled. 'I can take care of myself, you know that.'

Farandorn laughed gently, 'Yes I suppose you can.'

'As for happiness...' Scarlet trailed off, gazing towards the window at the blue sky. 'I'll find him, Father. I'll find the man that loves me as you loved my mother.'

Alessandra sat at the small table sipping tea from a porcelain cup. Mateo was seated across from her, and she watched as he fidgeted with his fingers while she drank. 'Am I making you uncomfortable, Mateo?' She smiled wickedly as he shook his head.

'Usually, you just take my money, and I leave. I wasn't expecting to be sitting here, my lady.'

'Well, I've decided to let you keep your coin today.' Her voice was pure velvet once more. Mateo looked at her with wide eyes. 'Calm down. I haven't taken a liking to you.' Alessandra enjoyed the moment his shoulders visibly fell at her words.

'Then why don't I have to pay?' He asked in a sullen tone.

'Because I need a favour.' She finished the tea and gently placed the cup back onto its saucer. 'Tonight, the princess will come to see me. I've promised her a soul mate, and she will do anything to find out who he is.' The look on Mateo's face had now changed; he was listening intently and had lost the pathetic demeanour she was used to. This must be how he looks to the outside world—the face he presents as one of the King's Knights. Interesting, she thought.

'I am going to rid the world of humans,' Alessandra smiled.

Mateo nodded for a moment before looking up with wide eyes. 'What?'

A slow smile spread across the court mage's face. The shock on his face was delightful. Speaking of such things as these would be considered treason, a crime punishable by execution and here she was. Telling it to a Knight of the King. Admittedly, Alessandra enjoyed knowing that Mateo wouldn't betray her. He would follow any command she gave him. After all, her people and his own were one in the same. United against humanity.

Alessandra continued. 'The princess will be given to Cadian Vordane.'

Mateo's eyes widened, and he unconsciously pushed his seat backward. 'The Necromancer?' His name was known to many of the elves. As far as rumours went, he had lived through Ilvanya Vo, seen the changing of the tides for the elven kind.

Alessandra nodded. 'The very same. And when he is finished with her, corruption will flow through her veins.'

'I don't understand how that destroys the humans.'

Alessandra sighed heavily. 'Cadian has been weaving magic through the cities and towns across the realm for centuries, connecting all of humanity by an invisible thread. We have waited patiently for the perfect specimen to attach the thread to, to hold them all together. Then our dear princess was born.' The cruel smile spread across Alessandra's lips once more. 'She *will* fall for him. No woman can resist his charms. None ever have.' Alessandra's eyes misted over for a moment as she remembered her own dalliance with the darkness. Shaking her head slightly, she continued, 'When corruption takes her, her very soul will blacken, taking humanity with it.' She leaned back in her seat. 'She will die, followed by her people.'

Mateo sat silently, and Alessandra stared at him, unblinking. After a few thoughtful moments, he spoke, 'So, why are you telling me?'

'Because the corruption begins here. You will educate the girl. After all, she wants to be ready for her soulmate.' She cackled as she spoke, 'You will please her, you will allow her to please you. But you will, under no circumstances, take her virginity. That is promised to Cadian as part of the magic. She must remain physically pure for him.' Alessandra stood and walked to his side, whispering in his ear. 'Do this, and you will owe me no payment for this week's affair.'

'You want me to bed her? Why?'

'The corruptions begins here. The virginal princess brought to orgasm by one of the king's knight? It's scandalous. And it will also allow us to see just how willing she is to accept love.'

Mateo nodded. 'Alright, I'll do as you ask, my lady.'

Scarlett sat through the second half of the parade, praying that someone would catch her eye, but she knew the truth. She wouldn't pick any of these men, not until she had been to Alessandra and found out who her soulmate really was. No other man could compare to the promise of a fated love. The day ticked by slowly as she tried to keep a smile on her face, but emotionally, she was drained.

Eventually, the clock chimed for the close of the parade, and the civilians trickled out of the palace and to their homes. The room was quickly rearranged to include long tables, which were then filled with food and wine. Scarlett watched as the royal court members took their seats. A table was brought in front of her, and the king, plates and jugs were gently placed in front of them, and her father cheered and began the feast.

Scarlett spotted the mage at once; she was difficult to miss, given the extravagant robes that clung to her tall yet slender frame. There was never any hesitation in Alessandra's walk. Her head was always held high and proud. She made her way to the royal table, bowed to the king, and took her seat beside Scarlett.

'Let me know when you tire of these festivities, Princess.'

'I told you to call me Scarlett.' The princess blushed.

'Very well, Scarlett.'

'I'm ready now.' the princess whispered. 'I cannot wait any longer.'

Alessandra smiled and rose to her feet. Scarlett followed suit and turned to the King. 'Please excuse me, father. The day has drained me, and Alessandra has kindly offered to walk me back to my chambers.' The lie slipped past her lips and Scarlett was amazed by how easy it was. It was something she had never done before.

'Of course!' Farandorn stood and hugged Scarlett tightly. 'Tomorrow is a new day. We will begin the search again.'

Scarlett nodded and followed Alessandra out of the grand hall as the bards began to play their songs to the dancing crowds.

The Preparation of The Rose

The door opened silently into the mage's workroom. It was a beautiful cylindrical room with ornate wooden workbenches built along the curved walls. Upon the tables were potions being brewed in glass bottles, ingredients that had been chopped or blended, candles sitting under glass alchemy bottles, bubbling with coloured liquids. It was spectacular to see the inner sanctum of a true mage. Scarlett had always been curious, and her reward was the truth behind the veil. Alessandra was the real deal. Now more than ever, the princess felt confident that soon she would know the true design for her life.

With a practised touch, Alessandra picked up a beautifully carved hand mirror from the workbench and sat herself down on a tall stool. 'This, child, is the Obsidian Window. Hand carved by the elder monks in the Era of the Stone over three thousand years ago.' She turned it slowly in her hands as she spoke, 'Only one was ever created and it was passed to me by Orelious Ethervane, the Grand Mage of the Stone Order.'

The way the obsidian caught the light held Scarlett in an almost trancelike state, 'It's beautiful.' She murmured. Alessandra smiled, 'The mirror is to be used to look through the veil. To see something that lies in your future.'

'Like my soul mate?'

'Precisely.'

Scarlett stood in silence and watched as the dark elf gathered dried herbs in a pestle and mortar and began to grind them. It was strange to see such practices in person. The secrets of magic have always been very closely guarded by the mages and at this moment, the princess felt almost like an intruder while she watched the master at work.

With a small flick of her hand, Alessandra set aflame the herbs in the bowl and a deep purple smoke rose up and filled the air with a sickly sweet smell. 'Allow the aroma to penetrate you. To settle deep within your soul.' She picked up the mirror and walked to Scarlett standing closer than she needed to. 'Here, take this and look into your own eyes.' Scarlett reached out and took the Obsidian Window into her own grasp.

It was heavy and for a fleeting moment she imagined the mage's reaction to her suddenly dropping it, the horror that would spread across her perfect features. The now perfumed air felt thick and she felt more than a little woozy. Holding the mirror up, Scarlett took in her own face. It seemed innocent, even by her own naïve standards. 'What do I do?'

'Just look and have patience.'

Scarlett stared into her own reflection's eyes while Alessandra began an Elven chant. 'Dorathu maenoro il-sandrav norfedthen.'

The words were repeated, over and over. The mage's voice crept louder with every repetition. Scarlett watched in awe as her own face began to change. Her red hair turned darker and darker until it became ebony. Falling straight and sleek, just past her chin. Her eyes darkened, turning almost black. Even her own ears elongated and pointed at the tip. The face in the mirror morphed until it was unrecognisable to her. She was suddenly faced with an elven man. Her heart began to pound as she took in his beauty. The smile that intoxicated her until she couldn't stand to look away, dark eyes that pierced her heart and the aura of power. If this elf was to be her soul mate, then Scarlett would love him for an eternity. 'I see him.' Were the only words she could muster.

Alessandra stepped carefully behind the princess. Scarlett could feel the movement behind her, but she didn't appear in the mirror. ‘By the Gods!’ The mage sounded so surprised that Scarlett finally managed to tear her eyes away from the mirror to look at the court mage.

‘I know him, Scarlett.’

‘How?’ Scarlett dropped her eyes back to the glass. Her breath quickened at the pure beauty staring back at her.

‘His name is Cadian Vordane. He...’ Her voice trailed off.

‘He what? Who is he?’ Scarlett sounded as though she were about to cry. She needed to know who he was, needed to see him, to meet him. There was an overwhelming urge to run into the night to find him. An urge that had never existed within her before and it terrified the princess.

‘He is a powerful elven sorcerer. He taught me many things about the arcane nature of the world in my youth.’

Scarlett lowered the mirror and turned to Alessandra. 'You were his apprentice?' She asked, her face a beautiful picture of surprise.

The court mage nodded. 'Yes. For many years.'

‘Can you take me to him?’ Scarlett was almost begging.

‘I can ensure your safe journey to him, Scarlett, it's just...’ Alessandra's voice trailed off yet again.

‘Just what? Please tell me!'

Alessandra motioned for Scarlett to sit on one of the stools and placed herself on another, facing the princess.

She took her by the hands, 'He's elven, Scarlett. Surely that much you could see.'

'Yes.' Her voice was quiet.

'He's ancient, even by our standards.'

'You think he won't want me?' Scarlett's voice quivered betraying how close she was to crying. There was a part of her that didn't understand this wave of emotion but the very thought of him not loving her was heart-breaking.

'I honestly don't know why he would.' The words were harsh, but the voice was so gentle, so caring.

Scarlett's eyes began to well up, 'What do I do?'

'You cannot make yourself into something you're not. The mere fact that you are fated to an elf shocks me to my core, darling. You must get him to look past your humanity. To see your potential.'

'How do I do that?'

'Well, he is known for his...unusual appetites.' Alessandra brushed a curl away from Scarlet's forehead.

'I don't understand.'

Alessandra took a deep breath. 'Scarlett, he is known for his sexual desires within the world of mages. It is said that no woman can satisfy him, yet every lady that finds herself in his chambers, will never be happy with another man.'

'What?'

Alessandra rolled her eyes at the princesses incessant questioning. 'Sleeping with him, it ruins a woman. You will spend the rest of your life craving him.' The mage looked away, just for a moment.

'Then what do I do? I need your help.'

'There is no part of you that is experienced enough to keep his attention.'

Scarlett's eyes dropped to the floor.

'Scarlett are you a virgin?' she asked the question she already knew the answer to, and the princess nodded shamefully.

Virginity was important to the royals, it was something that should be shared only with your husband but sitting here, in front of the mage made Scarlett feel more inadequate than she had ever felt before.

'It's alright. I can help you.' Alessandra's voice was gentle, soothing. Scarlett looked up with hope in her eyes, 'Really?

'Of course. After all, practice makes perfect.' Alessandra reached out and rested a hand on Scarlett's shoulder. 'Listen to me, Scarlett. Go back to your room, sit on your bed and wait. I will send my friend to you. He will take great care of you, pet. If you allow him to.'

'You mean...' Scarlett's eyes widened. She couldn't sleep with a stranger. 'I can't, Alessandra.'

'It's alright. He won't take you. He will just show you a thing or two. And when you are delivered to Cadian you will be as pure as you are now. You'll just have a better idea of how to please a man. Trust me, Cadian will thank you for taking the time to learn. He cannot be expected to teach you.'

Scarlett nodded but a knot of dread formed in her stomach as she watched Alessandra pick out a garment from a drawer and place it gently into a cloth bag.

'Here, take this and wear it while you wait for Mateo. Now off you go, Princess.

Scarlett stood, gripping the bag and shaking imperceptibly. Quickly she turned and left the room.

Alessandra picked the Obsidian Window back up off the table and looked at the image of Cadian.

'Very good, Alessandra.' He smiled. 'She believed every word.'

The dark elf smiled in return. 'Thank you, my lord.'

'I only hope your *friend* understands his place in all of this.' Cadian growled. 'I do not cherish the thought of anyone touching her. The magic placed on her soul is delicate. She is *mine* to defile.'

'He knows his place, my lord.'

'It is on your head if he doesn't, Alessandra.' A smile crept across Cadian's handsome features as the image in the mirror blurred into Alessandra's own reflection. His last words echoed in her mind as she realised just how fast her heart was beating.

It was fear.

Scarlett sat on her plump bed staring at the wall while her thoughts raced through her mind. She was nervous, sitting there in a sheer nightdress provided by the mage from her own personal collection. Scarlett had never felt so exposed before. After she left Alessandra, she had gone back to her chambers and bathed in rose scented water, pinned her red hair up and applied a red lipstick. The nightdress matched her lips but gave the princess no modesty. Under it she wore nothing.

The room was cold, and her nipples had hardened in protest. As a shiver ran down her spine she wondered if she should light the fire. In all honesty, Scarlett was just trying to busy her mind, so she wasn't wondering about what was going to happen tonight. The butterflies in her stomach wouldn't settle and she couldn't decide whether to sit or stand so instead, the princess opted for a glass of champagne. *For bravery,* she told herself.

Time passed slowly and Scarlett finished the glass and began to pour a second. A slight fuzz crept into the edges of her mind. As she poured there came a gentle knock at the wooden door. Slowly Scarlett opened it and there stood a high elf. 'I'm Mateo.'

Scarlett stood aside and let him in. He was good looking at least, the worry that Alessandra would send a creep completely faded away. There was no comparison to Cadian though and while Mateo was tall with dark hair, tanned skin and hazel eyes he was missing that ethereal quality that drew Scarlett to the ancient mage.

The princess stood speechless as she realised Mateo's eyes were slowly working their way over her, taking in every inch of flesh he could see through the sheer material. As he poured over her, his eyes stopped at chest height, staring at her pert nipples. Scarlett felt a rush of embarrassment and wanted to fold her arms over herself, to make him avert his gaze. 'Oh Princess, you are a beautiful creature.' He murmured as he licked his lips.

It was only then that she realised she recognised him. It never occurred to her that Alessandra would send one of her father's guardsmen to her bedchambers, or that he would come so willingly, so brazenly to the room of the Princess. Not for one moment did she think a guard would look at her in this state of undress. Stare at her hard nipples, then slowly lower his eyes. He took a step towards her, and Scarlett took an equal step back, reaching for a glass, 'Champagne?' She asked, her voice coming out higher than usual.

'If you insist.' He grinned

Quickly she turned, took up the bottle and poured it into the glass. As she did, she felt a strong arm snake around her waist. The shock of being touched made her jump, almost spilling the champagne. Steadying her hand, Scarlett tried to maintain control of her own body which was now trembling. Was it fear? nerves? She didn't know. But as she felt his warm breath on her skin her heart quickened. A gentle kiss was placed on her neck, it lingered as he pressed his mouth to her pale skin. A shock flashed through her body, a pulse that coursed through her veins. No man had ever held her before, her skin had never been kissed. She had imagined it, longed for it, but never thought she would feel it. A quiet gasp escaped her lips as she became weak to his touch. The glass slipped from her fingers, topping over on her vanity and spilling its contents onto the wood.

Scarlett turned in Mateo's embrace to face him.

'I'm nervous.' She whispered as she placed her hands gently on his chest, marvelling at how firm his body was beneath her touch.

‘Don’t be,’ Mateo smiled, ‘I’m going to take very good care of you, princess.'

A flush crept over Scarlett's chest, 'You can probably call me Scarlett.'

Mateo’s voice was slick, as his words tickled her ear. 'Lie down.' He commanded ever so gently, and Scarlett nodded obediently. With a hand on her lower back, Scarlett felt herself being gently led to her plush bed. As she reached the edge she turned and sat down, sliding into the centre and lying on her back. The carved ceiling above her seemed suddenly unfamiliar in light of what was about to happen. This no longer felt like her room.

'Good.' Mateo stood now at the foot of the bed, looking down at her. 'Now, I want you to do exactly as I tell you, Scar. I want to look at you. All of you.'

The princess frowned, he was already looking at her, what did he mean? 'I don't understand.' She whimpered, embarrassed by her admission.

A sigh escaped Mateo's lips. 'Turn over.'

She did as she was told, rolling onto her front.

'Good. Now onto your hands and knees.'

Scarlett felt her skin become hot as she thought about the position, she was in. With no idea about what was to come next, she pushed up onto her hands and knees. The headboard was all she could see now, but she knew Mateo was getting a view of her that no one had ever seen before.

'You're doing excellent, Scar.'

Scar. Not the way you would address royalty, but it made her feel less like a princess. Scar was a name for a woman that was tough and worldly.

'Open your legs wider.' Came his voice from behind her and Scarlett moved without thinking. The cool air in the room touched her exposed regions and it sent a shiver up her spine.

The bed shifted as Mateo climbed onto the foot of it. Slowly, he pushed up the sheer material, which was covering her behind exposing her fully. His warm hand caressed her round cheek gently, slowly and Scarlett found herself enjoying the feeling. As he stroked her, his fingers would gently brush against her lips, sending little waves through her body.

'Scar, I intend to make you feel something you've never experienced before.' He whispered, hunger filling his voice. 'Now, lie down and turn over.'

Once again, Scarlett did as commanded. Lowering herself onto the bed and turning so that the ceiling was again, her view. She had to bend her legs at the knees as Mateo was there. Suddenly his strong hands took hold of her legs and gently parted them, opening her up fully to his gaze. Scarlett trembled as he took in the view. Never had she been so exposed to another person. The cool air of the room mixed with the desire to be touched made her nipples painfully hard.

Another gasp escaped her lips as Mateo trailed a lazy finger from the top of her vagina, brushing softly through her neatly trimmed curls. Her slick folds glistened in response to his gentle touch, 'Have you ever felt pleasure before, Scar?'

'No.' She pulled in a sharp breath as his index finger slid through her freshly pooled wetness.

'Not even by your own hand?'

Her head moved slowly to the side, 'No. It didn't seem proper.' She whispered.

'Well, that just won't do.' He smiled as he grazed a finger against her swelling clit. Trailing down to her opening. Scarlett gasped again at the gentle touch to her most sensitive spot. There had been times, while reading some of the more romantic scenes in her books where Scarlett had considered plunging her hands into her undergarments to explore the warmth that grew there. But had never had the bravery to take the first step.

But now she lay, perfectly still as Mateo moved his mouth closer to her slit. 'If it's not proper, Scar, then why does it feel like this?' He growled as he pushed his tongue between her folds and flicked the bundle of nerves. Scarlett felt something new. The pulse from before had been replaced with a hot wave that rolled the butterflies out of her stomach. A shocked groan echoed through her chambers from Scarlett's own mouth.

A heat began to coil low in her body as the moist tongue danced gently over her, sending spikes of sensations into her thighs and stomach. Scarlett's hand reached up to her own nipple, she didn't realise until she felt the pressure as she squeezed the hard nub between her fingers. The sensations made the gentle pressure against her clit even more intense. Quickly she reached up with her other hand and began to roll both of her nipples hard.

It was painfully clear in that moment that if a little pressure felt this good, more must be better. So, in response to her body urging her forward, Scarlett arched her back pressing her slit harder against Mateo, almost grinding against his tongue and gasping as the feeling intensified more. Mateo growled as he devoured her which only spurred the princess on more. With little care about how she must appear, wildly fondling her own breasts while a man ravaged her with his mouth.

As the tongue swirled against her grinding, Scarlett felt something new. A pressure against her opening.

'What is that?' Scarlett gasps against the pleasure that was overwhelming her, hoping that it wouldn't stop but terrified it would go further than she was ready for. Scarlett sat up as she felt the pressure start to enter her. Looking down between her thighs at Mateo, she met his fiendish brown eyes. 'My finger...just one to start.' He grinned as he began languidly pushing into her tight opening while his thumb replaced his tongue against her clit. Scarlett felt her mind reeling, she knew this couldn't happen. It was Alessandra's one rule. Nothing must penetrate her.

'Wait, stop!' Scarlett panted against the pleasure as Mateo quirked his eyebrow. 'You're here to learn, Scar. Remember?' He chided her as his thumb continued to circle her clit. Pressing slightly harder, drawing another groan of pleasure from the princess. It was becoming increasingly difficult to process her thoughts.

'Won't that...wont it take my virginity? Alessandra said-'

'Oh, my sweet princess.' Mateo interrupted, 'This doesn't count.' He whispered. 'So lie back down and let me take you over the edge.'

Scarlett nodded softly. Mateo was the one with experience. He wouldn't knowingly break the mage's rules. Scarlett lay back, allowing herself to become lost again in the building pressure as Mateo swiped his middle finger inside her folds. He painted painfully slow circles around her clit as Scarlett once more began to grind against him. There was a release coming, she could feel it building in her more and more. Moans escaped her lips as she once more began to roll her nipples between her fingers. Scarlett was lost to the sensations.

Mateo turned his hand, adding another finger, slowly sliding them deep inside her pussy and curling them as Scarlett gasped in rapture. It was all he could do to stop himself ripping open his pants and rutting his cock into her hard. He imagined the way her virginal canal would squeeze him as he attempted to stretch her out. The idea of the Princess of Novastraad mewling beneath him as he fucked her into oblivion was too much for him, after all it was clear she wanted it. Her pussy glistened in the light, dripping with lust.

He looked her over as she writhed beneath his touch, grinding against his hand that was soaked by her juices. Smiling, he knew in that moment he was going to fuck her.

Drawing back his free hand, he released his hard length from the deep maroon constraints of his leather trousers and wrapped a firm hand around it. He began thrusting himself into his own grip, edging the tip slowly towards her leaking opening. Already he could feel how ready he was to cum, and he wanted it to be inside her. As he looked down at her perfect body, he gently stroked his cock, letting out an involuntary groan as the princess whimpered, lost in the building waves of pleasure.

Breathing heavily, Mateo moved closer to her pussy, pressing his length against her and sliding over her opening. Pressing hard against her drenched clit, he coated himself in her juices. The princess was now grinding hard against his member, oblivious to the fact that she was almost being impaled by his cock. A deep growl escaped Mateo's throat as his own pleasure began to build.

He watched as Scarlett's eyes fluttered open at the sound of his pleasure and smiled as she realised his hands were no longer working her over. Her eyes widened when she looked at his cock and he thoroughly enjoyed the moment she flinched as she realised how close he was to fucking her, it almost made him cum right there.

'No...' Her voice trailed off.

He hummed, licking his lips as he continued his thrusts. 'I just want to feel you.' He slid the head of his cock between her outer lips, nudging it once more against her pearled clit. The sensation drew a series of lewd moans from Scarlett's lips as the coils in her core began to tighten again, more intensely. There would be an explosion and when that happened, she wanted to be filled by this man, this stranger. She wanted him to take her virginity, to fuck her until the heat that threatened to explode in her core made good on its word.

'Please?' She whispered as she brought her fist to her mouth, trying to hold in her moans as he swirled his tip against her clit.

'Are you begging me to fuck you princess?' Mateo growled. He lined himself up with the dripping centre of her cunt, pushing against the tight opening.

Scarlett moaned in pleasure. 'Please, fuck me.'

Mateo smiled. He was much too big, and he knew this would hurt her, but he had no intention of going slowly. 'Alright, if you insist, Princess. But you must never tell a soul that I was here first.' *Just once, just to see* he thought as he licked his lips. He slid his tip up and down her opening, getting himself completely coated in her slick wetness.

As he began to add pressure Scarlett moaned again, she wanted this. Her back was arching, her legs widening to welcome him in. Mateo growled again, this time in frustration as Alessandra drifted through his mind. *She has to stay pure for Cadian.*

Why? Why can't I take her right here. No one would know? But Mateo knew the truth. If the magic was tied to her virginity, it would break the moment he fucked her. And The Necromancer was not a man he wanted to fuck with. Mateo let out a frustrated roar and Scarlett's eyes flew open.

What a lucky bastard being able to ruin such a beautiful pussy. Mateo pulled back, releasing Scarlett from his grasp. 'Get on your knees.' He commanded, pulling her from her position, her pussy was still dripping. *She must've been so close.*

'Those beautiful rose bud lips of yours are going to give my cock a kiss.'

'I don't know what to do.' She murmured, her voice quivering. Mateo had a thought in that moment, the poor little princess' clit must be aching for a release that would never come. A devilish smirk crept across Mateo's mouth as he realised, he didn't care. 'You are going to suck my cock until I cum.'

Grabbing the back of her head, he weaved his fingers in her long red locks and pulled her mouth towards his unyielding cock. 'Open.' He ordered. Scarlett was looking up at him, there was a tinge of fear as her lips parted and Mateo thrust hard into her mouth sniggering as she gagged against his length. This new cruel demeanour was his only way of covering how close he came to getting himself killed by the raging bitch of a court mage.

Relentlessly Mateo rutted into the mouth of the princess, desperate for his own release. He wanted to be gentle, to ease her in like the delicate flower she was, but his overwhelming desire won out. If he couldn't fuck her pussy, he would fill another hole. Tears formed in her eyes as he pumped into her harshly. Spittle dribbled out the corners of her mouth as he fucked her face, groaning as the sensations of her hot, wet mouth started to coax an orgasm from him.

Mateo felt his spend begin to leak, the moment was here. Letting go of the princess's hair he cupped her face, and his breathing became ragged. Slowly he bucked his hips as her mouth worked on his velvet shaft, sucking lightly. Looking down at the tear streaked face of the princess of Novastraad, her red lips wrapped around his cock, on the edge of his own orgasm was all too much for the King's Knight.

He pulled his cock from her mouth as his pleasure exploded out of his cock. Releasing ribbons of hot cum onto Scarlett's face and neck, accompanied by the loud, uneven grunts of Mateo as he milked the last of his cum onto her chin.

When he looked down at her again, she was a mess of a woman. her face covered in his hot salty cum. He ran his thumb down her cheek, collecting his seed and easing it into her mouth. 'Swallow.' He ordered and Scarlett did as she was instructed. In that moment Mateo knew he was going straight back to his chambers where he would fuck his own hand over the memory of the ruined Royal.

'Take a bath.' He commanded as he closed his breeches and stood to leave.

Fated Love

The slap took Mateo by surprise and was brutal, crunching his nose with the force of it. He was already on his knees, but the impact knocked him sideways, sending him sprawling to the beautiful hardwood floor.

'You penetrated her!' Alessandra screeched at the fallen elf as he pushed himself back up to his knees, blood dripping from his nose.

'I'm sorry I-' was all he managed to get out before her hand connected once more with his face and he landed hard against the floor while Alessandra sucked in a deep breath. 'I gave you one simple task, Mateo. Teach her how to pleasure a man. That should not have been a difficult job for you.'

'I got carried away. I'm sorry.'

The hand swung a third time, exploding his lip and sending splatters of blood across the floor.

'You had better pray to all the gods in the pantheon that Cadian still wants her after this.' Alessandra seated herself at her vanity, looking over the man on her floor with disgust. 'Your services will no longer be required. Pack your belongings, turn in your armour and leave the palace.' Her words cut and she turned her back on Mateo as he pulled himself slowly to his feet.

'Are you fucking kidding me?' He roared at the back of her head. 'I only went there for you! Because you practically begged me to!' As soon as the words left his lips, he regretted them. Alessandra slowly stood and turned on the spot. 'I am offering you the opportunity to leave this palace with your life. Utter one more word and I will hand you over to Cadian. And I promise, you will wish I'd killed you myself.'

Mateo looked away from her gaze, turned and left the room in silence.

The door clicked behind him, and Alessandra closed her eyes for a brief moment, allowing her mind to clear. A red mist had clouded her thoughts at Mateo's folly, and it was everything she could do to let him live. In truth, she knew he didn't deserve death. But his desires had almost destroyed years of careful planning. Scarlett had been promised to Cadian on the day of her birth.

Upon opening her eyes once more she lifted the Obsidian Window and glared into it. Her own face looked back at her, and Alessandra had to admit, she looked tired. Her skin was taking on an ashy quality that didn't suit her. *Once Scarlett is delivered to Cadian, my work is done* she thought to herself as she dipped her fingers into the little clay pot on the vanity then brushed them gently across the glass.

'Dorathu maenoro ilsandrav norfedthen.'

Over and over, she repeated the words until she watched her dark complexion become pale, her hair turned to black and soon enough the face looking back at her wasn't her own.

'Alessandra.' Cadian's voice was deep, and she felt herself falter slightly under his dark gaze.

'I wanted to let you know that the princess will begin her journey to you this afternoon.' Keeping her voice calm took a great deal of effort in his presence. Cadian Vordane was the most powerful mage that had ever lived. Slowly his lips began to curl into a smile. 'Very good, pet. Did you find out...is she pure?'

A stab of panic gripped Alessandra. 'Yes. She has not yet allowed a man's seed inside of her.'

Cadian gently shook his head and tutted slowly. Purposefully. 'Such careful words. Perhaps no seed has touched her womb. But was she not touched last night? His job was to prepare her for me. To teach her how to pleasure *me.* Instead, he left her shamed and covered in his...' Cadian paused.

'You know?' Alessandra whispered.

'I watched.' Cadian growled. 'You think I see only through the window *you* offer?' And with those words, Alessandra felt her blood run cold in her veins. Was she truly so arrogant as to believe she had control? *Cadian's will be so* was the mantra that played audibly in her mind. The words he drilled into her when she was no more than a child learning his black magic. Silence thickened the room as she averted her gaze, there was nothing brave about standing against Cadian.

'I have been watching since the day you came to me, the day you begged for my help. To show you how this war could be won without elven bloodshed. And I granted your wish, Alessandra.' Even as he said her name, chills ran through her. 'I told you then what I will tell you now. The magic that binds the princess to her people is fickle. Corruption only works on innocence and last night I watched as your *stain* had my princess begging to be filled. You almost ruined all of my work.' Throughout it all his face was calm but Alessandra knew better than to believe there would be no punishment for her misdeed.

'What would you have me do, my lord?' She asked, her head bowed low.

Cadian leaned in close to the mirror. 'I wish to see someone suffer for this. I will let you decide if that is to be you, or the stain.' As the last words left his lips, the mirror darkened, leaving only the court mage's own reflection. Alessandra choked back a sob and rose to her feet, straightening herself and wiping her eyes. Trying to erase the threat of tears.

Mateo would have to die.

The morning after Scarlett's debauchery she awoke with renewed vigour. She knew now what it meant to be used. The way Mateo had left her, dirty and unfinished burned at her. The shame she had felt as she walked to the copper bath and dipped herself into the cold water was overwhelming. True love wouldn't be that way.

There was one other thing she had learned, at that was how good it could feel to be touched, to be physically loved. She craved that feeling and knew there was only one way to fulfil that desire.

She needed to meet Cadian.

'Father!' Scarlett bounced excitedly into the Throne Room where King Farandorn sat, smiling warmly. With a smile she ran down the centre and up the steps to her father's seat. 'I have something to tell you!'

'By all means.' He grinned and Scarlett tried to contain her excitement. 'Father, I know who I will marry.' She knew this news would please her father greatly but she worried how he would feel about the man himself.

'That's wonderful news my sweet. Tell me, who is the future King of the realm?'

This is it Scarlett told herself. *No backing down now.* 'His name is Cadian Vordane. Father, he is elven.'

Silence fell. Scarlett knew her Father had dedicated his life to uniting the Kingdom, that he saw elves in a more favourable light than most. But she didn't know how he would feel about marrying off his only daughter to one.

'Child, are you certain this is what you want?' The king asked carefully, and Scarlett nodded in response.

'This will not be an easy life for you. Many of your people will turn their back on you for this. To marry an elf is to ensure the royal bloodline will always be a mix of both races. Many will oppose your decision.'

'I know. But since I was a child, you've told me of my obligation. I am to unite the realm. *So it was seen, so it will come to pass.*' She quoted from the tapestry in her room. 'Father, this *is* my duty.' Scarlett stood proudly as she spoke. This was the right thing for her people, she was certain of it.

'How did you meet this, Cadian? Was he at the parade?'

Scarlett shook her head. 'No father. Alessandra introduced us. She used her magic to find my soul mate.'

'Ah.' Farandon raised his eyebrows. 'So, this elf is fated to you then?'

'Yes.' She whispered. The joy on her face was apparent to any that glanced at her.

'Then the only question that remains is, when should the royal carriage be prepared to retrieve this...Cadian?' The King asked.

'Well, that's the thing. Alessandra feels it would be better for me to go to him.' Scarlett stood very still, looking at her father. This was the big question.

'I'm not sure I follow, darling. Why wouldn't you want us to bring him here?' There was a whisper of concern in his voice. 'Surely the offer of a palace is enough to tempt anyone.'

Scarlett stepped up to her father's throne and sat on the brass arm that had been carved with roses over the centuries. 'I've never lived outside the palace. I need to learn who I am outside of being the future Queen.' Scarlett picked up her father's hand and continued before he could protest. The words sounded like her own, but they had been suggested by Alessandra of course. 'It's only proper that a man and wife know each other alone. Learn who they are together, especially if they are to be the King and

Queen of an entire realm. If I am to marry him, father, I wish to know him.'

King Farandorn sighed heavily at his daughters words. 'When should the Royal Carriage be prepared to deliver you to your *temporary* new home?'

Scarlett smiled and wrapped her arms forcefully around her father. 'This afternoon! I have packed most of my dresses and I am assured he will have everything else I need.'

The King put in a great deal of effort to keep his misty eyes from dropping a tear, but it wasn't enough, and Scarlett wiped it tenderly. 'Oh Father, it's not forever. And I will come to see you often.'

'It seems so very sudden.' His voice was low, and Scarlett knew why. She was the only heir to the throne. If anything happened to her, chaos would reign throughout the realm while a new era was decided. It was a dangerous game to play, but Cadian was a powerful mage, as was Alessandra. They would keep her safe.

'Have faith in the magic that is bringing Cadian and I together, father. Alessandra is *your* mage. I trust her as you do.' Scarlett knew she had won. Her father had always told her to have faith in Alessandra, because he chose her personally to lead in his court. He trusted her implicitly. The king gently nodded his head. 'The carriage will be prepared for your journey two hours past the midday strike.

It's just a painting Mateo told himself over and over as he threw his clothes into a cloth bag. Castle guards don't have a great deal when it comes to personal belongings and Mateo was no exception. He had emptied his bunk in record time stopping only to look over the painting one last time. It was the ocean. A sight he'd never been afforded the luxury of seeing in person, but every day he would look at that painting and imagine life on the coastline. He wanted to rip it off the wall and take it with him. After all, didn't he deserve at least that? Considering he'd lost his home and his work in the span of a minute. He hadn't even wanted the job, it was all Alessandra's idea! And how was he supposed to know how serious she was about the rules she had set in place. In the end he hadn't even fucked the princess, although now he was beginning to wish he had. *May as well be hung for a sheep as a lamb.*

Deep down, he blamed Scarlett. The beautiful lips, flowing hair and innocent eyes combined were too much to take. He growled to himself as he hung his bag over his shoulder and walked to the door, stopping only to take in one last look at the ocean.

Novastraad's capital city, where the palace resided was called Ashton Glade, which sounded a lot nicer than it was. A thousand years ago, it was just that, A palace surrounded by fields and flowers with small huts and camps set. Over time, it had transformed and now Ashton Glade was a stone filled hell for someone like Mateo. While the elves held the majority within the confines of the palace wall, out here in the real world, they were still considered less than human by many. Finding a place to sleep would be near impossible in the city. He would have to leave, find a new town. There were those out there that would welcome him as a farm hand. It wouldn't be the best life, but it'd be far better than begging on the streets of Ashton Glade.

As the morning sun crept into afternoon, a beautiful carriage awaited Scarlett in the palace courtyard. Manned by a single driver and led by two perfectly white horses, it looked rich, but not royal. Scarlett smiled, her father really did consider everything. The journey to Cadian's home would take six days and her father had already made arrangements for Scarlett along the way to ensure she had a roof over her head each night. But sending her in the royal carriage would have been a terrible mistake. Such a folly would certainly result in Scarlett being held captive, or worse by those who lurk in the woods. Thieves and bandits are rife in the wilds and the King had wanted to send an entire escort caravan with her, to ensure her safety. He came to her room as she packed the last of her bags. But Scarlett had rejected the notion immediately. 'Father, I do not wish for all the world to know where I reside.' She smiled as she handed her bags to a waiting servant. 'Trust me, this way is better.' She turned to follow the last of her luggage as it was carried out of the room.

'But think of your safety. What good is a soul mate if you are killed before you can greet him?'

'Come now, father, I doubt the bandits care much for me when there are bigger caravans journeying on quieter routes. You've already added two days onto the journey by insisting we take the patrolled roads.' She began to walk out of the room. 'Come see me off.'

Once they reached the courtyard, Alessandra was waiting. She curtseyed as the royals approached and smiled up at Scarlett. 'Safe travels, your majesty.'

'Thank you. For all you have done for me, thank you.' Scarlett pulled the mage into a warm hug and felt the elf stiffen, even going so far as to let out an audible gasp. 'You're welcome, Princess.'

The princess stepped into the carriage and looked back at the palace and her father once more. Ahead of her was a new life, her first and only love, her soul mate. She waved and stepped inside the carriage, closing the door behind her.

As the princess began her journey, Mateo wasn't quite ready for his. His feet had brought him to the Low Quarter of the city. An area reserved for the poor, the useless and the broken. In this moment, Mateo was all three. An anger bubbled below the surface of his skin, which escaped through his mouth is short huffs of air and grunts as he trudged through the squalor. A couple of copper will get you a bed for the night here, but a single gold will get you an entire room. As he fingered his coin purse, he found what he needed. A shiny gold piece. A room in the tavern was his.

Dropping his canvas bag onto the wooden floor, Mateo sat on the edge of the straw-filled cloth that was to be his bed for the night and rubbed his eyes hard. All the humiliation he had faced on this day would normally have him hard as a rock, but the anger was overwhelming him and all he could think about was fucking the princess. His hand would not suffice, not tonight.

He supposed Alessandra was right about one thing, he had a fetish for humans. Particularly innocent, virginal princesses that begged for it.

With a grunt, Mateo adjusted himself slightly as he finally began to grow hard. None of this was his fault. He has simply done as instructed, he hadn't fucked her, he'd barely fingered the tight bitch. *She* was the one that wanted it. Lying there, moaning like a whore for it. He deserved a fucking medal for restraining himself, not complete rejection from his entire life.

As he pondered on the situation, Mateo found himself rubbing his bulge. There was still another gold coin in his pouch and that would buy him the cleanest whore this quarter had to offer. All he wanted right now was to fuck his frustrations away and clear his head ready for the morning. It was a long walk to the farmlands and there wouldn't be many maidens between here and there. This was his last opportunity for a while.

Decision made, Mateo headed down to the bar under the room he had paid for. The barkeep was a middle aged man stacking metal mugs on a shelf behind him. 'Can you help me, friend?' Mateo asked.

'Whatcha need?' The keep had a definite grumble to his voice.

'I was hoping you could furnish my room with a fair maiden. I have the gold to pay.' Mateo dropped the gold piece onto the rough wooden bar.

Eyeing up the coin, the man offered a toothy grin. 'Oh aye? Anything in particular?'

'Red hair. I want her to have red hair.'

The man nodded and Mateo turned to head back to his room once more hardening against his leather pants.

It was an hour before the woman knocked on his door and when he opened it, he couldn't help but smile. A lovely petite woman, no more than twenty years with large green eyes and long red hair smiled back at him. 'You asked for me?' Her voice was deep and not at all what he'd expected. He ushered her inside.

'Yes, my lady. I did.' He closed the door and smiled darkly at the decent facsimile of the princess. 'What's your name?' Mateo asked, already regretting the question.

She bit her lip, her eyes twinkling innocently. 'Whatever you want it to be, sir.' She replied in a husky voice. It wasn't quite as honeyed as the princess which did bother him somewhat, but he could work with that.

He took her by the hand and led her to the rough spun covered bundle of straw that this place called a bed. He was trying his best to focus on the similarities between Scarlett and this whore instead of fixating on the beauty mark above her cupids bow. Mateo shut his eyes tightly picturing his princesses swollen lips wrapped around his cock as she sucked on his velvety shaft.

'Where do you want me?' The voice snapped his out of his erotic thoughts. He opened his eyes to find the red head on top of the bed on all fours, her white linen skirts hanging loosely around her ankles. Mateo freed himself from the restraints of the leather that bound his shaft and wrapped his hand around his length, pumping it vigorously as he moved towards her, lining himself up with her opening. 'I want you just like that, beg for me to fill you, like you did before.' He growled.

Her slit was not quite as inviting as Scarlett's. The glisten of her leak didn't sparkle quite as brightly, everything in this room felt raw, unfinished. Mateo felt an anger deep in the pit of his stomach as he ran his land up and down his length. He might as well have fucked the princess for what it was worth, he would have found himself in the same place. A cheap room with his dick in his hand. But no, she was too innocent. She was off limits. 'Mateo scoffed.' Fucking innocent. The bitch begged for it.'

'Sir?' The woman turned, looking over her shoulder with those big green eyes. 'You fucking begged me for it.' Mateo squeezed himself tightly enraged with her mere presence. 'It's your fault! You wanted it as much as I did!' He spat.

Fear flashed in her emerald eyes, her mouth emitting a small frightened whimper. That was more like it, more like the princess. Acting like being fucked was the farthest thing from her mind, all the while getting wetter as she writhed for him. Mateo ran the purple tip inside her labia trying to gather as much of her pooled wetness as he could. Her sticky arousal wasn't enough which only infuriated him further. *The princess was practically dripping for him.*

Dropping to the foot of the bed he had planned to tongue her helping her wetness, but the tangy taste was tainted by the spend of countless patrons before him. Filling his mouth with saliva he spat violently on her opening, spreading it hard with his thumb. There was no gentleness as he shoved two fingers into her cunt. His lip curled in disgust as he realised, he could fit in another, and he did. He spat once more, coating her as he screwed his fist deep inside her cave. She wasn't Scarlett, and he couldn't pretend. But he had paid for her, and he was about to get his money's worth.

Fisting her furiously, imagining re-arranging her insides, Mateo revelled in her pained moans, watching his arm disappear inside of her. 'Stop.' She begged as she gasped for breath between each brutal thrust. 'Please, don't.'

That was better, now she sounded like Scarlett. 'This time, you take it Princess, whether you like it or not.' He snarled. The sound of her wetness around his wrist as he drew himself from within her was music to his ears. His cock ached to be inside her. Standing straight behind the woman on all fours, he lined himself up with her stretched opening and rutted himself deeply inside of her, dragging her hips closer and driving his cock painfully deep. The girl gasped, her arms flailing backwards as she lashed at him, trying to push him away.

'Sir! Please!' She wailed through a scream of strangled sobs. But Mateo didn't hear her. He had lost everything because of the siren princess. His whole world had changed because of her, because she had wanted him as much as he wanted her. But while she paraded round the castle, a secret slut with no shame, he was hiding in a filthy hovel. Not anymore, he had her now. The princess was wrapped around his cock, and he was going to fuck her raw.

But he wasn't fucking any more he was ruining, destroying. He wanted to watch her face as he rammed hard into her, he wanted to see the pain in her eyes. Swiftly, he withdrew, and the poor girl scrambled across the bed trying to escape his powerful arms. But he was much too quick and, in a moment he would reflect on later, he realised her struggle only made him harder. The fear in her eyes scored lines across her tear-stained cheeks like a brand. He loved it.

Grabbing her ankles he yanked her furiously to the end of the bed, pinning her feeble frame down by the throat, he forced himself deep into her bruised opening. As she gasped for air. Never had he pounded himself into something so ferociously in his life, every drop of rage that coursed through his veins fuelled his movements. Never taking his eyes away from hers as he thrust against her, again and again, brutalising her. He felt the fight begin to fade from her body as he held her throat tightly. And when the last gasp expelled from her little mouth, he pumped his load deep inside of her. The princess had truly been destroyed.

Except it wasn't the princess. Pulling himself out of the dead prostitute, a post orgasmic clarity struck the elf as he looked down at the dead whore lying on the bed and he realised his life was well and truly over as well.

Blinking hard Mateo stepped backward, away from his handiwork and shuddered. All this had served to prove is that it would feel so much better when he finished off the real princess in this way. Pacing around the room, he quickly realised he didn't have much time if he was going to escape Ashton Glade before the whore was discovered. Hastily he collected his clothes from around the room and quickly dressed, grabbing his bag once he was finished and throwing it over his shoulder. As he turned to leave the room he glanced back at the body of the poor girl with her new blank stare, 'Goodnight, love.'

With the hood of his cloak over his head, Mateo moved silently through the houses. If they were sending the princess to *him* then she would need to leave soon. Alessandra had made it clear that the deadline was tight. As he made his way towards the palace he heard the conversation of two older women, beating carpets in the street. He coughed slightly as a cloud of dust surrounded him and he pressed himself against the side wall of the rotund woman's house.

'Oh, didn't you see the carriage?' The fatter of the two ladies asked the other.

'No, our Arthur was having one of his moods, I missed the whole thing. Who did they say it was?' The other asked in response.

'Well, they were in the blue carriage, you know the one? It's the Kings own but not his fancy one.' The first woman explained, and Mateo thanked the gods that the city was filled to the brim with old busybodies that had nothing better to do than know everyone else's business.

'Oh yes, I do like the blue one.' The second woman smiled to herself as she whipped the cane she was holding against the rug.

'I don't know who was in it, but they went right past our Frank's house, up on the front. He watched the whole thing from his thatching. Sneaking ciggies up there, he was I reckon. Not that Cecilia will care, mind.'

Mateo felt his brain begin to ache from the sheer pointlessness of the conversation and he pushed himself away from the wall. If the carriage truly did have the princess inside, then it must be leaving through the south gates to have passed this district. A sinister grin spread across Mateo's handsome face. They were only a few hours ahead and the only town they'd reach before nightfall was Fellglow. He could make it there by midnight if he left the city now. A wave of determination spread through Mateo's skin as he began his march.

The Princess would by dead by first light.

The Adventure Begins

The roads were uneven, and the carriage juddered endlessly as Scarlett was bounced around. The sun was beginning to fade to a deep pink as they journeyed on. As the lands darkened, Scarlett stared out of the window, watching shadows become darker among the trees that lined the road. They would soon arrive at the small town of Fellglow where her father had arranged a tavern room for her. The owner, Oromore, was a friend of the crown and had assured the king that his daughter would be quite safe. In truth, Oromore and Farandorn's friendship dated back to childhood, but her father never spoke of why Oromore left the city to live in the small village he chose.

As the rocky tracks turned into straw and dirt, the ride began to smooth out and Scarlett could make out small stone buildings lit by glowing orange torches. The tavern stood tall in the small town, a building that was clearly cared deeply for by the small community. A large wooden sign hung above the door that read The Copper Cove Inn and Scarlett wondered what a Copper Cove was and if there was one nearby. It sounded like a place to explore. Not that would ever be allowed of course. It's not befitting of a princess to go rooting through dank caves seeking adventure.

As they got closer to their destination, it became clear to Scarlett why her father had felt this was a safe place for her. All the way up the road they had passed by the people that called Fellglow their home and not a single one had paid any mind to the carriage. They simply carried on with their lives. *They must see plenty of Lords and Ladies* Scarlett thought. It seems that to the people here, Scarlett was no more important than any other toff that came passing through.

It was a relief to her as the attention being a royal would bring on this journey was more than she wanted to deal with. As they approached the tavern doors, Scarlett relaxed. The first day on the road was completed without incident and she realised, this was the furthest she had ever been from the palace. The carriage slowed and a white-haired, well-kept man in an apron that Scarlett could only assume was the tavern keep stepped to her door and opened it up with a big grin.

'Welcome Scarlett!' His obvious familiarity caught the princess off guard, and she frowned. 'Sorry, princess.' He whispered. 'It's just that, your father and I were very close friends in our youth. I was one of the first people allowed to hold you.' As he spoke, he offered his arm to assist Scarlett out of the carriage and she accepted gratefully. 'My name is Oromore Greydan, and it is simply wonderful to see you.' He smiled warmly. 'Please, come in and I shall get you a warm drink. The nights can be biting here.'

The warmth of the tavern was a welcome change from the carriage that was getting cooler by the minute and as Scarlett allowed herself to be ushered in quickly by Oromore she shivered. 'Please, have a seat while you wait.' Oromore smiled and gestured to the tall stools that lined the bar, then he turned and started busying himself, making a hot beverage for his royal guest. Scarlett hopped up and tried to comfy herself on the wooden disk, watching as cinnamon and candied orange peel were added to milk in a pot over the fire. 'It'll be a few minutes!' Oromore called over.

Scarlett smiled in response and looked around the tavern for the first time. It was a huge space with the bar being a large wooden outline of a square sitting firmly in the centre, surrounding a large fire. Thick wooden tables and chairs were packed in tightly and almost completely filled with drinking patrons. There were those that were playing dice games for coin, those talking quietly over their drinks and then the more riotous tables with barely dressed dancing women that laughed as the male customers groped and handed over their coin.

There was one woman in particular that caught Scarlett's attention. A blond woman, dancing loudly on one of the tables, her skirt lifting higher along with the music from the bard. Scarlett watched, enthralled by the sheer brazen behaviour. It was entirely unbecoming of a woman, and yet Alessandra's words about her future husband echoed in her mind, *'It is said that no woman can satisfy him.'*

For a brief moment Scarlett believed a woman like the blond could satisfy Cadian. At least, she'd have a better chance than the princess did. As she watched her dance, a tall brute of a man lifted the blond off the table by her waist and sat himself on a wooden chair. The woman laughed. A throaty laugh that was deep and alluring. The princess couldn't tear her eyes away as the man placed the woman on his lap, unclipping a pouch and handing it to her. With more laughter she shook the pouch, Scarlett could only assume it contained gold when the woman's eyes brightened, and she lifted the ruffles of her skirt. The last thing Scarlett saw before she turned her head away, flushed with embarrassment, was the man's hand disappearing under the material and the blonde woman throwing her head back with a moan.

This was a world never explored by the princess and it was one she didn't know if she was prepared for. Her mind wandered back to Mateo, how his hands had crept closer to her core. Slowly. A shiver ran down her spine as she remembered his finger reaching her-

'Just a pint, my friend.'

Scarlett's eyes flew open. So involved in the world around her, and her own memories, that a man had taken the stool beside her without her notice. Turning to look, Scarlett came face to face with steely blue eyes. 'Good evening.' The man smiled at the princess, and she felt a blush creep over her cheeks as he glanced her way. Scarlett felt certain that her musings over Mateo and the blonde woman would be clear upon her face. As she looked at the man beside her, she realised he had a chin dimple covered by a sprinkling of light stubble. He wore a green cloak with the hood pulled up, but she could still see blonde waves peeking from over his shoulders.

'Hello.' Scarlett muttered in a small voice desperately hoping that this man with such kindness in his smile could not somehow detect the thoughts that moments ago were racing through her mind.

Oromore returned and gently placed a cup of spiced milk in front of Scarlett before dumping a tankard of ale in front of the blond man and snatching away the copper piece with a grunt. It startled Scarlett to see the change in the friendly barkeep, the animosity towards the blonde man was as clear as the Westfold Sea. She turned slightly to steal another look at the man beside her. He seemed so friendly; she couldn't imagine what he could've done to upset Oromore so much. But as she watched, the man took off his cloak. Underneath he wore green leather armour and his hair fell thickly past his shoulders. And then she saw it, the point of his ear peeking through the waves. The man was no man at all, but an elf. Surely that didn't warrant such hostility, after all the elves were treated well in the palace and that must bleed through to the communities. Scarlett sipped her drink while she looked at him.

'Would you care to sketch me while you stare?' He smiled as he turned away from his drink to face the princess. 'I'm sure I can find you some parchment and coal.'

'Oh, I'm sorry. I just...I wasn't...' Scarlett had no idea how to finish that sentence. Was she so accustomed to her own perfect world that she was unable to function outside of the walls of her home? 'I didn't mean to stare. I'm sorry.'

A look of surprise flitted across his handsome face for a moment. 'It's quite alright, you don't need to apologise.'

Scarlett still hadn't looked away, the curiosity burning inside her. Surely Oromore wouldn't hate someone simply for being an elf. It made no sense. So Scarlett did the thing she always did at home when she was curious, she asked an honest question.

'I was just wondering why Oromore dislikes you. He seems like a sweet man.'

The man beside her gently laughed and took a sip of his drink. 'If I didn't already know about the animosity, that might have wounded me, Red.'

'Red? What?' Scarlett asked before the dawning realisation that he was talking about her hair. 'Oh!' She toyed with a curl that had fallen over her shoulder. 'I didn't intend to wound, Sir. I was merely curious.'

'A human calling an elf *Sir*? I did not think I would live to see that day.'

Scarlett blushed slightly at his words. Normal people clearly did not behave this way and she needed to remember that if she was going to keep her cover intact. The blond-haired man continued. 'He doesn't like elven folk. Oromore, I mean. Normally won't even let my kind in but, I help out a lot in the town. I'm good muscle.' He chuckled to himself. 'And I guess for that I'm more tolerated than most.'

'That can't be true.' Scarlett shook her head. 'He told me he was friends with the king and the court houses many elves...'

'I think that's why he lives out here these days. It was shortly after the court mage was appointed by King Farandorn that he upped sticks and left the capitol.'

Scarlett stared down at her drink in contemplative silence. It was no secret that the elves were treated unfairly in life, her lessons had taught her all about the bias humans held towards their pointy eared counterparts. But she'd never seen it with her own eyes. Her entire life had been spent in the company of both humans *and* elves. She was practically raised by both, and to think that Oromore left because of Alessandra, after everything the court mage had done for Scarlett. For just an instant, Scarlett hated the barkeep.

But it passed quickly as the blond elf kept talking. It was difficult to understand for the princess, but he distracted her mind. It was a pleasant distraction but one she hadn't really experienced before.

'What's your name?' He asked, smiling warmly, before raising an apologetic hand, 'You don't have to tell me, in fact, if it makes you more comfortable, I can find another place to sit.'

'Oh, no it's alright. I'm glad for the company.' It was true, Scarlett was glad to have someone beside her to keep her mind off the journey ahead, and yes Scarlett was promised to Cadian but there was something very comforting about sitting beside the handsome blond elf and just *talking.* She didn't feel like a princess when he looked at her, she felt like a woman.

'My name is...' She paused for a second. The entire kingdom knew Scarlett Rose was the princess so that wasn't an option. Her mind whirled, *okay Scarlett, time for a new name. Just for tonight.* She thought.

'You can call me Red.' She grinned.

The elf laughed, 'Alright, a woman of mystery. I'll play along.' He held his hand out to the princess. 'I'm Finnadan Mayleen. But most just call me Finn. Sounds more human I suppose.' He shrugged to himself, and Scarlett took his hand and shook it gently.

'What do you prefer?' She asked.

'In truth, I don't mind.' Finn sipped his drink again. 'They both do the same job.'

Scarlett nodded along and raised her own cup to her lips. The milk was warm and spiced and it coated her mouth with the pleasant flavour.

'You don't seem as though you fit in with the humans, Red.'

What an unusual thing to say. Scarlett gazed at those steely blue eyes. 'What do you mean?' She asked.

'Well, it's not often your kind ask for the opinions of an elf.' Finn spoke bitterly and it stuck Scarlett that this was probably the longest conversation he'd ever had with a human. She deeply hoped it would go some of the way towards mending the hurt her people had caused. But it seemed unlikely that the kind words of one woman could undo a lifetime of bigotry.

All she could do was be honest. 'I'm sorry for the way they treat you. I wish I could change how things are.'

'It won't happen, Red. Humans and elves aren't meant to be friends.'

With a gentle smile Scarlett pictured Cadian's dark features. The anticipation of meeting him was sometimes overwhelming, but pleasant conversation with Finn was certainly helping to distract her. 'Perhaps they can be. I'm engaged to an elf so I have to hope.'

'You plan to marry an elf?' Finn huffed, 'Prepare yourself for a lifetime of bitter hatred and scorn from those who will never understand.' Finn shook his head. 'If it is an arrangement you can avoid, I would strongly recommend you do. Marry a human and live an easier life.' There was bitterness perhaps even a hint of anger.

'I do not wish to escape my obligation. Marrying him is my choice, he is my soul mate.'

Finn let out a choked laugh into his tankard as he drank, spraying ale upward into his face. He lowered the cup and started into Scarlett's eyes. 'Soul mates do not exist. When you let your heart take over your head, you will end up pained and alone. Trust me.' He drained his cup and slipped gracefully off the stool. 'I thank you for the company, but I think I've had enough.'

'Wait, I didn't mean to offend you!' Scarlett tried to explain but Finn was no longer hearing her. He had already wrapped his cloak around his shoulders and was marching purposefully towards the door. Sadness crept over Scarlett as he left. It was nice to have company, even just for an evening of conversation. She'd never had the opportunity to make a friend before and now she was realising that her social skills may not be up to the task.

'Do not worry yourself princess.' Oromore picked up the empty tankard, making Scarlett jump at his sudden appearance. 'He has been a bitter creature since his wife was killed.'

Scarlett looked to Oromore as he picked up her cup. 'That's awful, what happened?'

Oromore shrugged. 'No one really knows.'

'How can no one know?' Scarlett asked.

'Well, it's more like, no one wants to say. There are people here that know exactly what happened to the poor thing. But they won't speak of it. Murder is still a crime you know.'

Scarlett's mouth fell open. 'She was killed?'

'Aye, I reckon so. It's what she gets for marrying one of *their* kind I suppose. Such a shame, she was a real beauty.'

Scarlett felt her insides twist. This is how people would speak of her once she announced her marriage to Cadian. It wasn't right. 'Poor Finn.' She barely knew him; in fact, she would say they didn't know each other at all. But she felt a pang of sadness for him. No one should have to lose their love in such a way.

'You know, I think I've had enough company for tonight. I'm going to get some rest.'

'Suit yourself. Sleep well, alright?'

With a nod, Scarlett slid from the stool and left to find sleep.

The loud crack of wood echoed through Finn's room, and he sat up in his bed. A good few hours had passed since his conversation with Scarlett and he had thrown himself onto his bed, hoping sleep would quiet his mind. But the world had other ideas.

The crack sounded as though it had come from right outside the window so barefoot and wearing just his breeches Finn padded across the stone floor and pulled back the ragged curtain. It had once been a beautiful room, with two delicate lace curtains, a thick rug and paintings hanging from every inch of wall.

Not anymore.

The rug had become so threadbare that Finn had tossed it out, one curtain had fallen apart completely while the other clung on for dear life and the paintings...the paintings had been hidden away many years ago.

As he peered into the darkness, he saw the deep blue carriage that had been stationed outside the tavern. One of the wheels was now on its side on the ground and he could just make out the broken axle. Whoever that belonged to was going to have a hard time getting it repaired in this town. Best chance they have is a trip to the Capital, it's the closest place that could help but it wouldn't be easy on foot.

Finn turned to go back to the warmth of his bed, but something bothered him. A thought crept into the back of his mind. *There was only one new face in the tavern.*

'Dammit, Red.'

The pretty young human would be stranded, and he couldn't leave the poor girl to wander alone back to the city with only a carriage driver for protection. He thrust his feet into his favourite and only boots and threw a tunic on. The night air was cold as he crossed the dirt road to the carriage. *Always the hero.* Finn thought bitterly as he trudged over to the vehicle.

Curiously, upon closer inspection Finn found that the axle wasn't jagged, the wood hadn't snapped. It was a clean cut, right through. 'What the hell?' He muttered as a ran a finger along the clean edge. *Sabotage?*

The tavern sounds were dying down which told Finn it was likely nearing or just past midnight. He circled the carriage, looking for any more signs of damage and that's when he saw him. The driver, lying face down in the dirt with crimson pooling beneath him in the dry mud.

Fuck.

Click

Scarlett's eyes opened slightly. Was there a noise? Had something stirred her from slumber? It had seemed at first that sleeping above the tavern would be impossible with the ruckus that was going on downstairs, but as she reached the top floor and closed the hall door behind her, silence had descended. Which made the click all the more unusual. She was certain she had heard it, but now in the quiet darkness, she wondered if she had been dreaming.

Creak

That time she definitely heard something. Not the creaking of a house in the wind but the sound of a board underfoot. There was someone in the room. Slowly Scarlett opened her eyes and turned onto her back, looking down towards the door. She cursed the lamp that had burned out as she slept, thrusting her into darkness. But there was a shadow, moving silently closer. Scarlett opened her mouth to scream but, in an instant, there was a weight on her and a hand over her mouth. The shadow straddled her in her bed while Scarlett lay frozen in fear.

'Don't be afraid, it's not the first time I've been inside your bedchamber, *princess.'*

That voice...she knew that voice...as the hand gently slipped away from her mouth she whispered 'Mateo?'

'Yes, *your highness*.'

The way he spoke, not the words, but the inflection. They dripped with condescension, with distain. 'Why are you here?' Scarlett asked, barely audible as fear had gripped her voice. What was he doing here? What did he want? He had done as Alessandra asked and Scarlett had let him, but that was yesterday. The rising sun on this day brought with it a Scarlett that belonged to another. *Cadian.*

'You left without saying goodbye. I had hoped we could finish what we started.' His lips were against her cheek while he spoke. His smooth skin dancing against her own. *No.* Scarlett began to struggle, 'I don't think that's a good idea...' she gasped as she tried to push him away but, in a flash, he had her wrists and pressed them into the bed above her head.

'I didn't ask for your permission.' He growled and Scarlett's eyes widened. He released her hands but before she could even sit up, he pinned her down with a silky scarf pressed roughly against her lips, forcing her mouth open and tying it tightly behind her head. Tears stung her eyes as they fell. This couldn't be happening, not here.

He couldn't take what was promised to another. *Cadian would kill him.*

Horror filled her as he once more pinned her hands above her head with one of his own. She cried out through the scarf as she felt his hand trail down her body to her thighs, he began to gather the nightgown in his hand, almost gently at first but in moments he was ripping it up over her hips, exposing her to the cool air. Scarlett shook her head and prayed to all the gods that this wouldn't happen. A finger snaked against her opening, and she screamed as well as she could with the scarf covering her mouth. *I will not let this happen.*

Violently she twisted, moved, pulled her body from side to side as best she could. Mateo was strong but she was fighting for her life. There was no part of Scarlett that believed for one moment that Mateo would allow her to tell Cadian of what transpired here today. If her future husband truly was the most powerful practitioner of magic in the realm, then Mateo would be made to suffer. Scarlett wouldn't leave this room alive. While she fought, Mateo made an attempt to pin her with his knee on her pelvic bone, pressing so hard she felt sure the bone would crack. And suddenly, a finger, forcing its way in. She screamed again, it wasn't just the invasion of her body, but the pain that accompanied it.

Bang

The door flew open, almost off its hinges. As as Scarlett heard the sound, she found she was suddenly free from the weight of Mateo. There were no more hands, no more pressure, no more fingers. Sitting up, she quickly pulled the scarf from her mouth and pressed her back against the headboard, making herself as small as she could as she turned to look at her saviour. For a brief moment she believed *he* had heard her screams. *He* had heard her fear. Cadian had come for her.

Until she saw the blond hair.

Finn.

With a roar Finn threw Mateo against the wall and held him there by the throat, pressing firmly with his forearm as the disgraced former knight struggled and kicked. Scarlet felt vindicated. This was retribution. Seconds barely passed before two armed guards barged in and Scarlett pulled her blanket up quickly to cover herself.

'I will kill you princess!' Mateo screamed as the guards dragged him from the room. 'This isn't over! I will kill you!'

Slam

Finn shut the door forcefully, muffling the murderous threats Mateo screamed, then looked to Scarlett. Concern was plastered all over his face as she shivered from the shock. How had he known? Scarlett wondered. How had he known to save her? And what if he hadn't. It's very possible that yesterday's sunrise would've been Scarlett's last. The shock began to abate, the fear of what could have been set in and tears began to fall silently down Scarlett's cheeks. Quickly, she wiped the tears away, looking down at the bedsheets shamefully. Suddenly there was an arm around her shoulders and her senses were filled with the aroma of leather and something else...*lavender maybe?*

'It's alright, Red. He's gone and by the looks on the guards faces; he won't be getting free anytime soon.' Finn pulled her a little closer. 'You're safe, I promise.'

Who Dares To Touch Her

Alessandra paced her room, crossing the hardwood floor from bed to door and back repeatedly. If she continued in this manner, then she would surely wear a deep groove into the varnished surface. Her attempts to find Mateo had not gone well at all, it looked like he'd fled the city. The remnants of the locator spell components lay scattered. The visual representation of her frustration as she had thrown the table when she realised the bastard had slipped from her grasp.

Cadian would come for her, that much she knew. If he was unable to punish Mateo, then Alessandra would bear the brunt of his anger. She shuddered as she remembered how he had shown her effective methods of torture in her youth. Cadian had always had a penchant for violence and pain. It was almost like it sustained him. Many of the techniques he had shared with the court mage had become part of her bedroom repertoire. She supposed, quite correctly, that those skills were the main reason she was so popular with those who were desperate for sexual degradation.

'Alessandra...' The whispered voice trailed off. The court mage froze on the spot and her eyes immediately flew to where the Obsidian Window used to reside. An empty space that reminded her of her temper once more. But she knew Cadian didn't need the window. Her eyes squeezed shut and she took in a long, deep breath, preparing herself for what was to come. 'Cadian.' She replied.

The room was still empty, but she knew he could see her, smell her fear. And she knew he enjoyed it. Her dark skin erupted in goose bumps as she heard the whisper once more.

'He came for her.'

'What?' Alessandra's eyes flew open. 'Who did?'

'Your stain. Your Mateo.' Cadian growled.

'What? How?' Alessandra began her pacing once more. 'I don't understand.'

'He followed her.' The whisper was deeper with every word, vibrating through her as he spoke. 'Killed her driver and entered her room in the night.'

Alessandra felt her blood run cold. If something had happened, if Scarlett was dead then it was over. The humans had won, and she would be forfeit. She remained silent, willing Cadian to leave her alone. But the whispering continued regardless. 'He held her down while she wept, gagged her with her own scarf, *and forced his hand inside.'* The last words were inhuman as they hissed against her soul. 'He dared to touch what is *mine.'*

Mateo had cracked, he had broken. It was the only explanation for this. He wasn't heinous, this wasn't the man she used to entertain weekly. He was nothing more than a pervert wanting to be punished.

'I'm sorry.' She whispered. Not sure if she was talking to Cadian or Mateo.

'Keep your apologies. They are mere words. I require actions.'

A solitary tear rolled down her face. 'What do you ask of me, my lord?'

'I want you to remove my competition for the throne.'

'What?' Alessandra asked, confusion spreading across her face as Cadian sighed. 'I want you to kill the King of Novastraad.'

Alessandra gasped. She knew this would be the eventual outcome, but not by her hand. She had truly believed Cadian would deal with this upon his arrival at the castle.

'And while the kingdom mourns, I shall corrupt his precious heir with the darkness and the kingdom will fall. When I arrive at the palace it will be as the celebrated King of Novastraad, home of the Elves. Do you understand?'

'Yes.' Her voice shook. She was desperate not to show her fear, but it was impossible with Cadian. He had complete control. No one was able to fight against his will.

'Excellent. I'll be watching, pet. Do not disappoint me again.'

As the whisper faded Alessandra dropped down onto the floor and wept. Killing the King would be the end of her. This was the punishment. This was how Cadian would destroy her. He would allow her to do it to herself.

The tears flowed for hours. Her whole body shook as it expended all the energy she had left. Her life in this world was ending all because of the whims of Cadian. He would become the King. There was nothing more for her to do.

Unless...

The thought seized her, and she froze. There was still a chance for her. A way for her to survive. Scarlett only becomes the queen if Farandorn is dead because he leaves no male heir to take his place. A smile began to spread across her face. Marrying a king wouldn't be so bad. She could ensure his survival and the King's armies would protect her from the dark mage. She would need to be careful, Cadian couldn't know until it was too late. He would be watching her, to see her kill Farandorn. So she would need to let him believe that was what was happening.

The morning sun cast it's light through the small window in the tavern room. Scarlett blinked against it and rubbed sleep from her eyes as she sat up confused. She hadn't remembered falling asleep. Finn sat in a wooden chair across the room with a book in his hands and he looked up as she moved. 'Did you sleep well?'

'I, um...yes.' She coughed the morning out of her throat and took in the room. It looked perfectly normal. No one would ever know that she had almost lost her life in here mere hours ago. 'I didn't realise I'd fallen asleep.' She didn't think she would ever sleep again after what happened. Always thinking there was someone coming for her to hurt her. It was a fear she had never experienced before.

'That's the thing about strong women,' Finn spoke without raising his eyes from the book. 'They don't hold onto fear.'

'You think I'm strong?' She asked. No one had ever implied such a thing before.

'Of course. It takes a brave princess to leave the castle with only her driver and travel through towns like these.' Finn still didn't glance up from the book.

'You know?' Scarlett thought about the night before. The memory was fresh, but it had mingled into flashes of pain and tears.

'*He* called you Princess.' It was all very matter of fact. There was no informal chatter like they'd had at the bar. He still hadn't even looked at her and Scarlett felt annoyance swell inside her chest. After what had happened, she would have expected him to at least look her in the eye as she talked but instead, he was just cold.

'Is your book more important than our conversation?' She scolded 'Isn't it polite to look at a person when you talk to them?' She watched as Finn raised an eyebrow, still keeping his eyes on the book. 'It isn't customary for an elf to look upon a princess while she wears only her nightgown.' He smirked slightly and Scarlett's eyes widened as she pulled the cover up to her chin. Finn rose to his feet and stepped towards the door, still not looking at her. 'I shall be outside the door. Once you're dressed, let me know.' He opened the door to leave but Scarlett stopped him. 'Finn, wait. Why are you helping me like this?'

'Because you're the Princess of the realm, and you're alone. I will not see you come to harm.'

'But the way you're treated by humans, why do you care?' She asked. It was true that the throne sympathised with elves, but humans in general were not pleasant to their ancient cousins. He had faced enough prejudice in his life from her kind and it would serve her right if she got herself killed. Why would he protect her?

'My wife was human.' He sighed gently and stepped out of the door, closing it behind his with a quiet *click.*

She was *human.* Scarlett's mouth hung open as she stared at the door. There was a vague memory that danced through the fog of shock from the previous night. The memory of Finn's arm around her shoulders, holding her in a way she had never felt. It was protective, enough that Scarlett had fallen asleep in his arms. *I'm such a fool.* She chided herself as she climbed out of bed and pulled a dress from her case. Her travelling clothes weren't the extravagant dresses she usually wore around the castle. there was no corset or underskirts, just the thick material and a travelling cloak for additional warmth.

Quickly Scarlett dressed. There was a chill to the room as she pulled the clothes on, and a shiver ran over her spine. Once she was decent, and her nightgown was safely tucked into the case, Scarlett opened the door to see Finn leaning casually against the opposite wall. He looked up as the door opened and smiled. 'It's nice to see you princess.'

'Shhhh!' Scarlett hissed as she reached out and grabbed his arm, pulling him back into her room and throwing the door closed. Finn pivoted to face Scarlett as she turned, and they almost crashed. Scarlett steadied herself and looked up into Finn's elven features. 'You cannot call me princess. Not ever.'

A dawning realisation washed over Finn's face. 'I'm sorry, I didn't...It's expected to call a royal by their title.'

'I know, but I'm kind of incognito out here. I don't wish to have my identity revealed.' Scarlett moved past Finn and sat on the edge of the bed as Finn watched her. 'Alright, what would you like me to call you?'

Scarlett's mind raced back to the night before where they had sat at the bar together and she felt a smile creep upon her lips. 'You can call me Red.'

A laugh burst from Finn. It was deep yet musical. 'Alright, Red it is. Where are you heading, *Red*?'

'Briar Heath Manor. It's on the outskirts of the Oran Province. In fact, I should be going. Francis will likely have the carriage prepared by now. He doesn't like to dawdle.' Scarlett rose to her feet. 'Thank you for saving me, Finnadan.'

'Wait, Red...You can't leave.' Finn's face creased and Scarlett stared at the handsome elf. He looked pained. 'Why not?' She asked.

'The man that attacked you, he...he killed your driver and broke the carriage...I'm sorry.' Finn went to rest a hand on Scarlett's shoulder, but she took a step back to the bed and dropped down onto it, her hand flew to her chest and tears began to form. 'Francis...' She mumbled. He was a kindly older man who had dedicated his life to her family. His wife was one of the palace cooks, someone would have to tell her.

'I can escort you back to your home, if you wish?' Finn asked gently.

Home.

Where was home?

Was it back with her father? Back at the palace?

No. Scarlett knew where she belonged. The Obsidian Window had shown her the truth. Her soul mate was waiting for her, and she had to go to him. 'Could you take me to Briar Heath?' It was a lot to ask of a complete stranger.

'Red...It's a long way. Are you sure you don't want me to take you to the King? You can get another carriage.'

'Please, Finn. I need to get to Briar Heath. If I return to the castle my father won't allow me to leave a second time. I can make sure you get paid well for this.' This was her only chance. There was no feasible way for her to make the journey alone.

'It's not about gold, We'd be running on horseback and I've only got the one. So that means cutting the journey. No fancy taverns or quaint villages, we'd be sleeping rough.' Finn explained and Scarlett felt a pang of fear. *Sleeping rough?* It begged the question, how desperate was she to get to Cadian?

'How rough?' Scarlett asked in a quiet voice.

'In a tent in the forest with no amenities. Plus, all those cases you brought on the carriage, they're not making the journey. Whatever you need for the next three days is all you get.'

'That's this case, it's holding my travelling clothes. But what will happen to the things I leave behind?' Scarlett asked. Almost afraid to question as it seemed that Finn was getting on board with taking her.

'I'll store them at my house. Oromore can send word to the King and I'm sure they'll send an escort.' Finn paused for a second. 'Scarlett, I'm really not sure this is a great idea. I think I should take you back to Ashton Glade...'

'No. I'm not going home. Not until I've met Cadian. If you won't help me, I'll have to find someone who will.' Scarlett stood once more and picked up her case. It was heavy and she strained as she carried it to the door. 'I appreciate what you did for me last night. You will always find a warm welcome at the palace, should you ever need it.' As Scarlett turned to leave, she suddenly felt the weight of her case vanish. Turning she saw Finn gently lifting it from her grasp. 'I'll help you, Red.'

'You will?' Relief flooded her veins.

'Of course.'

Finn overtook her in the hall and led Scarlett down to the main tavern. With a tight smile he placed her case beside the bar. 'Get yourself a coffee and one for me. I'm going to pack your things up and prep Star. It won't be long before we're on the road. Let Oromore know someone will need to collect the rest of your things.'

'Who's Star?' Scarlett asked unsure if they would be taking a third travel companion.

'She's my horse.' Finn turned and left leaving Scarlett to search the bar for Oromore. He wasn't hard to find. Slowly he sauntered over to the princess and smiled. He looked exhausted and dark circles had formed underneath his eyes. 'What can I get for you, love?' He asked.

'Two coffees please.'

'Two? Please tell me you're not keeping company with that elf.' Oromore rolled his eyes as he pulled two metal mugs from a shelf and poured boiling water into them.

'*That elf* saved my life last night. Tell me Oromore, how would my father have felt if I'd been murdered in your tavern?' The words flew from Scarlett's mouth in annoyance. It certainly wasn't the way she had been raised to speak to others, but Finn didn't deserve Oromore's vitriol. The mere fact that the tavern keep was so derisive towards her hero was utterly disgraceful to the royal and for the first time, she was so very grateful to her father for his way of teaching her kindness towards others. For keeping company with the elves and for making sure Scarlett saw them as equals.

'You...you were attacked? It was *your* room?' Oromore had gone very pale, making the dark circles even more prominent. 'The guards, they said he killed the carriage driver, and that he'd made his way up...Oh Scarlett, I'm so sorry.' He placed the cups heavily onto the bar.

This wasn't pleasant. She despised seeing him look so sorrowful and it wasn't in her nature to keep someone in such misery if she could help it. She reached over and placed a hand on his arm. 'It's not your fault, Oromore. But Finn *did* save my life. I know you have your prejudice, most humans do. But please let this be a moment that you remember about the kindness of elves.' Her voice was so gentle, so kind and Oromore tightened his lips into a weak smile and nodded slightly. 'Here's your coffees. I'll send word back to your father about the driver-'

'Francis.' Scarlett interrupted and Oromore stuttered slightly before continuing, 'Francis. I'll also tell him that-' He took a deep breath, 'That you're continuing your journey with a new guide, a skilled and talented elf named Finnadan who I trust implicitly to take care of you.'

The mere fact the Oromore would be willing to pay even the slightest compliment to Finn was shocking to Scarlett. From what she had witnessed in the last twelve hours, she assumed he would have a hatred of the elves for life. But perhaps even the most stubborn human can change their mind.

'Thank you Oromore. Please also let him know that the rest of my belongings are at Finn's home. Please ask that someone collects them and brings them to me at Briar Heath.'

While Scarlett pondered the door opened and Finn strode in. He effortlessly slipped onto the seat beside her and picked up the other cup, took a swig of the hot, dark liquid inside and let out a satisfied sigh. 'Star is ready when you are, Red. But we should be prepared. I don't expect the weather to hold for the journey. We may see rain before we reach camp.'

Rain.

Damn.

Scarlett became acutely aware of how unprepared she was for this journey. Her cloak was thick, but it was woollen. It would soak up the water and leave her chilled to the bone. This wouldn't be a pleasant journey through the forests and fields of Novastraad. It would be cold, wet and difficult.

But it's worth it.

Horseback

'That's a big horse.' Scarlett mumbled as she looked up at Star. The ponies that lived in the paddocks behind the castle were minute in comparison to this beast. Her heart beat firmly against her chest as she took an involuntary step backwards and found the solid frame of Finn behind her, blocking her escape.

'Haven't you ridden before?' He asked as he gently stepped past her and patted the horse on her flank.

'Of course!' Scarlett felt her face flush. 'It's just, my ponies were a lot smaller than this.'

'Don't worry, she's a gentle old thing.' Finn grinned as he held his hand out to Scarlett, 'I'll help you up.'

This was definitely outside of her comfort zone and Scarlett had to steady her nerves with a deep, cleansing breath. *It's fine. Finn will keep you safe* she thought to herself as she reached out, allowing Finn's hand to grip her own. With remarkable ease, he pulled her up off her feet and hoisted her upwards. As he lifted her higher, Finn wrapped an arm around her waist and gripped firmly. Suddenly Scarlett found herself perched atop the horse. Instinctively, she reached out and grasped the reigns which made her feel a little better but there was still a moment where she wondered if she would slide right off.

Then Finn's strong arms securely wrapped around her frame and Scarlett felt safer in an instant. The rich smell of his leather armour surrounded her as Finn grasped the reins. A low rumble echoed through the clouds above and Star whinnied in response to the warning of an impending storm. 'You ready?' Finn asked, his lips close to Scarlett's ear. She nodded as her heart thumped. In reality, Scarlett was terrified of riding across the land on horseback with a relative stranger. But it would all be worth it.

For Cadian.

It's not that bad was the thought running through Scarlett's mind as they journeyed on. It was around an hour into their trip and she had started to grow used to the rocking motion. Though her legs had started to ache, and her back was sore. Long distance riding was considerably more strenuous than she'd imagined.

While she considered the pain in her thighs, a drop of cool water splashed against her cheek, making her flinch. it was followed by another that hit her forehead. Suddenly the heavens opened, and an icy downpour battered the riders. Scarlett let out a shiver as the once gentle breeze turned into the enemy against her wet skin. Finn pulled her a little closer, the rain washing away the scent of his armour, and he let out an almighty sigh, 'I'm sorry about this, Princess. I didn't think the storm would hit so soon.'

'It's alright.' Scarlett talked through chattering teeth and roaring rain. This was most unpleasant for the princess. Visions of warm baths and cups of hot chocolate floated through her mind as she closed her eyes. *I wonder if Cadian will have chocolate...*

As she thought about her future husband, Scarlett felt one of Finn's arms slowly retract away from her and minutes later, a cloak was being placed over her shoulders. A green cloak. 'Finn, you need protection from the storm as much as I do.' Scarlett had to raise her voice to shout over the beating of the rain. Her hair was now sticking to her face, and she begun to wonder if she looked similar to the palace pups after their bath, when their fur hung wetly, leaving streaks of water on the hardwood floor. She imagined she looked just as sorry for herself as they did.

'Don't worry. I've ridden through worse with less.' Finn shouted back as he pulled Scarlett closer. Then she felt the hood being pulled over her head. The relief from the downpour was immediate and Scarlett found herself wrapping the cloak tightly around herself.

As quickly as it started, the storm subsided. Going from thick heavy droplets to a fine mist in a matter of seconds. Scarlett didn't know if that was worse. The water filled her hood from every angle it seemed, and she wiped her eyes with her sleeves fruitlessly. As soon as she'd got her vision back, it was obscured by water once more. She had no clue how Finn could see where they were going.

It wasn't long before the mist too ebbed away leaving the riders cold and wet upon the horse. Scarlett felt every bite of wind that touched her soaking clothes and shivered relentlessly. This was going to be a long ride.

'So, tell me, Red. Why are you so desperate to get to Briar Heath? What awaits you there?' Finn asked. It seemed to be a vain attempt to distract her from the miserable weather and Scarlett was grateful for it. Her mind played the image of Cadian in the Obsidian Window for her once more and Scarlett felt a warmth spread through her and a wistful smile etched its way onto her lips. 'My fiancé is there. That's his home.'

'Surely the fiancé of a princess should be travelling to the palace. Not the other way around.'

It was the same point the king had made. And perhaps under normal circumstances they would be right. But how could she bring an elf to the castle, to sit as her husband when she didn't even know him? Scarlett already knew she needed to be ready to defend Cadian to all the humans that lived in their city. Acceptance would be difficult for her people, but surely those who believed in the prophecy would understand how their union would, in time, come to unite their people. A wry smile crossed Scarlett's lips.

'You sound like my father.' Scarlett mumbled and Finn let out a soft chuckle. 'Well then the king is a smart man indeed.'

That comment alone earned an eye roll from Scarlett that Finn couldn't possibly see. 'I know what I'm doing, Finn.' She snapped.

Silence followed that comment. It hung in the air between them. *I know what I'm doing...*

Except she didn't. Already a man had died, and another was in prison because of Scarlett's desire. And now Finn was spending three days travelling across the continent on horseback to escort the silly little princess to her new home. How childlike she must seem to an elf. And for the first time Scarlett didn't feel quite so confident. The words Alessandra had spoken echoed through her mind, *you must get him to look past your humanity.* But how? Scarlett's heart sank as she considered the fact that her own soul mate might not want her.

The two journeyed in silence for a while, eating dried fruit leather and nuts as they went. Finn seemed keen to continue, to cross as many miles as possible on this day. By the time the dusky sun began to sink towards the mountain tops, Scarlett's entire body ached. She pleaded internally for Finn to stop and make camp. Exhaustion was creeping in, and she knew he hadn't slept a wink the night before. *He has to need a rest* she thought. But as he pulled Star to a stop and gracefully dismounted, Scarlett could see he still looked wide awake. She dreaded to think what she looked like. Her curls had dried from the downpour into a mess of frizz and her clothes were wrinkled from the cloak. Finn reached his arms up towards Scarlett. 'Let me help you down.'

With a nod, Scarlett allowed herself to be lifted gently and lowered to the soft ground below. Finn had chosen a rather nice spot to rest. Nestled within the depths of the forest was a stunning clearing, encircled by towering, protective trees. Its soft, moss-covered ground, dotted with white daisies, seemed to beckon weary travellers, as if it had been crafted just for them. There was a stream glistening in the last of the late afternoon sun. Scarlett eyed it carefully and wondered if a quick bath might make her feel more human again. 'It might not be a bad idea.' Finn offered, as if he had read her thoughts. 'Aside from today's storm, the weather has been clear and warm for weeks. It'd probably be quite pleasant.'

She didn't need too much convincing. 'Thank you for today, Finn. I'm sorry I was...' She trailed off trying to think of a good way to say bitchy without sounding unroyal. Luckily, Finn finished the sentence for her, 'Snippy?'

'Sure.' She laughed slightly. 'Snippy. I was just cold and miserable.'

'Don't worry. You go take a swim, and I'll light us a fire and set up camp, okay?' Finn smiled down at the princess, and she nodded. 'Alright.'

The stream was fuller than usual due to the unexpected rainstorm, and who could complain about the fresh spring water? Certainly not Scarlett. With a smile she slid her feet out of the leather boots and wriggled her toes before dipping them into the cool stream. It felt so refreshing against her skin. Carrying her boots, she made her way carefully downstream. Picking her way over rocks and flinching slightly when she stood on a particularly uncomfortable stone.

The stream led to a quiet tranquil pool and Scarlett's eyes lit up. This was perfect. It was shrouded by trees and as the sky was darkening, Scarlett noted the tiny glow bugs that were beginning to fill the air. The place felt magical, special, like nothing she had ever experienced.

Working quickly, Scarlett shrugged off her sodden wool cape and her dress and slowly began to sink into the water. She gasped as the cool liquid lapped at the bare skin of her legs and shivered. With a deep inhale, Scarlett plunged herself into the pool up to her shoulders. While the cold was biting, it also made her feel more refreshed and awake. It was invigorating and she could feel her heart rate increase as she paddled around. It was unlike anything she had ever experienced. Scarlett was often bathed by her handmaidens in a bronze tub that stood in front of a large ornate fireplace that blazed with heat.

But this wasn't the princess in her bath, this was Red. Bathing herself in a cool stream in the forest. *I'm a new person.*

'Hey Red, are you decent in there?' Finn's voice echoed through the tranquil paradise and Scarlett turned instinctively to face in the direction the question came from, covering her chest with her arms. When she looked down, she was quite relieved to note that the darkening water was offering her a great deal of modestly. The only visible part of her was her shoulders and head, and honestly that seemed alright for travelling companions.

'Decent enough, I think.' She called back as she checked again. When she looked back up, she saw Finn approaching with Star by his side. 'My girl needed a drink, and I figured I could fill our canteens as well.' He smiled as he led Star to the pools edge then crouched down and scooped up some water in his hand. He gulped it down then used some more to rinse his arms and face. Star happily drank from the waters as Finn let himself drop from crouching to sitting. He was looking at the horse, or more specifically, *not looking at me,* Scarlett thought.

There were so many questions she had for the blond ranger but found that holding a conversation while naked felt remarkably uncomfortable. And also, rather mean considering how Finn was trying to look in any direction except hers. 'I think I'm ready to get out now, Finn. If you don't mind?'

He only glanced at her for a moment before whipping his body round so that his back was facing her. 'Not at all, Red. I'll take Star back to the camp. Do you want me to wait for you?'

'Thank you, yes.' The sun had begun to set, and Scarlett was beginning to feel a little exposed to the darkening forest. She paddled quickly to the edge and as the water level lowered she revealed more of herself to the world. In a few moments she had wrapped the woollen cloak around her wet body, picked up her dress and slipped her feet back into the boots. 'Alright. I'm as decent as I'm going to get for now. Scarlett imagined sitting in front of the fire and allowing the heat to warm her naked skin. But she could never, not with poor Finn here. She took his arm as they walked back to camp, her on one side of him and Star on the other and it wasn't long before they were back at the mossy clearing.

There stood a small tent beside a large fire. Finn had obviously spent some time starting things up here while Scarlett had bathed and it looked cosy and warm. As they approached, Scarlett saw her case was tucked beside the open tent, inside which were two bedrolls. Her heart skipped for a moment when she realised they would have to share. It was unreasonable to expect this poor man to sleep in the elements after she was the one that had dragged him out here. No, if she was too uncomfortable then she would have to sleep outside. It was only fair. She knelt beside her case and pulled out a dress. It was the thickest one she had packed but even still, it wasn't designed for horseback travel through goodness knows what weather. However, it would have to suffice. Slipping inside the tent and dropping the flap she realised it was actually alright in here, they'd be close but body heat may serve them well if the temperature dropped any further. It took her a few minutes but soon Scarlett was in dry clothes and her woollen cloak was tossed outside alongside the dress she had worn today. After a few more minutes she ventured back into nature and sat by the fire.

The grass had warmed and it was quite pleasant to sit under the open sky as it turned from a deep purple to an eternal black. With a glance around she noticed Finn had tied Star to a tree on a long rope, long enough that she could reach the heat of the fire if she wished, but not the flames themselves. She also saw her cloak and dress hanging over a branch to dry. She realised then just how it must have looked from his perspective when she had simply tossed her clothes outside and expected them to be dealt with. She hadn't actually thought about it, because she never had to think about it before. But somehow it seemed worse now. Reality spoke clearly in moments like these. Scarlett was spoiled but the surprising part was the pang she felt as she hoped Finn didn't see her that way.

'Thank you.' She offered, not really knowing which specific thing she was thanking him for.

'For what?'

'I don't know...all of it. Just, thank you.' Scarlett felt her cheeks redden. This was probably the most time she'd spent with a man that wasn't her family and she really didn't know how to behave anymore. Each passing moment seemed to get more awkward. It didn't help that in the darkness, with only the flames for light, Finn was a strikingly handsome elf. She found herself pondering the woman in the tavern the night before, who'd raised her skirt for the man who had given her gold, his hands reaching further and further towards their goal-

'Scarlett? Did you hear me?' Finn asked and Scarlett's eyes widened. 'Sorry, I was...' What? Thinking about what that might be like with Finn? *You are spoken for Scarlett Rose. Now act like it.* She scolded herself. 'I'm just tired I think.' She smiled weakly.

'Well, dinner is more fruit leather I'm afraid. The bread was a casualty of the weather.' Finn held up the loaf which dripped onto the grass and shrugged slightly before handing the princess the pouch of dried fruit.

'That's alright, I like fruit leather.'

'No one likes fruit leather.' Finn laughed as he took a bite. 'But it's great for the road.'

Scarlett ate her fill of the sweet, tough fruit and sighed heavily, watching the flames. One thing still bothered her about the night before. 'How did you know to come help me?' She asked. 'Last night I mean. How did you know I was in danger?'

Finn shrugged slightly. 'I heard the carriage fall. My home is across from the tavern and I guess I'm a light sleeper. I figured it had to be yours so I went to check. That's when I found...well you know.'

'Francis.' Scarlett nodded sadly.

'Yeah. I thought someone was after you so I couldn't just ignore it. It's not in my nature.' He sat silently for a minute and Scarlett could see his jaw clenching tightly then releasing. After a few minutes of silence he spoke again. 'You're a sweet woman Red, but you're naïve. That may work in the palace, but out here it'll get you killed.'

Scarlett's mouth dropped open. Was it so clear that she was hopeless? Were the elves so old that she was nothing more than a silly little human girl? Would Cadian see her that way? It was a struggle to hold back her tears as Finn poked the fire and instead, she stood. 'I think I'd like to get some sleep.'

Finn's demeanour changed in an instant at he rose to his feet with a horrified look on his face. 'Wait, Scarlett! I didn't mean that.'

'Yes, you did. And you're not wrong. Please, let's just sleep.' She turned to the tent and before she could even take a step, Finn was standing in her way, gently gripping her arms. 'Listen to me, this whole journey is a damn brave move on your part. You've been through too much already and truth be told, I'm just worried something will happen to you before I can get you to your new home.'

'You're worried about me?' Scarlett asked.

'The king would have my head if I let anything happen to you.' He grinned and Scarlett felt herself smiling in response. 'It's not easy to stay angry with you, you know.' She chuckled and Finn released her arms. 'My wife used to say the same. Perhaps she had a point.'

A silence fell between them as they looked as each other until Finn stepped aside. 'After you, *Princess.*' He grinned and Scarlett offered an eye roll he could've seen from miles away. The tent suddenly seemed much smaller than it had a few hours ago as Scarlett made her way inside and dropped gracefully down onto the bedroll. It was just a blanket on the soft grass with a layer of leather to keep it dry, but it was more comfortable that she expected. Finn gently climbed beside her, and Scarlett could hear his breathing as he lay close. She found herself being draped in another blanket but still shivered against the cold. 'Please don't think I'm being forward, Red.' Finn whispered as he placed an arm over her waist and pulled her close.

'You're shivering, I'm just gonna keep you warm, okay?' Finn whispered as Scarlett nodded.

There was a hand hanging over her waist as she lay on her side and Scarlett could feel the entire length of his body against her own. He'd taken the hard leather off and she could feel how warm he was. As he held her the worries of the day began to ebb away as the soft ground and warmth lulled the princess into a peaceful sleep in the arms of her protector.

Finn's day

Finn lay there, arm draped over the Princess of Novastraad, listening to her breathe. The soft, sleepy moans echoed gently around the glade in a hypnotic melody. For one moment he felt at peace. Why does she fit so perfectly?

Finn had to assume it was the feeling of having a human woman in his arms again. It had been just over a decade since his wife Ellie had been taken from him. The hole it left in his heart had never fully healed and he often found pushing her out of his thoughts helped him to function in his daily life. He always knew he would live a thousand years or more without her, she was human after all, but he never expected to have so few years with her first. Finn had hoped for fifty or sixty. She deserved that life full of children and laughter. He sighed heavily as he shuffled to try and quiet his mind. But there would be no peace for his overactive brain this night. Once he allowed his mind to wander to what might have been, he would be awake for the duration. He pondered about the woman currently lying in his arms. Another human woman. One that reminded him a little too much of Ellie. The eye rolls at his bad jokes, the grace she carried herself with, and the fact that she was beautiful.

Beautiful?

He hadn't wanted to notice that. It was obvious, he knew that, but he wanted to pretend it wasn't. Continue with the pretence that she was just a normal woman that he was escorting out of the goodness of his heart. But if he really let himself dwell on it, he knew the truth. He had chosen the seat beside her in the bar because she was unique. Her hair, her freckles, her smile. Stop it he chided himself. He was delivering her to her husband to be. She is not his. She will never be his.

She will never be mine.

The thought swam around in his brain. Bouncing as the corners of his mind started to dim. Finn felt the sleep begin to take him and surrendered to his exhaustion. But just as he was about to fall into oblivion he heard a voice, 'Finn...' It was like honey. His eyelids fluttered open, and he realised Scarlett had turned over in his arms. Her face now inches from his own. 'Scarlett? What-'

'Shhhh.' She soothed as she buried her face into his neck. Her warm breath sent goose bumps across his skin. What is she doing? His hand was still draped across her waist and as she snuggled into him, Finn allowed his arm to tighten around her. To feel her not just sharing his heat, but truly in his arms. She smelled like red berries, sweet and ripe. Finn sighed happily into her flaming hair.

Just as he felt like he could lie this way for an eternity, Scarlett readjusted, pulled her face away from his neck and her gaze met his own. A gentle smile slowly spread across her red lips as Finn ran his fingers up her side, following the path of her curves, slowly trailing up her neck until he was close enough to run his thumb along her bottom lip. It was like fire against his skin, and it ignited something in the elf. He watched, almost in awe of this woman as she nestled her face into his palm, placing a chaste kiss there.

It was time to make a choice. Finn knew he had to either stop this and go back to sleep, dealing with the awkwardness in the morning, or just relax into it and let it happen. It'd been years since he'd allowed a woman to touch him, to kiss him. He knew his judgement was clouded by the way her soft lips danced along skin of his wrist.

Fuck it.

Finn began tracing the contours of her jaw. The desire to have her as his own was an ache he could not ignore. Gently his fingers continued to the peak of her lips, feeling the warmth of her breath on his skin. With his heart racing he leaned in slowly, looking into her eyes as he savoured the moment. Their lips pressed together softly, meeting for the first time and feeling like lightening. Finn pulled away, to gage the reaction from the princess in his bed. As he searched her face, her fingers twisted into the hair on the back of his head and pulled him in. Their lips crashing together in a passionate embrace.

As he held her, Scarlett's mouth parted, letting his tongue slip in to dance with her own. A heat started growing inside him, hardening him as his hands began roaming, exploring the unfamiliar curves of the woman in his arms. His fingers found Scarlett's nipples through the material of her dress, and he gently swirled over the material. Feeling her respond with a moan, Finn whispered, 'Tell me how it feels, Princess.'

Another moan, 'It's...amazing.' Scarlett was breathing heavily, and Finn went back to the kiss once more, deepening it, enjoying the feel of her in his hands as he rolled her hard nipple through the material. 'Finn...' She moaned into his mouth

Fuck.

This woman, this angel was moaning his name in his arms at his mere touch, he wanted to please her. To give her everything she deserved from love and more.

Finn wanted to make love to the Princess of Novastraad.

The moans of encouragement were enough for Finn to break the kiss and slowly trail kisses down her neck, his thumb still working her nipple through her dress. Gently, he rolled Scarlett onto her back and continued kissing those perfect lips. The feel of her was overwhelming and Finn was becoming lost to her, losing his mind as the princess wrapped her arms around his lower back and pulled him closer, lifting her hips to meet his bulge. The feel of her grinding against him elicited a low groan from his throat. He felt an animalistic urge to tear Scarlett's dress open and plunge himself into her warm depths.

No, this has to be gentle.

As she writhed against his hardness, Finn felt the heat rising in his loins, he hadn't been this hard in a long time and he allowed himself to fall into it. His fingers moved lower, dancing over the material of Scarlett's dress as he reached for the hem of her skirt, drawing it back up her thighs, feeling her skin beneath his touch. He was inches away from her opening, the tops of her thighs already slick with her spreading wetness. As his fingers crept closer to their goal, Finn felt the world fall away. The lips faded, the roaming hands vanished, and he was lying once more on his side, the princess sleeping soundly in front of him. The wisps of Scarlett's curls fluttered against Finn's breathing as he tried to control his heartbeat. But his mind went straight to the stiffness between his legs. The thick veiny bulge that was pushing against the confines of his breeches. Suddenly the realisation hit that his tryst with the princess was in his own head, his subconscious mind playing a cruel trick. He couldn't let Scarlett see him like this or feel it. After all, she was an engaged lady. A royal for fucks sake!

Quickly he rolled away from her and fled the tent hastily yet thanks to his elven ancestry, in complete silence. Shame spread across his face in the guise of a red flush as his mind wandered over the image of Scarlett writhing beneath him. The next two days were going to feel like an eternity.

With his back to the tent, Finn started working on the fire. The sun had begun it's ascent into the sky and the dawn chorus had well and truly started. He heard Scarlett moving around under the blanket and a few minutes later, her voice filled the air. 'Good morning.' She groaned sleepily, followed by a yawn. Finn didn't turn to look at her. He couldn't. 'Morning, Red.' He muttered. 'You sleep okay?'

'Yeah, but I think I must have slept on a rock.' Scarlett announced and Finn finally turned to look at her, standing in the door of the tent in her long dress, rubbing her lower back.

'Right...well, we should make it to Redstone by nightfall, there's a tavern there and the owner owes me a favour.'

He turned back to the fire as he continued, 'I'll make sure you have the comfort of a real bed.'

'That sounds great.'

Finn poked at the beginnings of the fire, urging it to life so they could warm up before their journey began. He watched out of his periphery as Scarlett sat beside him and held her hands over the small flames. 'I'd better take Star to water and then I'll pack up.' Finn rose to his feet and began to move away.

'Finn, wait.' Scarlett called after him and he froze, still unwilling to look the poor woman in the eye after his subconscious attempt at defiling her.

'Is everything alright? You're being more quiet than usual.' She asked and Finn could hear her rustling as she stood, moving closer to him as he reached for Star's reigns. 'I'm fine.' he replied but she continued to close the gap and placed a hand gently on his arm. Turning him slowly to face her. 'Have I done something to offend? Because it seems likely and if you don't tell me what it is...' She paused and her face turned thoughtful for a second. 'Well, if you don't tell me then I'm very likely to continue doing it.'

How could he tell her? What was he supposed to say? I want you to fuck me. I want to hold you in my arms and hear you scream my name Scarlett, I want you to flood me while you ride me. I want us to ruin each other. Say the word and I will get down on my knees and worship every inch of you.

He couldn't, that was obvious. But she was a damn perceptive creature. He couldn't keep ignoring her. Not for another two days. 'I'm sorry. You're right, I'm just tired and a little grumpy this morning. I'll do the chores and I'll be much better when we're due to go, alright?'

He watched her face for a sign that she didn't believe him but instead a smile spread across her face. 'Alright. can I help?'

He laughed in response and admittedly, that may have been a mistake. 'This isn't royal work. You sit down, have some rations and we'll be ready before you know it alright?' Even as he spoke, he could hear the patronising tone in his voice. What in the deepest hells are you doing, Finn? He asked himself but it was too late. A look of defiance spread across Scarlett's face as she turned away and stalked back to the warmth of the fire.

It was going to be a long day.

The New Queen

King Farandorn had remained in his chambers since Scarlett left the palace grounds. It wasn't unheard of for a King to keep his privacy for weeks on end, but this wasn't just a king simply keeping his own company. This was a father who missed his daughter.

Alessandra paced outside his door. This was the time to strike, while he was vulnerable. Weak. If she was to slaughter the King, there truly was no time like the present. For a moment she considered it. After all, it would be at least an hour before he was discovered that alone would give her a good head start...

No. That wasn't her plan. Her fingers gripped the stone around her neck tightly. Earlier that day she had sat on the hard floor of the arcane library with her eyes closed. She knew well enough that the dark magician could see through the eyes of his victims. That much had become clear to her in the past few days. So she would have to do this blind.

With closed eyes it had been difficult to find her way. Running her hands along walls and doors to find the right one. Stumbling over chair legs in the library and almost falling into the reflecting pool in the centre of the hardwood floor. That was her destination, the stone circle of water that sat beneath the glass domed ceiling.

Three hundred years ago the centre of the dome had been replaced with a lens, specifically designed to allow a magnified glimpse of the moons that sauntered through the night sky. But at midday the sun shone through into the pool, intensified by the specially built dome. The water would quickly boil, bubbling and steaming as the light passed overhead. She knelt beside the small pool and dipped a finger into the water.

Still cool.

There was time yet, but not much. Quickly she fished a smooth stone out of the pocket in her cloak and placed it in the palm of her hand, holding it up towards the glass ceiling, over the water. In a few moments the sun would be overhead.

Alessandra took in deep breaths, trying to calm her nerves. What was coming would be excruciating and yet she couldn't make a sound. If Cadian was watching, he couldn't know what she was doing and an old mage like him would be able to add up the parts to determine the spell.

Soon her palm felt the initial sweep of the sun's heat, gentle and warm against her skin. The natural light was uncomfortable for Alessandra anyway. The dark elves had always preferred the south of the continent where the snow fell daily, and the sun was rarely seen. But this wasn't unpleasant at first, it was akin to warming your hands in water. Soon though, it became a raging fire, bathing the stone in its purifying light and burning her flesh. Alessandra could smell her own body cooking in the heat and gritted her teeth as tears poured down her cheeks.

And then it was over. The sun passed and Alessandra's eyes flew open. The spell she has cast would keep Cadian out of her head, it would shroud her in the sun's blazing light for as long as she had the stone. Looking down at her burned skin, Alessandra finally let out a cry of pain. The agony would stay with her for a while, but it was worth it.

It would heal in time.

She gently pulled the stone from her melted palm and tucked it safely into a decorative metal locket designed as a cage. She clasped it closed and allowed it to hang round her neck. Minutes later she was in her room, bathing her hand in aloe and gently wrapping it in a bandage. A very noticeable bandage was needed to cover the extent of the damage caused. With a sigh, she pulled on black leather gloves, wincing as they settled over the injury.

For now she was safe.

And that was how she had wound up standing outside the King's room with a letter from Oromore, the tavern keep from Fellglow. He had sent word to say Scarlett had been attacked while spending the night in his tavern, but was safe and continuing her journey with a skilled ranger. Alessandra had burned the letter. This was the perfect opportunity to destroy the king's heart, So instead, she would claim it held word from the road patrol guards. A terrible accident had befallen the small village of Fellglow. It had been burned to the ground with no survivors. They'd seen it all from miles away and sent word as quickly as they could.

Lies to tangle myself in.

Sending a miscreant from the streets of Ashton Glade to burn the village was simple enough. Alessandra had paid him enough gold that he'd never want for anything, it would buy his silence. And there would be no witnesses. For all intents and purposes, Scarlett was dead. And Alessandra would be surprised if she ever made it back to the palace. Cadian was known for his appetites and the princess was a little too delicate, too easily broken. Perhaps this plan would be better. If Alessandra married the king, she could bear a child for him, a new heir. Half elf and half human, with the title of royal, and magic in their veins.

Yes...this will work.

Alessandra knocked on the king's door gently. 'My lord, may I enter?' Her silky voice penetrated the door, and she heard the muffled grunt of approval from the king. As she entered, she took in the space. It was clean enough, but the windows needed to open, to freshen the air. Farandon sat on a chair reading a children's book. He barely glanced up at her. 'My King, I'm afraid...I come with news.'

King Farandorn slowly raised his eyes from the book. 'You bring word of Scarlett?' He asked hopefully. A normal soul would probably flinch, knowing what was to come, knowing the grief the king would feel. But Alessandra simply nodded and knelt before him. 'I do, your majesty. But the news is not good.'

'Speak it.' The King commanded, his voice suddenly low, threatening. It was very unlike the man Alessandra knew and for an instant she felt like fleeing the room. 'There's been an accident. At Fellglow. My King, there was a fire.' Alessandra looked to the ground, her performance as the devastated court mage was impeccable and she heard the air escaping from King Farandorn's lungs. 'My Scarlett? Is she...' He asked tentatively. But Alessandra just shook her head. 'I'm so sorry, Farandorn.' She whispered as the King's sobs echoed through the chamber. The mage held her king as he wept, shushing him gently as a mother would comfort a child. On the outside it was the perfect image of grief, but no one could hear the thoughts racing through Alessandra's mind. The irritation at the tears spilling onto the velvet dress she wore, the discomfort from sitting on the floor and the intense pain in her hand.

Nevertheless, this was the start. Her plan was in motion and by the time anyone realised the Scarlett was safe, it would be too late. She would be the new Queen of Novastraad.

Fated To Meet

Scarlett awoke with a start. The sun shone into her room in the tavern and outside the horses had begun to whinny. The sound burst into her room, and she smiled. Today was the day she would meet Cadian. It was barely more than five hours travel and she was ready for it.

Slowly she crawled out of bed and stretched, her aching body protesting as she did. Riding Star for almost three days had made her aware of muscles she didn't realise existed within her, but she had no intention of letting the pain win. She skipped to the vanity and sat down in front of the mirror, smiling at her own face. Soon Cadian's visage wouldn't be just a memory of his reflection. It would be real. Real enough that she would be able to reach out and touch him, caress his flawless skin, run her fingers through his hair, kiss him...

Oh, to kiss him...

There was a twinge low in her abdomen and her eyes drifted closed as she imagined what it would be like to press her lips against his. She thought about how he would smell, how he would feel, and began to lose herself in her fantasy.

'Hey Red!' Finn shouted through the door. 'Are you awake?'

Scarlett's eyes flew open, and she sighed dreamily. 'Yes, come in.' The words left her lips, still tingling from the imaginary kiss before she'd even really thought about it. As the door clicked open, Scarlett realised too late that she was still in her nightgown. 'Wait!' She cried out as Finn walked in and caught sight of her. 'Red!' He stuttered and turned away quickly. 'Would you mind, maybe, putting some clothes on?'

Scarlett hurried to the case beside her bed and pulled out a dress. Perhaps she would have been more aware if she'd known of Finn's own fantasy, his dream of her. Maybe she would've been more careful to cover herself. In a few moments a new dress was pulled over her head and the nightdress tucked safely back into the case. 'Alright Finn, you can turn around now.'

As he did, she noticed the slight flush that was quickly fading from his cheeks and smiled to herself. He really was quite adorable. 'May I?' He lifted the case.

'Of course, thank you.'

'I asked the tavern keep to run you a bath this morning, I figured you'd want to start the day as fresh as possible.' Finn held the door for Scarlett, and they made their way downstairs. 'That's very thoughtful.' The princess smiled.

They made their way downstairs and Finn dropped Scarlett's case beside a table in the corner. For a moment she stood awkwardly, looking between the table and Finn as he sat himself down, seemingly oblivious to the Princess' confusion.

'Finn?' She asked gently and the elf looked up at her. 'Yes, *your highness*?' He whispered back. It was suddenly clear to Scarlett that he'd chosen this seat for privacy. Just as she opened her mouth to shut him up, she realised his eyes were glinting with mischief. 'What am I missing here?' She asked, the confusion spreading through her mind.

'Nothing. I'm just feeling...a little chaotic today.' Finn grinned back. 'The bathhouse is just through that door.' Finn pointed to a wooden door near the back of the room. 'I paid a little extra for privacy.' Scarlett turned to look where he was pointing then back to Finn. 'Can you promise that by the time I get back, this mischievous side of you will have dwindled?' She asked with a smirk. She actually liked this side of her travel companion, seeing a real smile on his face really brought out his features.

'I'm not promising anything, Red.' Finn grinned as Scarlett turned and wandered to the bath house.

After a wonderfully hot bath, provided by the tavern keepers wife with fragranced oils and candle light, Scarlett wrapped herself in a towel and went to stand in front of the mirror in the room. The words *drowned rat* came to mind as she looked over her visage. Rolling her eyes at herself, she wrapped another towel around her head and rubbed her curls vigorously, intent on drying them as much as possible. Once they were only slightly damp, she ran her fingers through them and looked once more in the mirror. *A little better* she thought to herself. Scarlett no longer looked like she had ridden across the land through storms and forests for four days, but she certainly didn't look like her usual, well-kept self. It took a little longer to finish drying off and change back into her clothes but soon enough she was walking back through the tavern to Finn's table. He hadn't noticed her yet and was sitting, his side to her, sipping his coffee and reading from a small pocketbook. With a wicked grin, Scarlett formulated a plan. Finn had decided that today, chaos would reign, and she was more than willing to be swept along in it. Especially since her mood was already high.

Quickly, she darted towards the wall, just enough to be out of his eyeline should he glance over and snuck along the edge of the room until soon there was only a foot between them. if he turned now, it'd be all over. Quick as a flash, Scarlett reached out, grabbing Finn by the shoulder and shouting his name.

'What the fu-' The elf practically jumped out of his skin and dropped the book he was holding. He whirled round in his seat to come face to face with a giggling princess. He took a second to catch his breath and then, thankfully, found the humour. 'You're a menace Scarlett Rose.' He whispered as she slid into the seat across from him.

The barman brought over a metal cup filled with hot, black liquid and a platter of fresh baked bread and some cheese. Finn tossed him a coin as he placed the food in front of Scarlett. 'We'll get going once you've eaten. It's a big day for you.'

Scarlett smiled as she tore into a piece of warm bread. 'Finn...' She began then paused, not really knowing how to say what she wanted to. This elf had so far, safely transported her across the land. A job that he didn't need to do. It was a kindness not many beyond the palace walls would have offered and she wouldn't be quick to forget it.

She stuffed some bread into her mouth and Finn raised his eyebrows. 'Do you just enjoy saying my name or do you want to finish that sentence?'

Swallowing the bread, Scarlett smiled and took a sip of the coffee. It was bitter and a little harsh, but it felt good as it washed the bread from her throat. 'I just wanted to say thank you.' She blushed slightly. 'What you've done for me...I cannot tell you how much it means.' Another sip of coffee. 'I won't forget it, Finn. You will *always* have a friend in the palace, and a place there should you ever wish it.'

As soon as the words were out of her mouth, she stuffed more bread into it. Talking so openly to someone, anyone, outside of the palace, it was unheard of, and she was afraid of how he would react to her words. Since technically she'd just invited him to live in her home after knowing him for four days. But she hated the idea of him returning to Fellglow and being treated like a lesser being just because of his elven lineage. It wasn't fair.

Finn was smiling. 'I didn't know you were such a softie, Red.'

'Are you making fun of me?' She asked, narrowing her eyes. Surely he could lay off the mischief for five minutes while she tried to be genuine.

'Yes, I am. But only because I don't know what else to say. I appreciate what you're offering me and if I ever feel the need to leave my home, then the palace is as good a place as any to live. But I don't imagine it happening for a long time. I'm okay in my little life, Red.' He reached out and placed a hand on the princess' holding it tightly. 'You're a good woman. With a good heart, and after spending the last few days with you I can honestly say that, Cadian is a lucky man.' Finn released her hand and leaned back as Scarlett's mouth fell open in an O. *If things had been different...*she almost allowed her mind to wander to a world where she'd never known about Cadian. Where she'd met Finn and only Finn. He was kind, and fair. Excellent traits for a King to have...

Stop it, Scarlett, she scolded herself. That wasn't the life she was choosing. Cadian would be her King.

'Finish up, we should get going.' Finn's voice dragged her back out of her own head, and she began to eat her breakfast with gusto. *Only a few more hours.* She thought.

The beautiful old mansion loomed over the small hamlet ominously as Finn and Scarlett approached. The dull yellow glow from the windows looked brighter than it should against the dark façade of the house. By Scarlett's inexperienced reckoning, it was still over an hour away, but it could be seen as soon they crested the hill. As she took in the view, Scarlett's heart beat a little faster. The large manor house dominated the smaller buildings below it, it reminded her of the palace that sat on top of the hill in Ashton's Glade with the city below. A smile crept onto her face at the thought. *This may not be so different after all.*

Rather than a city sitting below the palace, it simply looked like a small village, little houses with smoke coming from their chimneys, a few bigger buildings, perhaps a tavern or two, maybe even a schoolhouse. Oh, what a year this could be, spent in a lovely quaint town, getting to know the locals and living with her future husband.

This would be her perfect home.

As they got closer, Scarlett could start to make out more details of her new residence. The manor house stood, looming over everything else, it's dark stone walls covered with green ivy giving it a rather haunted look, reminding Scarlett of the old ghost stories she used to read. If life there was anything like those books, it would be nothing if not an adventure.

The windows that glowed slightly, weren't just glass. Now they were getting nearer, the princess could make out colours shimmering and she quite correctly reasoned that it must be stained glass in the panes. All around the base of the house was greenery, a garden that looked like it overflowed with bushes and grass. It wasn't the immaculate home she has expected, but her father often said she had inherited her mother's talent for gardening. There was never much need for it in a palace with staff that kept things immaculate, but here...here she could put her skills to good use.

I'm almost home.

When they approached the outer edges of Briar Heath, Finn leaned in close to Scarlett's ear as they rode, 'Are you certain about this, Red? This place gives me some really bad vibes.'

Oh Finn, he had become so protective of her in the days they had spent together. It was a unique experience for Scarlett, having someone with her that wasn't on the payroll. It meant he was by her side because he chose to be which filled Scarlett with a warmth. The princess of Novastraad had made her first ever friend and she intended to nurture that friendship.

But not in this moment. In this moment she needed him to know that she knew what she was doing.

'I'm certain. This is my home, Finn' She whispered as she took in the buildings around them. There *was* a tavern, it was small though. Definitely dwarfed by Oromore's place in Fellglow, but it looked cosy. A nice place to take a drink after a pleasant evening stroll through the village. Small houses dotted around the place quite haphazardly and a marketplace stood in the centre with four little stalls. It really was a tiny place, but it seemed to have everything Scarlett could need for a simple life.

People milled about, glancing up occasionally at the visitors on horseback but none looked for too long and no one spoke to them. It clearly wasn't unusual for them to have visitors here. A few children ran through the marketplace as they passed, playing some sort of game. Scarlett watched them, trying to understand the rules. One would chase the others until they touched them, then that person would become the chaser. A sad smile spread across the princess' face. She had never played like that as a child. There wasn't exactly an abundance of children in the castle, and she had mostly played with the maids when they weren't too busy.

Soon they reached the gate of the manor house. *Home.*

Finn pulled Star to a stop and climbed down, reaching up to help Scarlett. Once she was safely on the ground, they began to approach the intimidating house. Excitement bubbled through Scarlett's veins as she took the lead, smiling while Finn followed behind, leading the horse by the reigns.

Just as Scarlett reached the steps that ascended to the large, ornate double door, it opened. The princess froze on the spot, one foot on the bottom step and one still on the path below. As the door slowly creaked open, a figure stepped out. A man with long pointed ears and hair so black it seemed to absorb the light around him. His eyes were dark as they bored into Scarlett. She could physically feel his gaze as it wandered over her. He was tall and wore an immaculate suit that hugged his frame. Scarlett could see the slight bulge of muscle beneath the fabric.

As his gaze settled on her face, her breath caught in her throat. Cadian looked into her eyes, and he spoke the first words he would ever say to Scarlett.

'Welcome home, darling.'

Welcome Home

There he was.

Cadian.

Cadian...

The princess was holding her breath and she could feel her lungs as they burned in her chest, begging for fresh oxygen to flood her body. But she didn't dare move. It felt as though she had journeyed so far, endured so much for this dream and if she moved even one inch, her bubble would burst, and he would be gone. It was as though perfection stood before her with a perfectly chiselled jaw and eyes that set her core on fire with a mere glance. And those eyes never left her face.

'Thank you for bringing her safely to my home.' The words were directed at Finn, but they seemed to be little more than an afterthought. The one that brought her here was no longer useful and wasn't worth his time. Before she could protest, he continued 'Princess, please, come in.' Cadian stepped aside, seemingly breaking the spell between them and Scarlett could finally breathe again. As she went to take a step forward, she faltered for a moment before turning to face the elf that had brought her this far, that had kept her safe and warm on the road, that had treated her as a gentleman would.

Her protector.

Finn.

Smiling softly, she took a step away from the threshold and reached out to take Finn's hands in her own.

'Thank you, Finn. From the bottom of my heart. You are a friend I will not forget.'

'It's aright. It was an honour.' Finn smiled warmly back at his travelling companion. 'The road will seem a little lonelier without you.'

'Let me write a letter to my father.' Scarlett continued, 'If you deliver it then he will pay you handsomely for what you have done.'

Finn shook his head and sucked in a little air. 'I didn't do it for coin, Red.' He glanced at Cadian, back to Scarlett and then lowered his voice. 'Be safe, alright? And if you ever need me, send word to Fellglow.' He shifted from one foot to the other, looking back up at the master of the house. 'Look after her, Sir.' It was polite, but Scarlett heard the unspoken words. Look after her or you'll answer to me.

'I'm fairly certain I can care for my own future bride.' Cadian smiled and slipped an arm around Scarlett. It was the first time he'd touched her, and she felt a jolt in her stomach. As if an ache had existed all her life, and only now was it sated. The princess melted inside. 'Come, we have much to discuss.' He whispered to her and turned her away from Finn. Together they stepped into the mansion and gently, seemingly without intervention, the door closed.

This was it.

My new home, she thought. The beauty of the manor didn't escape the princess and while it didn't have the extravagance of the palace she called home, it did have a certain antique opulence that felt familiar to her. The door had led them into the entrance hall which was vast and had a large spiralling staircase in the centre, leading to the second floor which was nothing more than a balcony, lined with doors that were sure to lead to the other wings of the house. The floor was a dark hardwood covered in flawless rugs patterned with deep red roses. A décor choice that Scarlett hoped he had chosen due to his admiration of the flower that was her namesake. Her mind drifted off to an image of a Cadian that had always loved roses, but never known why.

Soul mates.

The wood panelled walls were lacquered to a shine and held ornately framed painted portraits. As Scarlett peered closer to a painting of Cadian her brow furrowed. The style of the art reminded her of the older royal portraits that hung in the palace, but they had been painted hundreds of years ago and Cadian looked in this painting as he did at this moment. It wasn't a secret that the elves lived extended lives and Alessandra herself had said Cadian was ancient. But for the first time Scarlett truly wondered, how old is the man I promised to marry?

'Join me for a drink.' Cadian whispered into Scarlett's ear as she stared at the artwork. It wasn't a request, that much was clear to the princess and to her own amazement a shot of fear travelled up her spine. His tone was commanding, and she found herself nodding silently while she followed Cadian through the entry hall and into another room. Comfort awaited in this space, a level of lavishness that she had missed while on the road. A fainting couch that was overstuffed and covered in a thick velvet, armchairs that looked as though you could vanish inside the plump, patterned cushions and a roaring fire that scared away any traces of cool air. Scarlett watched as Cadian approached a mahogany corner table laden with crystal bottles that held some sort of amber liquid. He picked up one of the glasses and filled it from a bottle, then turned and looked at Scarlett. It felt as though his dark eyes were probing every inch of her soul.

'Sit down.' His voice had such an air of authority that was rarely seen from elves. They were usually so submissive to humans. Not this one though, Cadian was clearly unlike any elf she had ever met. A wave of defiance washed over the princess. Not once in her life had anyone commanded her to do anything, not even her father demanded of her in this way. Her hands found her way to her hips, and she raised an eyebrow, meeting his dark gaze. 'I'll take my drink standing, thank you.'

A grin spread across Cadian's face, and she couldn't tell if she had just made a huge mistake or not. It seemed as though these two soul mates were locked in a dance of dominance that neither was willing to lose. 'I could make you.' Cadian's voice lowered as he went from polite smile to playful grin that lit up his eyes. 'If I chose to.'

'You could certainly try.' Scarlett felt her own lips part as her smile matched his own. Before her stood a man that wouldn't bow down to her royal title or treat her as a glass vial that could break any moment. Excitement began to dance through her as Cadian stepped closer, conceding the battle and handing her the glass. 'Welcome home, Scarlett.' Cadian leaned in and placed a gentle kiss on her cheek and suddenly, Scarlett felt the world around her explode as heat surged from within her. She knew in that moment that only her royal upbringing had stopped her from hitching up her skirt and wrapping herself around him. He smelled like the forest and Scarlett breathed him in as his lips touched her skin.

'Perhaps we should discuss our arrangement, princess.' Cadian growled against her cheek, 'Before you do something you may later deem as undignified.'

Scarlett felt her skin flush and watched as her future husband crossed the room and sat on one of the armchairs. *Please tell me he cannot hear inside my mind*, Scarlett silently prayed. With a deep breath, she downed the drink he had given her and sat in the chair opposite. With great effort on her part, Scarlett summoned all of the regal training she could and spoke. 'Tell me what you know of soul mates, Cadian.'

The elf sighed, 'Not a great deal, I'm afraid. They are rare among elves and more so for humans. Never have I heard of the soul connection crossing between the races. I believe you and I may be the rarest of all, Princess.'

Scarlett nodded along. 'Alright, then tell me what you know about our connection. What did Alessandra say to you?'

'Only that you looked into the Obsidian Window and saw me.' Cadian leaned to the side of the seat and brought a hand to his lips, drawing a finger across the bottom one thoughtfully. 'And that is enough to convince me.'

'Really? Why?' Scarlett asked. Surely the most powerful and ancient elven mage would need more than an anecdote from a court mage.

'Because I have known Alessandra for a long time. I was the one that passed the Obsidian Window to her.' He smiled almost wistfully. 'I had no idea that it would bring about my own mate. That I would find myself...pledged to another living soul. And yet here we are.'

A pulse ran through Scarlett as his words surrounded her as silk would, gentle and soft. When he spoke of committing himself to her, she felt as though the world would fall away. No, do not allow yourself to be raptured so easily, Scarlett, she chided herself.

'What are your intentions with me, Cadian?' Scarlett asked and there was almost a flicker of surprise on his face before Cadian caught himself and smiled warmly. 'Princess,' He began as he rose to his feet, 'It is my intention to discover you, as a woman and a wife.' He crossed the room and knelt before Scarlett, taking her hands in his own as Scarlett found herself holding her breath once more. 'I intend to know you, every inch of you.' He pulled the Princess forward in her chair and lifted a hand to her cheek. 'And I intend to love the woman I discover.' He whispered. and Scarlett became surrounded by him, his scent, his aura. His very existence was intoxicating and as he leaned closer, she allowed his lips to gently brush her own. The taste of him was pure heaven, like nothing she had ever experienced. A warmth spread to her core at his gentle touch and Scarlett felt her skin tingle.

Leaning into the kiss, Scarlett wrapped an arm around Cadian's neck and pulled herself to the edge of the seat. Without her even realising it, her legs parted to bring him closer as she deepened the kiss. Opening her lips to allow his tongue to explore her only intensified the heat inside her.

Quickly, both of his arms were wrapped around her waist and his kiss began to devour her. It was a hunger that joined them, and Scarlett could feel the wetness soaking into the cloth of her underwear. It was suddenly so clear where this kiss would lead. Was she ready for that? Was she truly prepared to allow a man to take her body? Especially a man she had known for barely an hour?

Her mind wandered to Mateo, the way he had her mewling the night they met, and the monster he turned into the day after.

Wait... The word danced through her mind but didn't made it out of her mouth as Cadian's lips left her own and began to dance along her neck, drawing a moan from the Princess instead.

It's now or never Scarlett.

'Wait.' She moaned breathlessly, moving her hand to his chest and pushing him slightly. 'I can't, I'm...I don't think...' Scarlett struggled to find the words. He was her soul mate, her future husband, and by far the most exquisitely handsome man she had ever seen. How could she say no? He would think her crazy. What if he sent her away? Perhaps prudish women weren't his type.

'You're not ready.' Cadian's forehead came to rest against her own, his breath had quickened, and Scarlett couldn't mistake the hardness that pressed against her. Cadian was fully ready to take her right here on the chair.

'I'm sorry, I just need a little time.' Scarlett pulled away from him, moving backwards on the seat, studying his face intently as a smile broke across it. 'Darling, it appears as though I'm not getting any older. I have all the time in the world to wait for you.' He took her hands in his own once more and lifted them to his lips, kissing them gently as he tried to slow his breathing. 'Allow me to show you to your room.'

Broken

'What do you think?' Cadian's voice came from behind Scarlett as she stepped through the door into her beautiful new room.

'It's perfect.' She whispered.

A four poster bed sat in the centre with deep purple curtains adorning the wooden frame that were swept back. A thick, soft carpet spread over the floor and practically begged Scarlett to kick off her boots and squish her toes into it. Against the wall stood a beautiful, hand carved wardrobe with golden filigree inlaid into it. It was magnificent. Candles lit the entire space and the warm yellow flicker, coupled with the orange glow from the ornate fireplace, gave the room a cosy atmosphere.

And the best part? There wasn't a tapestry in sight. Scarlett turned to Cadian. 'Thank you. I love it.'

'Your happiness is my only priority, darling.' Cadian placed a hand on her lower back and Scarlett felt the warmth creeping in between her thighs once more. In an effort to ease the burning she stepped away, walking into the room. 'I'd better unpack and take a bath. Could you bring me some water?' Scarlett asked as she glanced once more around the room. 'Wait, where's the bath?'

Cadian grinned. 'Come with me.' He held his hand out and the princess took it in her own allowing herself to be lead down the hall slightly and into another room. As she stepped inside, she gasped. 'Oh my goodness. This is...incredible.'

The whole room was a white marble mixed with rose gold and in the centre sat a pool of clear water. A large opening sat on the far wall, spilling fresh water into the pool. Around the edges, the water overflowed into slits in the marble. A constant flow of fresh water. Scarlett's mouth fell open, never before had she seen such a large and elegant bathhouse. Even in the castle, she had a copper tub in front of the fire. It was a beautiful tub, but a tub none the less.

Cadian waved his arm and the candles in the room flickered to life and Scarlett's eyes widened at the display of magic. Such casual use was forbidden in the castle, but she supposed, in his own home, Cadian made the rules.

'Take your time in here, my pet. Dinner will be ready whenever you like.'

Scarlett turned in time to see Cadian leave, closing the door firmly behind him. And for the first time, Scarlett felt as though she could breathe again. In his presence it was like there was something in her soul wrapping around her. Perhaps that's what soul mates felt like. Heavy, connected, grounding. Although now, she felt as light as air. With a smile she pulled off her layers, dropped them onto the marble and stepped to the edge of the water. Dipping her toe in, she expected the chill of a fresh stream, like the one she bathed in the night she camped with Finn. She smiled at the memory of her friend, but her mind was pulled back to reality as her skin touched the water.

It was warm.

'Oh, by the gods...' She muttered as she slipped in and let the heat enter her muscles. They ached from the journey, but the water quickly helped. Soon she had washed but wasn't ready to leave the water. It was too warm and pleasant. Scarlett closed her eyes and relaxed in her new home. This was possibly the most wonderful experience of her life. The passion the romance...it was perfect. Except, she didn't seem willing, did she?

The man of her dreams was downstairs, willing and able to take her, and yet here she was. Bathing alone because she was too afraid to let him in. Courage must come from somewhere. How was she supposed to find hers? Finn said travelling across the continent to meet Cadian was brave, and maybe it was. But being afraid to let him touch her made it seem as though this was all worthless. What was the point of finding your soul mate if you can't let him touch you.

With a shiver, the princess eased herself from the warmth of the water and stepped across the cold marble, being extra careful not to slip. There were fluffy towels waiting and she wrapped herself in them to dry before dashing back to her room.

Dressing for dinner was a quick affair, Scarlett had opted to be as willing as she could be, wearing her favourite green dress that draped to the floor and held her cleavage up. It was really the only thing she had that made her feel even slightly sexual. She wasn't certain of what would happen tonight, but she at least wanted to make him feel *something.* While she dressed, she thought about how he made her feel, the warmth that emanated from his touch, the way it burned as desire in her. That was the effect she wanted to have on him.

The dining hall was another stunning space with mahogany lined walls, more beautifully old paintings, cabinets filled with ornately painted porcelain crockery and a large table that stretched the length of the room. Two places had been set at the far end, facing each other and separated only by candles. Cadian rose to his feet as Scarlett entered and smiled, he reached out to her as she crossed the room and took her by the hand, placing a gentle kiss on her skin, just above her fingers. 'You look beautiful, darling.'

Scarlett felt herself blush at the compliment and then the embarrassment crept in. *Grown ladies don't blush, sheltered princesses blush.*

'Are you alright?' Cadian asked, his smooth voice danced around the room as he spoke, surrounding Scarlett and in response she nodded awhile sitting herself at the table. 'Yes, thank you.'

'I trust your bath was adequate?' He asked as he uncorked a bottle of deep red wine and filled their glasses.

'It was wonderful. How do you get warm water to run constantly?' It was a question that had been annoying Scarlett since she'd slipped into the bath. It functioned perfectly but she had no idea how. Cadian winked, 'Magic, love.' He handed her the drink and Scarlett sipped. It was delicious, akin to the finest wines her father served at the royal banquets.

Meat and vegetables cooked to perfection were placed so perfectly upon the platter before her, it reminded her of home. So beautifully made that Scarlett had to question where it came from. 'Did you cook this?' She asked and Cadian nodded. 'Cooking has always appealed to me. It's very similar to magic.' He smiled as he lifted a piece of carrot on his fork and eyed it carefully. 'You see, both spells and recipes call for specific ingredients. Some are easy to come by, available in any market in the land. But others...' He smiled and ate the carrot, his eyes sparkling. 'Others take time and dedication to find.'

'Do you practice magic often?' Scarlett asked. She knew he was a powerful mage but, no more than that. Cadian nodded once more. 'Magic is like a muscle, the more you use it, the stronger you become. But if you allow it to stagnate, if you ignore the gift, then it will fade from you. Once upon a time, all elves could weave their magic. Now, only a handful remain that remember how.'

'All elves?' Scarlett's eyes widened as she thought of Finn and Cadian nodded. 'It is our birth right. But being chased from our home meant that the few who remained focussed on survival. By the time we reached the humans, there was only a handful of us still casting.' Cadian's face had darkened while he spoke, and Scarlett suddenly realised what he was saying. 'You were there? You were one of the refugees?' Her voice shook. It was impossible, the elves arrived on human shores over a thousand years ago.

'I was young, no more than a child by elven standards. But yes, I was there. Stubborn enough to keep my magic through the oppression, and the war that followed.'

Scarlett sat open mouthed at the revelation. Her future groom was over a thousand years old. *A thousand.* It made sense now that Alessandra was concerned, after all Cadian must've had hundreds of women in his lifetime, there could be nothing he hadn't experienced. What could Scarlett possibly offer a man like that? She took a big gulp of her wine and averted her gaze to her plate.

'I've made you uncomfortable.' Cadian's low voice surrounded her again and it felt like a blanket. When he spoke, she felt soothed.

'It's not that, it's just...'She paused. How could she possibly say what she was thinking? That a man like him couldn't possibly want an inexperienced virgin as his wife. 'Perhaps the Obsidian Window was wrong. Maybe we're not really soul mates.' She glanced at him as she spoke. A flicker of curiosity followed by confusion crossed his face and her heart fluttered again.

'I prefer to think that after a thousand years of loneliness, I have finally met the woman that will complete my soul. Scarlett, darling, you are all I have wanted for a thousand years.'

'Oh.' Her voice came out as a squeak as Cadian rose to his feet and slowly stepped around the table, it was almost predatory, the way he walked, and Scarlett found herself standing to meet him as he approached her. 'I wish to know every inch of you, Scarlett.' Cadian leaned in and gently kissed her neck, sending shivers through her body. 'I want to taste you.' He whispered as he pressed her backwards against the table edge.

'I want to fill you.' His lips moved against her skin as he spoke. 'I want to give you what no other man ever has.' His hands began roaming her back over her dress, but it still felt electric to Scarlett. Her breath quickened as she felt herself dampen for him. 'What's that?' She whimpered.

'Pleasure, my princess. Pure, orgasmic pleasure.' He lifted her onto the table and parted her legs with his own, pressing against her warmth with his hard bulge. His lips met her own and Scarlett melted into his embrace, closing her eyes against the sparks that fluttered across her skin, eliciting moans from her that hardened Cadian even more.

If she had opened her eyes she would have seen the darkness that emanated from Cadian, the corruption that flickered as black tendrils, wrapping around her as they kissed. Prickling at her mind, she could feel it. The oppressive darkness that almost made her want to cry as Cadian's fingers began to unbutton the back of her dress masterfully.

Not yet. Her inner voice whimpered.

A tear slid down her cheek as her eyes fluttered open to look at her future husband, he was suddenly across the room, crashing into the cabinet and sending delicate dinnerware crashing to the floor. Scarlett gasped at the speed in which he moved. 'You're crying.' He muttered between heavy breaths. 'Did I hurt you?'

Scarlett reached up and touched her cheek, wiping away the tear. 'No.' Scarlett thought hard, she couldn't place her finger on what had happened but for a few minutes there, she had been quite terrified. 'I'm sorry, I don't know what happened.'

Cadian straightened himself and crossed back to where Scarlett stood, wrapping his arms around her. 'It's alright my love. You're safe here.' He kissed the top of her head. 'Perhaps now is the time to rest? We can talk more tomorrow, and I'll show you the town?'

Scarlett nodded. 'I would like that very much.'

'Alright. I'll bring your dinner and maybe some books. You can spend the evening getting comfortable here. And if you need me, for company or...anything, call for me. I will always hear you.' Cadian had walked back to her side and reached behind her, picking up the plate of food in one hand and holding his other arm out for the princess.

It didn't take long to put Scarlett to bed and within minutes she was engrossed in his stories of romance and handsome princes that slayed dragons for the woman they loved. Cadian smiled as he closed the door to her room and slowly made his way through his home to his study and finally, to his favourite chair. It was a puzzle to him, this situation. The princess was physically begging for him, that much he could feel. And as he expected, as the passion built, the corruption had begun to flow between them. The magic was working. So, what had upset her? Could she feel the darkness? The tendrils? The moment her eyes had opened, he had the overwhelming fear that she might see them. But it was impossible, they were ethereal, visible to him only. They shouldn't have caused her fear.

The magic required her to be a willing participant in this, he couldn't take her by force, she had to be completely his. But something was stopping her, making her afraid of him. Making her afraid of sex. The mage had a limited amount of patience, and this was beginning to wear it down. The lust she felt should be enough to have her whimpering for him. So why wasn't she?

Cadian watched the fire burn as he pondered. She had been willing for Mateo to fill her, mewling for him like a little whore. He balled his fists as he remembered listening to the sounds she made while she writhed beneath the stain of an elf. The sounds that filled him with a jealous rage. Scarlett was his and his alone, and now no one would ever touch her.

But, somewhere along the line had come a blockage. Something that wouldn't allow her to give herself completely over to pleasure, to Cadian. Was it Mateo? His behaviour in the tavern, his attempt on her life? It was possible that his attack had left Scarlett more protective of herself. Which made Cadian's work more difficult. His fingers swept aimlessly over his chin and bottom lip while he thought.

The woman needed to believe she was safe here, under his protection. Not only that, but that she was capable of protecting herself if she ever needed to and the only way was to teach her how to kill. Scarlett needed to be convinced of her own strength and it was clear that she had plenty. No woman had ever said no to Cadian, no woman had ever wanted to. The princess was a unique creature.

It's a shame she must die.

Cadian caught himself quickly as his mind played over the plan. For a moment there was a pang of something. Was it guilt? Or perhaps regret?

No.

This would not be tolerated. Cadian could not grow to like the target of his corruption. She is an ingredient in his magics. Nothing more.

And back to the matter at hand, there was something in the basement of his home that Cadian intended to use to teach Scarlett just how strong she could be. By sundown tomorrow, Scarlett would be his. Body and soul.

Sweet Revenge

Amber leaves drifted past the window as Scarlett opened her eyes to the bright morning light. It already looked like it was going to be a lovely day, warm as pie her father used to say on particularly nice days. It brought about a pang of sadness to think of the King and Scarlett sucked in a long breath. Missing her father was inevitable, it had been just the two of them for her whole life. He was her entire world.

Not anymore.

Now there was Cadian, with his dark eyes that bored into her, the intensity that swirled around him was palpable. With newfound excitement for the day ahead, Scarlett practically leapt from her bed and prepared herself for breakfast. Before long she was skipping down the stairs, following the smell of freshly baked bread. What she found in the kitchen took all of the air out of her lungs.

There stood Cadian with his usual straight backed, serious demeanour. But he was up to his elbows in flour as he firmly kneaded a lump of dough on the counter. He faced away from her as she walked in, but she had made no attempt to hide her approach.

'Good morning, darling. I trust you slept well.' He didn't turn as he spoke, just continued his work.

'Oh, it was lovely.' Scarlett sat herself at the counter and picked at the fresh berries that sat in a bowl. Popping one into her mouth. 'I have to say, chef Cadian is quite the sight.' She chuckled and for the first time, Cadian stopped and turned slowly, a smirk plastered on his face. 'Oh really?' He asked, his voice still low but with a slight hint of joviality. Scarlett wondered what it must sound like when he laughed.

'Yes really. I could get used to this.' She popped another piece of fruit into her mouth and almost choked on it as Cadian swept across the room to her side. He was so fast, it took her breath away. Gently, slowly, he placed a kiss on her cheek and Scarlett felt the familiar butterflies take flight inside her at his closeness. He paused for a moment, his lips edging closer to her own before sighing heavily and going back to the bread.

'Tell me, Scarlett. Did you receive schooling in the palace?'

Scarlett felt her head whirl at the speedy change of pace and suddenly found herself thinking about Mrs Crenshaw. Her old teacher at the castle. 'I did. My father considered education of the Royal family to be a top priority. He used to say that intelligence made the difference between a king and a politician.'

'What did you learn? Arithmetic? Science?' He paused for a moment and turned to look at Scarlett.

'A bit of everything, I suppose.' She answered and yet he didn't look satisfied. What is he probing for? She wondered.

'I adore the specificity of your answers, princess.' Cadian's voice had taken on a somewhat sarcastic note that Scarlett did not appreciate one bit.

'If I am to be your wife, Cadian then I would expect you to say whatever it is you want to say. If there's something you want to know then just spit it out. I do not wish to play games with you. I'm not a child anymore.' Scarlett sighed and ate the last berry from the bowl. When she glanced at Cadian, he seemed frozen, one eyebrow raised staring at her. 'What?' She asked. 'Do you think I'll sit here like the quiet obedient little woman? If that's what you're looking for then perhaps I should return to my father.' Scarlett turned away and began heading for the doorway. Whilst she had never been a rebel or a dissident, she wasn't exactly a wallflower and she had never expected a husband that would treat her as a trophy or decoration. Perhaps she had allowed herself to become so caught up in the search for love that she was willing to ignore the red flags. Truthfully, her desire for Cadian was so fierce that she didn't feel like her choices were her own when he was near. He had a hold on her, and that couldn't possibly be a good thing for the future Queen.

As she reached the open doorway a hand wrapped gently around her wrist. She allowed him to slow her but didn't turn to look at him. If she had any chance of getting through a conversation with him without giving in to lust, then she absolutely must not look at him.

'I'm sorry.' His voice was so low it was almost a growl. 'I have lived for many years, and I have never had a woman leave me without words.'

Scarlett pondered for a moment, she knew that he had known many women before her, but he seemed perfectly capable of speaking right now. It seemed unlikely that she could have any such hold over him. 'I don't believe you.'

Cadian edged closer to her. 'You...intimidate me.' He whispered. 'You are the future Queen, Scarlett. I'm a lot of things, but I'm not Royal. I don't know how to love you.'

It hit Scarlett at that moment that she had been so wrapped up being awestruck by this beautiful, ancient creature that she hadn't realised her own power here. She sighed heavily as she turned to face him. 'You can start by just being honest with me. When you asked about my schooling, what exactly did you want to know?'

'I was curious if the royal family prepared their children for war.' Cadian looked at the ground while Scarlett absorbed what he just said. War? Why would that be on his mind? What possible reason could he have for asking about her ability to kill innocents in a mindless war. Scarlet was many things, but she was not a murderer.

'I can see why you didn't want to ask.' She muttered.

'My reasoning was twofold. Please, come sit down with me, let me explain.' Cadian pleaded as he pulled her arm back towards the kitchen. She allowed herself to be moved across the room and sat back on the stool with her arms folded.

'Our union may well reignite the bitter rivalry between humans and elves. We cannot say that having an elf as a king will unite both sides, Princess. There may be dark times ahead and I wanted to make sure my wife would be safe.' Cadian sat on the stool beside her and took her hands in his own. Scarlett felt her stomach flip as his skin touched hers. It felt like fire.

'I know, Cadian. But there's nothing I can do to change the will of my people except show them that no matter what, I am still their Queen.' She paused studying his face that didn't seem to change. 'What was the other reason?' She asked gently and watched as his face darkened.

'The other reason...is revenge.' Cadian looked into Scarlett's eyes, and she felt suddenly exposed. Like he could see inside her. His grip on her hands tightened slightly and she saw his jaw clench and unclench. Anger was taking over him.

'What do you mean?' Scarlett was frozen to her seat, too scared to look away from her fiancé who was beginning to look like a caged animal.

'Someone hurt you, Scarlett.' Cadian growled. 'He was going to kill you.'

'Mateo.' She whispered, the realisation hitting her. 'But, I'm safe now and the guards have him. We don't need to waste our thoughts on a creature like that.'

'The guards don't have him.' His voice was low as he looked away. 'I do.'

'What?' Scarlett finally freed her hands from Cadian's and slid off the stool slowly. 'He's here?' Anger began to flood her veins. 'You brought him here? To our home?' Her voice was raising, how could he do this to her. Mateo assaulted her, tried to kill her and if it wasn't for Finn, he would've succeeded. 'Get him out of this house!' She screamed at Cadian who hadn't moved an inch.

'He will not leave while his heart still beats.' Finally, Cadian rose to his feet. He suddenly seemed far taller than he had ever been. 'And it's your duty to finish him, Scarlett.' He gripped her wrist firmly and pulled her through the kitchen once more. This time, no amount of defiance would help against his strength. Scarlett found herself being dragged through a door at the far side of the room and down a set of wooden stairs into the darkness below.

It took a few minutes for her eyes to adjust to the environment but soon she could see him. Mateo. His arms were pulled above his head and held in metal cuffs. They in turn were chained to the ceiling and Mateo hung there, in the centre of this stone walled dungeon. Scarlett froze and Cadian turned to her gripping her by both shoulders. 'This man tried to defile you. To kill you. And you wouldn't have been the first.'

Scarlett's eyes widened. 'What?'

'They found a dead woman, a night worker that had been called to the chambers he had paid for. She had been raped and murdered, Scarlett. And her hair was red, like yours.' His voice was silk again, his grasp of the princess had become gentle, there was genuine concern showing in his eyes and Scarlett let herself get wrapped in the comfort it provided. 'The tavern owner said that Mateo had asked for a woman with red hair specifically. She died a painful and violent death, simply because she looked like you.'

Scarlett stole a glance at Mateo. He was watching them talk but looked weak, like there was no fight in him. He was simply waiting to die. When she looked back to Cadian, she felt his soft hand gently cup the side of her face. 'He needs to be punished for what he has done, my love. He is a killer, he deserves to rot in hell for his crimes.'

'You're right.' She heard the words slip past her lips and grimaced. 'But I can't...'

'Yes, you can, Scarlett. You are a saviour of a woman. Anyone can see that. You're pure of heart, my love. But you're also filled with passion, and you can turn that into fire to burn the wicked.' He pressed the handle of a dagger firmly into her palm. 'He has committed atrocities against you, against the poor woman in your own city walls. He tried to force his way inside you, Scarlett.' Cadian growled slightly at his own words. 'I want you to end him.'

'I... I can't.' She muttered, stepping away from Mateo.

'If you don't do it, my love, then I will.' Cadian stepped closer to the bound man. 'I will rip his still beating heart from his chest for what he did to you.' Cadian turned quickly to face Scarlett. 'You are mine and mine alone. No one touches you.'

The feeling that spread through Scarlett was one of defiance. She was Cadian's. His love, his soul mate, and Mateo had tried to rob them of that. He had killed a woman, just like Scarlett. He was the evil one.

She looked down at the sharp blade. 'I can do this.'

'Yes...you can pet.'

Scarlett looked to Mateo and stepped closer. 'You told me I could trust you.' As she spoke, she felt like she was trembling all over, but the words came out clear, commanding.

Mateo looked up at her, his brow furrowed. 'Please don't, I can be better, I promise. I'll never hurt anyone.'

Scarlett took another step. 'If Finn hadn't been there, you would have raped me.'

'No, no, I wouldn't! I didn't mean it! I'm sorry, please Scarlett!' Tears rolled down his face as the princess stood before him. 'Please, have mercy.'

And there she stood. A dagger in her hand and a heart filled with hate for the murderer before her. She wondered for a moment if the woman he killed had begged for her life, pleaded with him to have mercy. But he didn't, there was nothing but evil inside Mateo. Destroying him now would rid her kingdom of it. Her hand shot forward and the blade plunged deep into Mateo's chest. He gasped in pain and looked down to where the handle protruded.

Blood trickled slowly from his lip as he looked back up at Scarlett. It only took a few seconds for the life to drain from him and he hung limply from the chains.

Scarlett let out a long breath and turned into the open arms of Cadian. 'I'm so proud of you, my love.' He whispered into her ear.

Making a Move

'Your Majesty, I extend my deepest condolences for the profound loss of your beloved daughter. Her passing is an immeasurable tragedy, and my heart aches alongside yours in this time of grief. As your court mage, it is my duty to offer solace and aid in any way I can during these difficult days.' Alessandra stood before King Farandorn who sat in his chair, a broken man. Three days had passed since Alessandra had broken the news to the king and his grief could be felt throughout the palace.

Farandorn's puffy red eyes met with the court mage's gaze, and he nodded while letting out a deep sigh. 'I know, Alessandra.'

'My liege, I am here to provide guidance should you seek it. Your wisdom and strength have always inspired those around you, and I am certain that you possess the resilience to overcome this sorrow. Your daughter's memory shall forever remain a cherished part of your kingdom's legacy. Should you ever require counsel or support in matters both personal and regal, I humbly offer my expertise. It is my sincerest wish to see you find solace and to contribute to the well-being of the realm in any capacity you deem fit.' She paused and closed the gap between herself and the King, kneeling before him and taking his hand in her own. 'Please know that my allegiance lies with you, Your Majesty, and my services are at your disposal whenever you may need them.'

'What am I to do now? I'm an old man, Alessandra and I've lost my daughter and only heir to the throne. The Era of the Rose dies with me, and I have to plan for what comes next.' Fresh tears fell down his round cheeks. 'I made no preparations for such a thing as this.'

'I know.' Alessandra gently wiped the tears from Farandorn's cheeks with a lace handkerchief. 'If you might indulge me for a moment, your Highness, I have lived through a great deal of the Era of the Rose, and during your reign, you brought elves into your court. You brought me into your world. You trusted me.' Alessandra replaced the handkerchief with her own hand, gently caressing the king's cheek. 'Throughout our years working together, I have witnessed first-hand your vision for our realm and the depth of your dedication. As your court mage, I have strived to uphold those principles and share in your aspirations. My unwavering loyalty, knowledge of the kingdom's affairs, and deep understanding of your desires make me confident in my ability to support you as both a trusted companion and-' She paused moment while she inhaled deeply. 'A Queen Consort.'

Farandorn looked down at the mage for the first time in the entire conversation, his eyebrows furrowed, almost meeting in the middle and his mouth falling open slightly. 'What?' He asked.

'Consider the prophecy. *She will come to unite the world.* We all believed this meant Scarlett, but we were wrong. Maybe it's me. I came here after the Era of the Stone, I watched the Rose grow and now, as an elf, I can unite both our peoples and prevent a war. We are on the brink, Farandorn. I can give you an heir, both elf and human. Together, we can save Novastraad from itself.'

Alessandra was on her knees, one hand on the King's cheek and the other clamped around the kings own, flinching slightly from the pain of the burn that would not heal. 'The Era of the Rose does not have to die with you.'

Silence fell upon the room. Alessandra knew she had overstepped, but this was the one time she had to be willing to go further than she ever had before. She had to secure her place by the King's side before Cadian's corruption began to influence humanity.

Farandorn looked down at Alessandra and nodded slightly. 'Perhaps you're right.' his voice came out defeated. Beaten down by life itself. 'The Era of the Rose could live on with our heir.'

While the King mourned the loss of his daughter, Finn crested the hill that would lead him back to Fellglow but instead of seeing the familiar sight of the small town in the distance, the elf could only make out the smouldering remains of what was once his home. Smoke still rose from the blackened, charred bones of the houses and shops and Finn's heart sank.

It wasn't too far-fetched to believe someone had once again made an attempt on the life of the princess. Somewhere out there was a person that wanted her dead. Finn gritted his teeth.

They'll have to go through me.

He and Star rode hard for the next few hours, reaching Fellglow as dusk began to fall upon them. Where once stood charming houses with thatched roofs and vibrant gardens, there were now only charred ruins. The flames had reduced Finn's once-happy home to a crumbling blackened structure, it's walls scorched and collapsed. The spirit of the village was extinguished as the fire ravaged through the entire community, leaving no survivors in its wake.

The tavern it had been a place where the villagers would gather as the sun set to share stories, laughter, and camaraderie. It was the place he and Scarlett had met. But now stood as a hollow shell. Its roof had caved in, and the charred beams that once supported it were a harsh reminder of the destructive force of fire. The warm glow that once emanated from its windows had been replaced by darkness and silence.

The air was heavy with the scent of burnt wood and lingering smoke. The village had been wiped out entirely. As he walked through the remnants, Finn called out desperately hoping to hear a voice calling back. Even just one solitary survivor. But he was met with only silence. Fellglow was no more.

Finn blinked back tears as he climbed back onto Star and began the ride to the Palace. It wouldn't take more than a few hours if he could keep up a good pace. Someone had to report to the King about Scarlett and the danger she was in. If needed, he would lead the guards to her new home and bring both her and her fiancé back to the safety of the Palace.

Losing Herself

Scarlett stared at herself in the mirror. She still looked the same, still looked like Scarlett Rose, Princess of Novastraad. But she wasn't just that, a new word applied to her now. A dark word.

Murderer.

Scarlett tried to shake the thought away as she turned away from her reflection. She had to focus on the words Cadian had used.

Powerful

Beautiful

Exquisite

She shook her head at the concept of Cadian finding her exquisite. There was still this feeling in the back of her mind that someone as old and powerful as him couldn't possibly see anything to love in her. She was too young, too naïve, and now...

Murderer

Scarlett frowned as she began to pace the room. She needed something to take her thoughts away from what she had done. Something to drive the vision of Mateo going limp from her mind. She needed Cadian, he'd know exactly how to help her, how to make her feel human again.

Anxiously, Scarlett opened the door to her room and began searching the house, her heart beating faster with each passing moment. She checked every room in the house except one. The one she was avoiding on purpose, his bedroom.

Nerves prickled across her skin as she made her way through the manor and quickly found herself standing outside the wooden door. Cadian was on the other side and Scarlett knew one thing for certain. In this moment, she wanted to see him, she wanted him to hold her in his arms. But on his bed? In his room? She knew where that would lead. She took a deep breath and held it. If she went into that room tonight, she wouldn't come out the same. She would be his.

Letting out the breath, she knocked gently on the door.

'Come in, pet.' His voice crept through the wood.

There he was, lying on his bed in just his breeches and a linen shirt, reading from an old leather bound book. He looked at her as she creaked open the door and smiled warmly at her arrival. 'Please, make yourself at home.'

The room was much like her own, panelled in deep mahogany with a four poster bed sitting against the far wall. There wasn't much in the way of decoration besides a few oil paintings and a large ornately carved wardrobe.

She tried not to look at Cadian as she sat down on the edge of his bed and stared out of the window and quickly a feeling of awkwardness washed over her. She didn't know how to tell him that she was here for comfort. That she wanted to be in his arms. The sound of the book closing gently drew her attention and she felt the bed shift behind her as Cadian edged closer. 'What brings you to my room, love?' That last word was whispered into her ear followed by a gentle kiss on her neck. Scarlett let out an involuntary gasp at the feel of his lips on her skin. Desperately her mind searched for words, but all she could come up with was. 'I'm a murderer.'

The gentle kisses stopped, and her body ached at the absence of Cadian. She stuttered as she tried to explain. 'I mean, I'm here because I can't stop thinking about what happened today.' Scarlett turned and knelt on the bed facing Cadian. 'I know that I was ridding the world of him, and that he doesn't deserve my pity but...'

'But it's the first life you've taken.' Cadian sighed as he wrapped Scarlett in his arms and pulled her onto his lap. She straddled him and rested her head on his chest as he held her. She could hear his heart beating. 'I doubt there's a single person in the world that could do what you did today and be unaffected.' Cadian placed a gentle finger under her chin. 'Just know, Scarlett Rose, that you are brave, you are beautiful and in my thousand years I have never met someone that could take my breath away like you do. There isn't a bad bone in your body. You're no murderer. You're a hero, my darling.'

The words swirled around in Scarlett's mind, and she felt her heart beating faster as she looked into his eyes. She lifted herself slightly and pressed her lips to his, sharing a soft kiss.

A sigh escaped her, one of contentment. Of all the compliments she had ever been given, hero had never been one of them. For the first time she didn't feel like the little princess, innocent and sweet. She felt like a woman. For years Scarlett's beauty was the object of peoples fascination. She was referred to as the Porcelain Rose, beautiful and delicate. But no one had ever spoken of her heart, her nature before. Until Cadian. He saw her for the woman she was and slowly, Scarlett was starting to see the same.

'Say it again.' She whispered against his mouth, trying not to break the kiss and she felt a smile creep across his face.

'You are...' He placed a chaste kiss on the corner of her budding lips before moving slowly down to her neck, kissing her skin. He applied a little pressure and let his tongue slide against her, tasting her skin, 'A hero.'

Scarlett moaned as he nuzzled into her neck, wrapping her arms around him. The warmth in her core slowly began to spread and she wanted to feel him against her. She wanted to feel that pressure.

His evening stubble scratched slightly at the peak of her breasts as Cadian trailed kisses towards the neckline of her dress. Her heart was beating so fast she was certain he would be able to hear it. Her heart always beat quicker for him, usually because she was slightly afraid. But not tonight. She had no fear of her fiancé and allowed her hands to roam the sides of his body, pulling his shirt free of his breeches. As she slid her hands beneath the fabric, she felt the warmth of his skin. He felt like he was on fire.

Like he was burning for her, she felt him growl against her skin and her stomach filled with butterflies.

In one swift, fluid movement Cadian had gathered her frame into his arms, turned slightly, and lay her gently on the bed. Scarlett relaxed against the pillow, tendrils of her loose curls decorating the steel grey fabric of the pillowcase. Cadian's mouth pressed against hers once more, using his tongue he parted her lips and deepened the kiss, manoeuvring himself between her legs. She could feel his hardness press against her, the pressure she so desperately wanted. She let out a moan as she lifted her hips in an effort to grind against him but felt him move away slightly onto his knees. He ended the kiss and rested his forehead against her own. 'Scarlett.' He whispered. 'If I allow this to continue, then you will leave this room a little less virtuous in the morning.'

'I know.' She whispered back. 'I knew the moment I stepped into the room. I'm yours, Cadian. Completely.'

He didn't say another word.

Instead, one of his hands roamed down her body as he leaned back down, kissing her with a passion she had never experienced. His fingers began gathering the fabric of her dress. It seemed to take him a while and suddenly the kiss was broken, and he was looking into her eyes with a smirk. 'How much fabric does a princess really need in her dress?'

Scarlett smiled as he slowly made his way down her body, coming to rest between her legs as he finally lifted all of her underskirts away. Scarlett looked down, her view blocked by the ruffles. She was blind to his next move and held her breath, waiting for him to touch her.

She felt Cadian slowly graze his fingers down the inside of her calves, lifting them slightly, one at a time, to bend at the knee. The sweet smell of her arousal began to fill the room as her legs gently parted for him. Scarlett still wore her undergarments but could already feel how ready she was for him as her wetness seeped through the thin material. Slowly Cadian pulled down the soft cotton garment that covered her innocence and she knew then that there would be no turning back.

Her skin was buzzing with a mixture of excitement and nerves. Scarlett instinctively allowed her legs to fall back open exposing her slick pink core to him. The air was cool against the moisture that pooled there as her clit throbbed impatiently waiting to be touched. Then suddenly, electric flashed through her body as Cadian swiped a finger between her swollen lips. Scarlett let out a gasp as Cadian swirled a finger in her juices, bringing them up to paint her engorged bud. 'That feels good, doesn't it darling?' Cadian hummed while Scarlett began to writhe beneath his touch. 'It's unlike anything I've known.' Her breathy voice quivered as she spoke.

This was new. The things Mateo had done to her felt good, but Cadian's touch was pure ecstasy. She needed more.

As Cadian drew painfully slow circles with his wet finger, Scarlett raised her hips, trying to find his hand, desperate to see where this feeling would lead. 'I'm going to have to clean up some of this sticky mess you are making, my sweet.' Cadian's voice echoed around her mind, had he said that out loud? Scarlett didn't know anymore. her toes were beginning to curl as she became lost in the ever rising swells of warmth inside her.

Suddenly the finger was gone as Cadian leaned closer. She felt the soft touch of his tongue as he began lapping from her opening to her clit. He chuckled against her flesh. 'You taste exquisite, my pet. Comparable to the finest wines.' He purred and darted his tongue into her as Scarlett let out another moan. She was getting closer to the edge, grasping the bedsheets tightly so she wouldn't float away. Cadian worked against her pert bud, building the pressure inside her until she felt ready to burst. But she didn't want this to end, not without feeling him inside her. Never before had Scarlett been this close to what felt like an approaching explosion, and she didn't know what would come after. The only thing she knew for certain is that she wanted him to enter her. Right now.

Scarlett pulled up onto her elbows, looking down over the folds of her dress. 'Cadian,' She moaned. 'I want you to fuck me.' Slowly she felt the tongue slip away and saw the beautiful elven man rise up from her. 'Oh Scarlett, you don't know what it does to me when you use language like that.' He grinned as he crawled up the bed and placed a kiss on Scarlett's lips, she could taste herself, it was new. As her lips parted, his tongue found its way back into her mouth and she pressed herself against him as they kissed. Quickly, Cadian rose to his knees, pulling Scarlett with him and effortlessly pulling apart the lace backing of her dress, destroying it completely and rendering the garment useless.

She didn't care.

The material slipped away, leaving Scarlett naked and exposed to Cadian, her budding nipples painfully hard and crying out to be licked. His eyes devoured every inch of her as he slipped the remnant of her dress from under her knees and tossed it off the bed. Cadian was already pulling his shirt over his head and Scarlett's eyes widened at the bulge that was straining against his breeches. He reached down and freed himself as he pulled down his pants and tossed them aside. Scarlett allowed her eyes to roam his body. He was tightly muscled and pale skinned. When her eyes dropped lower, she saw for the first time his length and wondered for a moment how it was going to fit. Nerves tickled down her spine as her mouth went dry.

'Will it hurt?' she asked barely above a whisper, tearing her eyes away from his meaty cock. Cadian paused for a moment, as though he was considering a lie. 'Yes darling, but only for a moment.'

With care, Cadian lay Scarlett down and looked her over. Her breasts sat beautifully, begging to be devoured and as Cadian took one in his hand, Scarlett roamed the chords of muscles on his arms with her soft dainty fingers. Her back arched as he rolled her pebbled nipple between his thumb and index finger, still slippery from her arousal.

He positioned himself between her legs, opening them with his knee. This was it, this was the moment. Scarlett looked up into her lovers eyes and smiled. Cadian grabbed his solid cock, and let it slide over her wetness, rubbing it against her clit. Scarlett moaned slightly as he did, biting her bottom lip. He edged slowly into her opening, stretching her and pulling a gasp out of Scarlett while her eyes prickled with tears at the new sensation.

It did hurt. Not excruciating, but enough to make her very aware of what was happening. To accommodate him,

Scarlett allowed her legs to fall completely open as he pressed deeper.

'Breathe, love.' Cadian commanded and Scarlett inhaled a slow, ragged breath. As he slowly pushed further, her opening began to stretch more. Scarlett found herself digging her nails into his back. The word stop sat heavily on her tongue, but she choked it back. She truly didn't want this to end, she wanted him inside of her, she wanted to know where the building pressure would lead. Cadian would be her husband soon enough, she was safe with him.

The initial pain of stretching turning into a dull burn, followed by a sharp sting. Cadian was smiling down at her, softly. He was being purposefully gentle but there was more to him, he looked restrained, as though he wanted nothing more than to thrust vigorously into her. But he was being so slow, so gentle with her.

The tightness of her virginal walls were like a vice around his cock as Cadian moved gently in and out. Slowly at first, until she began to mould to him, squeezing him, but the initial friction was easing helped by her arousal. He moved painfully slowly, lifting his body enough to slide his hand between them and to her clit. He pressed his thumb against the nub and Scarlett brought her hips up quickly to meet him. The change in her moans brought a growl from Cadian's lips which only made her wetter. To see how much he wanted her made her slick and he was sliding in and out of her easily now, still adding pressure to her clit. Her hips moved to meet his every thrust, and the pressure was building once more, deep in her abdomen.

'Will I bleed?' Scarlett asked, her voice hitching as she tried to keep her composure. Cadian bowed his head picking up the pace and drawing a low moan from her lips. 'Perhaps, but I will drink it all.' He said lost in his own rapture. There was a fleeting moment of fear that sparked across Scarlett at his dark words, but the pleasure was building so quickly in her now that she allowed the thought to pass.

With his thumb pressed against her pulsing clit Cadian began to delve harder, her walls contracting around him. She knew she was close to her own perfect release, whatever was coming was coming now. It was as if he knew how her body was reacting and in response, Cadian thrust with more force, Burying himself as deeply inside her as he could. 'Come now my queen, don't hold back.' His voice had become deeper, more animalistic.

Scarlett's moans were erratic, her body overcome with an array of primal sensations, her stomach feeling tighter and tighter. There was a sharpening deep inside her core, but it wasn't painful, it was just new. And each time Cadian jutted into her, paired with the added pressure on her clit she felt like there was about to be an explosion. Waves of pleasure crashed over her as her entire body tightened then released. Scarlett cried out in pleasure and Cadian held her tightly, slowly pumping into her through the pleasure, adding more sensations. Her sweat soaked forehead pressed against Cadian's damp shoulder as she gave out, drenching him in her fluids. It was simply too much for Cadian who became lost in his own pleasure, ploughing forcefully into her as he groaned. Scarlett felt his whole body judder as he exploded inside her.

They were one.

Slow Corruption

As Cadian lay with Scarlett for the first time the threads of his magic that had been woven over centuries began to come alive. They pulsed with a darkness that came straight from his blackened heart and delicately weaved around the princess.

Scarlett had marred her soul when she killed Mateo. It wasn't self-defence, or the protection of the innocent. It was revenge. The cold blooded murder of a guilty man. Cadian pondered this as Scarlett slept beside him. The very act of violence that had been so cathartic for Scarlett had also opened her up to Cadian's spell. It gave the corruption something to cling to. He smiled. Humanity couldn't survive this. *She* couldn't survive this. A smile crept across his face as he gazed down at her. The ruination he had planned for her body hadn't happened yet. A gentle fuck to break her in was enough, next time she would be devoured. Next time, Cadian would play.

With newfound vigour, he rose from the bed and left the room, following the shadow filled corridors of his home until he reached his grand study. Once inside, he locked the door and flicked his hand. The movement ignited a spark and all the candles suddenly burst into flames bathing the book filled space in a warm glow. Cadian was here with a purpose. He had done his part, he had made the human love him and now, he needed to ensure that Alessandra had removed the King from his throne.

Cadian pulled open a cabinet and removed from it a large cast iron pot filled with silvery liquid. Placing it gently upon the table he waved a hand over it and closed his eyes, picturing the dark elf court mage, allowing his mind's eye to hone in on her. As the image of her became clear in his mind, Cadian opened his eyes to the silvery liquid and saw the Palace of Novastraad becoming clear. As the image became clearer it began to float towards a window in the castle, to where she was. But as it did, a burning light emanated from the image leaving explosions of stars in the mage's eyes. Cadian growled, *how had she done this? How had she blocked his vision?*

It didn't matter, he would break her magic and then he would break the mage. A practiced hand waved over the image casting a shadow over the liquid that settled gently.

As Cadian peered once more into the bowl the shadows dissipated.

But the blinding light remained.

Cadian growled again, a low rumble from the back of his throat, and he lifted the heavy liquid filled pot with one hand, roaring in anger as he thrust it across the room. Breathing heavily, he stumbled backwards and dropped into a soft chair, his chair. 'That bitch.' Cadian muttered as he leaned back into the chair. She had found a way to protect herself from his sight. There were only a few spheres of magic that were out of Cadian's grasp, and Alessandra had found one. 'She will die for this.' He growled once more.

Nevertheless, the corruption had begun. The magic had solidified the connection between the princess and her people and as Scarlett became overwhelmed with darkness so too would her people, and as she slowly died in exquisite agony, *so too would her people.*

And as he pictured the Princess writhing in pain, Cadian felt something new. A shot of pain in his blackened old soul. Conjuring the image of Scarlett dying in his mind had hurt his heart. A frown spread across his handsome face. That was a pain he hadn't experienced in almost a thousand years.

What has she done to me?

Was this love? Had he actually begun to feel for the human? *Absolutely not.* She was nothing more than a mortal pawn to him. Perhaps the slow corruption of the Rose would have to be cast aside. As much as he enjoyed the torture of human women, the potential threat must be extinguished. It was time to solidify their relationship. They will marry and he will be King.

Then Cadian can speed up the corruption, power it, make it fiercer. Scarlett Rose must die.

The Princess stretched and let out a yawn as she rolled over in the big soft bed, her red curls contrasting against the grey bedspread. She had expected to feel different, more mature somehow. But the version of herself that would greet her in the mirror that morning looked exactly the same. Except for the smile. She couldn't rid herself of the smile if she tried. It felt like all the worries she had ever had, had simply melted away.

Cadian was missing from the bed as she stretched out and she wondered if he was once again making breakfast for her. This time it would not be marred by a fight or interrupted by Mateo. The day was theirs to spend together. Slowly Scarlett dragged herself from the bed and sat in front of the mirrored desk. As she pondered on the pleasure from the night before, she began to pull a comb through her hair. That's how Scarlett noticed the dark strands that sat nestled within her own curls. She knew that growing old brought with it the perils of silver hair, but she never expected that sleeping with someone could turn your hair black.

It was just a small section, but it was enough to worry the princess. Perhaps elves and human's weren't supposed to mix. It was possible that someone as magical as Cadian could change a woman simply by being with her. Was it worth asking him? It seemed like the smart choice, but Scarlett was afraid of the answer. No, she would keep it to herself for now. There were enough books in this house, surely somewhere within them there would be answers.

As she arrived at the kitchen she found Cadian there, pouring boiling liquid into an earthenware cup. He turned at her arrival and smiled, handing her a drink of fresh coffee as he kissed her cheek gently. 'Good morning, my love. Please sit. We have much to discuss.'

Scarlett placed herself on the kitchen stool and sipped the hot beverage. It was sweet and rich. He has added something to it, chocolate maybe? She sipped again. *Definitely chocolate.* Suddenly, Cadian was at her side, taking the mug from her hands and holding them within his own. His dark eyes pierced into her own. It felt different now. If felt like he was a part of her.

'Scarlett last night was...' He trailed off, smiling as he remembered. 'You take my breath away.'

'I feared I wouldn't meet your expectations.' Scarlett spoke quietly, embarrassed by the words that fell from her lips, but she couldn't silence the memory of Alessandra, telling her how she would never satisfy him.

'Why so formal? If I am to be your husband, you can talk to me from your heart.'

Scarlett looked down at her hands, gently entwined with Cadian's. 'The first time I saw you, in the mirror, Alessandra told me that someone as inexperienced as I would not be able to...that you wouldn't enjoy...' Scarlett sighed, she might as well tell him the truth. 'Alessandra said that I would never be able to keep your attention.'

Cadian clenched his jaw then relaxed it quickly. 'Scarlett Rose, no woman has ever left a mark on my heart like you have.' Cadian lowered himself until he was kneeling before the princess. 'I know we are fated. I know that there is an expectation that we shall marry. But I need you to know that I am here on my knees asking that you be my wife, not because a mirror told you I was your soul mate, but because I have fallen in love with the woman that you are.'

Cadian reached a hand into his pocket and pulled free a black, velvet covered box. He slowly opened it to reveal a black diamond set into a platinum ring. 'This belonged to my mother. It was crafted in Eridar, the home of the elves before Ilvanya Vo. It is with this ring that I ask you, will you be my wife, Scarlett Rose?'

A proposal. A proposal from Cadian. Scarlett's heart was beating so hard in her chest that she fully expected it to come bursting out. This was the romance Scarlett had dreamed of for years. The love that was so intense that nothing could ever extinguish it. This wasn't being done out of duty, this was real. She held out her hand and smiled as her eyes welled.

'Of course.' She whispered as the first happy tear slipped down her pale skin. Cadian took the ring from the box and slid it onto Scarlett's finger. The fit was perfect. He rose to his feet and pulled Scarlett close to him, pressing his lips against her own. 'My wife.' He whispered against Scarlett's lips as she felt herself becoming ready to take him into her once more.

As morning turned into afternoon, Scarlett found herself craving Cadian's touch. But he had taken his leave of her for the day. Said he had many tasks to complete before night fell and with Scarlett by his side, he would get nothing done but filling her with pleasure. He had kissed her hard before he left, and Scarlett hoped for more, but the door closed and he was gone.

She took the opportunity to roam the house, looking at the books and the beautiful oil paintings that adorned the walls. She made herself a cup of tea and a sandwich and settled with an old book. She had wanted to find books on elven magic, but the library Cadian had was simply filled with story books. She chose one about love and passion in the face of certain peril and began to read. As the afternoon wore on, Scarlett decided on a walk. She had been cooped up in the house since she arrived here, and the grounds looks magnificent from the window. So, she left to walk the gardens of Cadian's Manor.

As the late afternoon sun began its descent, casting long, dramatic shadows across the land, the gardens surrounding the manor house seemed to transform into a mysterious and hauntingly beautiful realm. Nature's elements danced in perfect harmony, creating an atmosphere both enchanting and foreboding. The gardens were an intricate tapestry of lush vegetation and twisted, gnarled trees. The air was heavy with the scent of damp earth and rich, moss-covered stones. Dark, velvety petals of black roses unfurled in stark contrast against the deep green foliage, their beauty tinged with an air of darkness.

A small, murky pond nestled in a secluded corner of the garden, it's still waters reflecting the fading light of the sun. Dark lilies with midnight-blue petals floated on the surface, their delicate beauty concealing a hidden danger. Wisps of mist rose from the water's edge, creating an ethereal atmosphere that sent shivers down Scarlett's spine.

Gnarled trees, their branches reaching out like skeletal fingers, cast twisted silhouettes on the ground below. Moonflowers, their pale blossoms glowing softly in the fading light, bloomed among the shadows, their fragrance imbued with an otherworldly allure.

Scarlett made her way along the stone pathway, stopping to smell flowers and take in the beauty of the early evening blooms. As she walked, the stones beneath her feet slowly began to fade into the grass, leaving her to wander along the beaten path into the woods behind the manor. She didn't exactly know how far Cadian's land stretched on for and as the trees grew thicker around her, blocking out the last of the evening sun she decided it was time to make her way home. But as she turned, she wondered, which way had she come into the woods? Darkness was changing the way the landscape looked and a horrible realisation struck the princess.

She was lost.

Why is the house empty? Cadian wondered as he stepped quickly into his study. There were traces of Scarlett, a teacup and plate sat beside an open book on the table. But their owner was nowhere to be seen. 'Scarlett?' Cadian called out as he began to go from room to room. But he already knew she wasn't here. He could no longer feel her presence. An ability that unnerved him at first. It made him uneasy to believe he was connected to the human in that way, but ultimately put it down to the magic he had woven. It wasn't love, it was power.

As he walked to the kitchens, he saw the patio doors sitting open to the night air, moths had found their way towards the flames of the kitchen candles and Cadian steadied himself. *She's run from me.*

That was not acceptable.

Cadian gave chase. The princess could not be allowed to escape him now, if she was to find a way to break the connection, to save humanity...Cadian shook his head as he ran. A thousand years of work, gone in an instant. It wasn't worth thinking about.

He must find Scarlett.

Sharp thorns began to tear into Scarlett's ankles as she walked through the dense woods. The chill of the night air had penetrated the light shawl she had wrapped over her shoulders, and she shivered. Darkness had surrounded her and no matter how hard she tried, she couldn't make out a source of light anywhere. Her skin burned where it was ripped open by the aggressive plant life and Scarlett failed to hold back the tears. *I'm going to die out here.*

No one knew where she was, she'd left no note, no explanation. Cadian would think she had simply left him, jilted him. She wiped her face quickly as the cold made her tears sting. Quite suddenly Scarlett found herself in a clearing. Open space in which she wasn't under constant assault from the forest and while there was still some bracken and exposed roots beneath her feet. The ground seemed a lot easier to move over. *Maybe I can sleep here.* It was as good a place as any. She was going to be cold no matter what, but by the light of the morning, she may be able to find her way back. As her eyes drifted over the clearing, looking for a decent enough area of grass to lay down in, Scarlett noticed something new. A sound she hadn't heard before. A low rumble permeated the air, almost animalistic, almost like a growl. She turned quickly to see where the sound was coming from and was faced with two very large, very angry looking wolves.

Her heart beat faster as adrenaline pumped through her veins. Scarlett held very still, her body seemingly taking control away from her mind. She wanted to scream, to run...anything at all. But instead, she remained frozen in fear as the beasts approached her. As they stepped closer, Scarlett found her feet and stepped backwards, eliciting a deep growl from the wolves. They dropped low, preparing to pounce and Scarlett turned, filled with fear she ran as fast as she could. But as her foot caught one of the roots, she fell to the ground hard. The wolves would be on her any second, she closed her eyes and held in a breath. This was it.

Then came the blinding flash of light. Scarlett's eyes flew open, and she saw leather boots step past her. She turned her head to follow and found herself looking at Cadian, almost inhuman in his rage he looked at the wolves and growled. 'She is *mine.*' His arms swept through the air, seeming to gather dark energy which was quickly thrown at the beasts. They crumpled to the ground silently as Cadian pivoted and looked down at Scarlett.

It was almost as though a switch went off in his mind, his face went from contorted with rage to filled with concern. He dropped quickly to his knees and scooped Scarlett into his arms, and she held him tightly in return. Her heart was still hammering against her ribs, and she could not believe she still lived. 'How did you find me?' She whispered.

'I can feel you, Scarlett.' Cadian replied gently, stroking her hair and holding her against his chest. 'I can always feel you.'

The copper tub was filled with hot water and Cadian poured oils and swirled the liquid inside. Ordinarily he would've put her in the master bathroom to take care of herself, but he didn't want to let her out of his sight. Instead, he had returned home with her, wrapped her in a warm blanket and placed her on his bed. She would bathe in here where he could keep her safe.

Why do you want that? He found his mind asking and he grimaced.

She has to be protected until the connection has had chance to grow. He answered himself.

What happens then? When the corruption has taken her fully? His mind asked again.

Then I kill her. Silence followed, his brain had quietened. But only for a moment.

Are you sure about that?

He shook his head. Of course he was sure, it had been the plan all along. The human woman would be overwhelmed with the corruption and as she died, so would all of humanity. Then Cadian will step forth as King of the elves and lead his people to a better life.

You were scared of losing her.

Cadian clenched his jaw. He was afraid of having to start again, having to wait for another opportunity. His mind flashed back to Scarlett lying on the dirt with the wolves closing in and he felt his chest tighten. The vision of her brought with it a cold sweat. He thought he would lose her, right there in the clearing.

I do not love her.

'Cadian?' The voice gently wrapped around him, easing his internal turmoil. *Oh, how easy it was for her to calm him with just the mere mention of his name.*

'What?' He grunted back.

'I think the water is well mixed.'

Cadian looked down at his arm which was now elbow deep in the warm scented water and for the first time in centuries, he felt his cheeks flush. 'Of course. I'll be outside the door.' He turned to walk out of the room but stopped when he heard her voice once more.

'I thought you were to watch me while I bathe. To keep me safe.' She dropped the blanket and began to peel away her dress. Cadian felt himself harden in response and inhaled sharply as he stepped towards her. Taking her by the shoulders, he stopped the dress from falling away. 'If I were to watch you bathe, you would have no hope of resting tonight. You've had a difficult time.' He placed a gentle kiss on her forehead. 'I will be outside the door. Call me when you're finished and I will put you to bed.'

Scarlett nodded as Cadian left the room.

How much of that was for her benefit? How much of it was for yours? 'I don't...I don't think...fuck.'

Cadian Vordane was in love with the human.

Into the Palace walls

As dusk approached, Finn arrived at the King's city and bedded Star down in the stables. It would keep the beast warm and dry for a few days while Finn decided how his life was going to look. Scarlett had promised him gold if he reported back to her father of her safe arrival and while he hadn't expected to take her up on that offer, his newfound homelessness made it seem like the only viable option.

As he ventured further into the heart of the city known for its harmonious blend of architectural marvels and natural beauty, he became lost in his surroundings.

The city's layout was a captivating fusion of elegance and functionality. Cobblestone streets meandered gracefully, lined with ornate lampposts that illuminated the pathways with a warm, ethereal glow after dusk. Elaborate archways, intricately carved with symbols of ancient lore, connected bustling districts, each with its unique charm and purpose.

The streets were quieter than Finn expected. He was anticipating a vibrant tapestry of people, both human and elven but instead found only a few people meandering along the cobbled streets, whispering in hushed tones.

As Finn continued his exploration, he looked up at the palace that sat above the city on a stone plateau. From all corners of the palace walls black material flapped in the breeze and Finn realised that they were black flags adorning the Palace of King Farandorn. They symbolized a time of mourning and solemnity. It was possible that the city was morning the loss of Fellglow, but ultimately unlikely. Such a small village would hold no bearing to the citizens of the city. This was something else.

An older woman, hunched over with a black scarf meandered down the street towards Finn holding a netted bag filled with green apples. She manoeuvred to walk past the elf, but he sidestepped into her path. 'My lady, please can you tell me why the palace is in mourning?'

The woman looked up at Finn, her blue eyes glassy from recent tears. 'You don't know?' She asked as she looked him over. But her face changed quickly as her eyes wandered over the points of Finn's ears. 'I wouldn't expect an *elf* to care.'

Again, she tried to move past him, but Finn continued to block her path. 'Please, if this is about Fellglow...it was my home'

The woman's eyes widened. 'You survived the fire?' She took a step towards him, surprise turning into anger. 'An elf survived while our...' She choked on a sob while she tried to get the words out. Finn felt his blood run cold as she tried to continue. '*You* should've died in the fire and our Scarlett should still be here.' More sobs burst from the woman as she shoved past Finn and made her way down the street. Scarlett died in the fire? That was impossible, she was safe in Briar Heath Manor. Finn frowned. If the King mourned his daughter, then he would simply explain to the king that she was alright, and then awkwardly ask for his payment. Finn rolled his eyes at himself. This felt ridiculous.

The wall that surrounded the Palace was designed to protect the inhabitants of the castle from a siege. It was built in the Era of the Stone while tensions were running high between the humans and the elves. The King at the time believed that the palace was large enough to house all the humans in the city and protect them from the horrors of war. And he was right. No one ever expected that it would be a human that ran a sword through the chest of the King and ended the Era.

Guards patrolled the top of the wall with crossbows in hand and the main gate was protected by four men that raised their swords as Finn approached. 'Good morning, fellas.' He called out but they didn't flinch. 'You must know an unarmed elf when you see one.' Finn held his arms out, 'I am here with a message for the King.'

'The King is busy preparing for the wedding.' One of the guards called back.

Wedding? 'What wedding?' Finn asked as he closed the gap.

'The King has chosen a new Queen.' The guard replied.

'Yeah, one of *your* kind.' Another guard muttered.

Finn stepped back involuntarily and ran his hands through his hair. 'He's getting married because he thinks he's lost his heir?'

A guard at the back rushed forward towards Finn, stopped only by the guard in front holding his arm out. It was clear the mention of Scarlett was a touchy subject. 'She's not just *an heir.* She was our princess!' He cried out.

'I'm sorry, I didn't meant to-' Finn tried to apologise but was quickly cut off. 'You need to leave.' The guard's voice was low. We don't want *more elves* here.'

Finn sucked in a deep breath, this might even get him beat up by four guards but it needed to be said. 'Scarlett's alive.'

An uneasy silence fell. No one quite knowing what to do or say. Finn broke it. 'I need to see the King. Now.'

'No.' The voice was quiet and seemed overwhelmed with emotion. Finn glanced at the guard that spoke. 'Your lies will not be tolerated, elf. Let the King mourn his loss in peace, or you will find yourself impaled by my blade.'

The face of the guard was red and angry, it was clear he was trying to keep himself in check but was barely managing. Finn took a step back hands raised slightly. 'Alright. I'm sorry, I'll go.' Turning away, Finn began the walk back to the market district. He would need shelter for the night and was going to need to find work. It was going to be a rough time for the elf. It was often said that the royal city was a welcoming place for his people and Finn had held that belief for all of his years. But perhaps in their grief, the humans true nature became apparent. His mind raced with a mix of disappointment, confusion, and determination. The city that had once seemed like a beacon of hope now revealed a darker side, clouded by grief and resentment. Yet, he refused to give up on his mission to deliver the news of Scarlett's survival to the King.

Nightfall draped the city in a cloak of shadows, but the lamplights continued to cast their warm glow, guiding Finn's path through the cobblestone streets. He sought refuge in a modest inn, its wooden sign creaking with each gust of wind. Inside, the atmosphere was sombre, matching the prevailing mood of the city. The innkeeper, a middle-aged man with weary eyes looked up as Finn entered. 'What do you need?' He asked as Finn approached the bar.

'A room for the night, nothing more.' Finn placed a silver piece on the bar. One of the few he had left, and the barman nodded. 'Alright. Down the hall to the right. Door marked GUEST. It's yours until noon tomorrow.'

A few moments later Finn was laying on the bed, staring at the ceiling, contemplating his next move. The thought of Scarlett and the mourning flags gnawed at his thoughts. If he couldn't reach the King directly, he needed an alternative approach, some way of getting word to the King of his daughters survival. A letter perhaps? Although if he's planning to marry out of grief, it's unlikely he'll take the time to read it. plus, there's always the risk that he won't believe it. No, this would have to be face to face.

'Come on Finn, think.' He muttered. And suddenly it seemed so obvious. A royal wedding meant planning, guests and workers all coming and going. And Finn needed legitimate work. He sat up quickly, a smile spreading across his face. At first light, Finn was going to get a job.

A Celebration of Love

The quaint chapel nestled in the heart of Briar Heath exuded an enchanting aura, beckoning all who passed by. With its weathered stone walls draped in ivy and a thatched roof adorned with wildflowers, it seemed like a timeless sanctuary of love and devotion. As evening approached, the warm glow of lanterns began to illuminate the chapel's entrance, casting a golden hue on the cobbled pathway.

The silhouette of Cadian's manor stood in the distance, reminding the people of the village who they could thank for their protection. Briar Heath had stood strong against the warring armies of both humans and elves, thanks to the magic of Cadian Vordane. The reason for that protection was known only to the dark mage himself. Nevertheless, the people of the village respected the man who saved their homes long before they were even born.

Entering the church through the intricately carved wooden doors, guests were greeted by an intimate space filled with an air of anticipation. Sunlight filtered through stained glass windows, painting vibrant hues of ruby, emerald, and sapphire on the polished wooden pews below. Fragrant tendrils of incense wafted through the air, lending a serene ambiance.

At the front of the chapel, a simple yet elegant altar awaited the bride and groom. The altar, adorned with delicate lace and garlands of blush roses, served as a symbol of purity and the blossoming love between Scarlett and Cadian. Candles of various sizes, arranged in graceful clusters, flickered softly, casting dancing shadows upon the stone walls. It was designed to delight the Princess, to keep her enraptured by Cadian.

To the side of the altar, a small ensemble of musicians positioned themselves, tuning their instruments with delicate precision. The soft melodies of violins and the gentle chords of a harp filled the chapel, weaving a tapestry of harmonious anticipation.

In preparation for the dusk wedding, the chapel's pews had been adorned with roses, perfuming the air. Every detail had been carefully attended to, from the silky ribbons tied to the pew ends to the rose petals scattered delicately along the aisle. With less than forty eight hours' notice, the people of Briar Heath had created the perfect wedding.

As the sun dipped below the horizon, casting a warm glow through the windows, the chapel was filled with an atmosphere of anticipation and joy. The stage was set for the union of Scarlett and Cadian, their bond was to be forged beneath the twilight sky in this enchanting sanctuary of Briar Heath.

Scarlett held her breath as she stepped out of the Manor and into the carriage that awaited her. She didn't know how Cadian had put all of this together so quickly. That morning she had been eating toast in bed and reading a romance novel when suddenly her room was filled with handmaidens carrying dresses and jewellery sent by her fiancé. Scarlett's eyes widened and she pulled her blanket over her nightgown, giving herself flashbacks to the morning she awoke to find Finn in her room. Buttered toast toppled down the bedspread leaving oily marks as she straightened up.

'What on earth is going on?' Scarlett asked the women in the room. 'Who are you people?'

One of the women, the one carrying a black suede case turned to the princess. 'I'm Arleya. Master Cadian requested our assistance this morning, your Highness, to prepare you for your wedding.' The woman smiled cheerfully and placed the case on the chest of drawers and opened it to reveal seven diamond necklaces.

'My wedding?' Scarlett asked? Cadian had only proposed yesterday. How were they talking about the actual wedding already? The woman nodded. 'Yes, it is the day of Aur'Iya today. It is a sacred day among elven kind.'

Scarlett glanced at the woman's ears but found them hidden by a headscarf. 'Are you...' Scarlett started.

'Elven?' She smiled again. 'Yes. One of very few here.'

Scarlett was stunned into momentary silence by the cacophony of noise in her room. She looked for words but only managed to ask, 'What's Aur'Iya?'

The maiden moved to Scarlett's bedside and sat gently. 'Aur'Iya is a day of celebration. My father used to say that back on our own Isles it was a day of great magical energy. It is important to our kind, almost celestial in nature. Weddings held on the day of Aur'Iya would be blessed for eternity. Ensuring the couple in love would be prosperous and have lives filled with joy.'

'That all sounds very nice.' Scarlett mumbled.

'You don't seem happy, love. Is everything okay?' The handmaiden asked and Scarlett blushed in return. 'Yes of course. It's all just unexpected. Is Cadian here?' Scarlett moved to get out of bed and the maiden stood up. 'He's down at the church. Preparing for tonight.'

Scarlett couldn't contain her disappointment as it spread across her face and the maiden put a hand on her shoulder. 'I know you're excited to see him. But in a few hours, you'll be by his side. I promise. in the meantime, let's get you ready.'

Several hours of bathing, essential oils and massages went by in a blur followed by hair and make-up by the handmaidens. As they pinned the copper curls up, Scarlett noticed more dark strands creeping through the red. She closed her eyes, as powdered colour was applied and soon she was being put into a dress. And oh, how she loved that dress.

It was a breath-taking vision of elegance and delicate beauty. Crafted with meticulous care, the gown was a testament to the skilled artistry of the finest designers. The ivory lace fabric, with its intricate floral patterns and delicate scalloped edges, adorned every inch of the gown, creating a sense of ethereal grace. Scarlett had no idea how it had been made so quickly, but it fit her perfectly.

The dress featured a classic A-line silhouette, fitted at the bodice and gradually flowing out into a sweeping skirt. The sweetheart neckline, framed by delicate lace straps, accentuated Scarlett's shoulders with a touch of understated allure. The bodice, expertly tailored to her figure, hugged her curves in all the right places, exuding a sense of timeless femininity.

Completing the ensemble, a cathedral-length veil, crafted from sheer tulle, gently framed Scarlett's face, cascading down behind her like a gossamer waterfall. Delicate lace appliques adorned the edges of the veil, harmonizing perfectly with the intricate lace of the gown. She looked at herself in the mirror and smiled. She wasn't just another human, she was the woman that stole the heart of an ancient elf.

With her head held high, Scarlett slipped into the carriage that awaited and smiled as they pulled away from the manor house. Cadian was waiting for her and by the time evening falls, she will be his wife.

Cadian stood at the altar of the church in a dark suit made of soft cashmere with a deep red silken cravat. His dark hair fell to his shoulders and framed his sharp features. The minister stood behind the decorated alter, preparing a batch of herbs and oils to be burned during the ceremony and Cadian watched him carefully. Before yesterday it wouldn't have mattered when they uttered their vows, they were a sham after all. A ploy to put Cadian in power as a prince. But now...things were different. He loved her. The plan needed to change.

The corruption was designed to kill fragile humans and Scarlett was the first intended victim. Instead, he was going to use the sacred power of Aur'Iya to connect her life to his own. She wouldn't die until he died. In the old days, elves used the ancient magic to ensure that soul mates would never have to live without each other. Cadian and Scarlett would be joined and the nothing would be able to take her from him.

The minister finished adding the herbs and began lighting candles while burning incense to purify the space and to allow the elven ancestors to watch the bonding of two lovers. Soon, the harp and violins filled the air with their music and Cadian turned to look at the door. Silhouetted against the setting sun was the most beautiful creature he had ever seen. His heart beat faster as she stepped down the aisle towards him, smiling the most perfect smile he'd ever seen. He was infatuated by this woman and couldn't understand why.

As she reached his side and he took her hand, Cadian leaned down and kissed her on the cheek. 'I love you, Scarlett Rose.' He whispered. And for the first time, he truly meant it.

The minister touched a flame to the herbs and a plume of blue smoke rose from the chalice. He lifted it high. 'Ancestors of elven kind, we ask that you witness this union on Aur'Iya and offer your most powerful blessing. That of eternal love.' He moved around the alter and placed the smoking chalice on the edge, allowing the fragrance to permeate the air around the couple.

'Today is a day of joy, for Lord Cadian Vordane has chosen a wife and blesses us with witnessing his union. My Lord, now is the time for you to commit yourself entirely to this woman. To vow to her your love.' The minister stepped back as he spoke and Cadian reached out, taking Scarlett's hands in his own and gazing into her eyes.

'Princess Scarlett Rose, in this moment, as the last of the dusk light weaves its magic upon us, I stand before you, as an elf consumed by a love that defies the boundaries of light and shadow. I vow to protect you, not only from the perils that lurk in the shadows but from any adversity that dares to threaten our unity. With every fibre of my being, I will be your shield, your guide, and your constant companion.'

The minister stepped forward once more and held out a ring. A simple band of platinum. Cadian took it and slipped it onto Scarlett's finger. 'With this ring, I bind our destinies together, intertwining our lives in a tapestry of passion and understanding. I offer you my heart, scarred and hardened by the trials of my past, trusting that your love will heal the wounds. I am your protector, your King and your love.' Cadian watched a tear make its way slowly down Scarlett's cheek and smiled as he wiped it gently away.

The minister turned to Scarlett. 'And your vow to Lord Cadian...'

Scarlett looked between the Minister and her husband to be with widened eyes. 'I wasn't prepared...' She whispered. Cadian smiled in return, 'You're simply meant to say what's in your heart.'

He watched as Scarlett took in a deep breath and nodded. 'Alright. Lord Cadian Vordane. My duty has always been to the Kingdom of Novastraad and its people. My purpose was to marry a man and make him the king. Though all my life I wished that I would find someone I could love, but I think I always knew I would marry out of obligation. And then I found you. Magic brought us together and our union will save the kingdom. But more than that, you have saved me from a life without love.'

The minister held a ring up to Scarlett and she gently placed it onto Cadian's finger. 'When my father placed a ring upon my mother's finger, he said it binds them together. So, I bind us, Cadian. In love, in loyalty, in life and in death.'

As she finished speaking, Cadian leaned close to Scarlett and pressed his lips gently against her own. The scent of her perfume intoxicated him. 'I wish for nothing more than I wish to rip that bodice from you and plunge into your depths.' He whispered. 'My wife.'

'Then we'd better hurry back to the manor.' Scarlett smiled wickedly.

As they stepped through the door, Cadian lifted Scarlett into his arms and carried her over the threshold. It was a human tradition but one that he believed Scarlett would hold dear to her now immortal heart. Eventually he would have to tell her the true effects of their union, but not today. What comes next for them is sacred, the physical bonding to finish the union magic. And Cadian did not intend to hold back.

'Can I get you a drink, my love?' He asked as he gently lowered Scarlett to her feet.

'Yes, that would be nice.' She smiled and his old heart ached. The poor girl had no idea what was to become of her this night and her innocence to his tastes made him stiffen slightly in his finely tailored trousers. Oh, how he would enjoy this, and the way she mewled when she was horny left Cadian confident that she would be amenable to his desires.

Taking her hand, he pulled Scarlett to his study. *A drink first, to loosen the morals* he thought as he poured two large glasses of brandy. Scarlett took one and sipped, looking up through her eyelashes at Cadian. 'So, what do you plan to do with me tonight, *husband?'*

Does she even know how she effected Cadian? He would bet both of their lives that she didn't. The audacity the woman had to just ask that of him, his desire was definitely firming. Quickly, Cadian attempted to keep his face still. To hide his need to be inside her. There was no rush, he had the entire night to devour her.

'Oh, my wife, tonight you discover anticipation and pleasure in ways you have never experienced.' He sipped his drink as her eyes widened slightly. The expectation was that her meekness would show, and he could dominate her, but a flash of excitement filled her eyes instead.

'I need to feel you in me again, Cadian. I'm empty without you.' Scarlett pleaded, running a hand slowly over his chest, playing with the buttons on his shirt as she did. Oh, this infernal woman was perfection in every single way.

Cadian drained his glass completely and threw it into the fireplace. That was tomorrow's problem. Tonight, he was focussed solely on the woman standing before him.

A slight gasp escaped her lips as the glass shattered but it was quickly silenced by Cadian's mouth on her own, his hands cupped her face as he kissed her, their tongues swirling together. Nothing in the entire world could taste as divine as Scarlett Rose's lips. As they embraced, his hands roamed to her bodice. It was thick material and steel boned, removal would include unlacing the entire damn thing. There were two choices laid before him. Cadian was more than strong enough to rip the corseted dress from the body of his wife where she stood, leaving her standing naked before him. Alternatively, he could be more careful, allowing her to keep the dress in tact as a memento of their matrimony.

Cadian growled as he pulled away from the kiss. 'Turn around.' He commanded and Scarlett did so without hesitation. It was good to know that she could follow orders, and that she trusted him. While her back was to him, Cadian stepped away slowly opening a drawer in his desk and removing an athame. It felt weighty in his hand as he stepped back towards Scarlett. 'Ribbon can always be replaced.' He whispered as he slid the blade into the corseted back of the dress and sliced through the silk string that held the back so tightly. The dress fell and gathered around his wife's perfectly soft legs, and he smiled.

'Do not be alarmed.' He whispered again as he let the cool steel touch Scarlett's back.

'What is that?' She asked, a quiver in her voice.

'It is to be our entertainment this evening my pet.' He stepped closer to Scarlett and wrapped both arms around her, the dagger in his right hand landed gently against her throat and his wife let out a gasp.

'Shhhh Scarlett, I don't intend to cut you. But accidents happen to careless girls.' Cadian allowed his left hand to trace down her stomach, lower and lower until it reached her underwear. As he did, he turned the knife, allowing the sharp edge to rest against Scarlett's neck. There was no pressure behind it, but she certainly couldn't move without having her head removed. Cadian was in complete control.

Slowly, his fingers made their way to the damp spot on the fabric that presses against her intimate spot. If nothing else, Cadian could tell this was exciting her. 'You love the danger, don't you.' It wasn't a question and Scarlett didn't answer, the blade had frozen her to the spot.

Smiling now, Cadian lowered the knife, slipping it into the fabric.

'Cadian!' Scarlett gasped. But he merely shushed her as he sliced into the garment and dropped it to the floor.

'I will draw blood, only when you beg me to.' Cadian growled as he brought the dagger up to her breasts, pressing the cold metal against her left nipple. The flat side of the blade was teasing her, hardening her under its presence.

A finger slid between her folds as Cadian placed a kiss on her neck and Scarlett sighed in response. This was his wedding night. Scarlett had already been deflowered, had already had Cadian at his most gentle. Now he would show her what real pleasure could be. His finger slid deeper into her slick entrance, and Cadian made sure he had wet his digit before sliding back out and circling her nub. A moan escaped his wife's perfect rosebud lips as her head fell back onto his chest. There it was, her neck, totally exposed. With a grin Cadian dotted kisses along her flesh as she moaned softly, his finger still making exquisite circles around her clit.

Then he bit her. Not hard enough to break the skin, but certainly enough to hurt. Her eyes flew open as she gasped, but Cadian held her tightly. She would have no respite from him. As he bit down, he swiped his finger across her most sensitive spot. Touching it for the first time and eliciting a lewd cry from the woman in his arms. This was what he wanted for her, the mixture of pleasure and pain.

Tantalisingly slowly he slid the blade down her skin while he massaged her clit, by now Scarlett was panti-ng, grinding herself against his soaking hand as a bruise formed on her neck. Then he pressed the very tip of the blade against her nipple, enough to sting. The sound that came out of Scarlett as she came on his fingers almost sent the elf into a frenzy. The urge to rip his own clothes off to fuck her where she stood was overwhelming.

No, first we play. Then I will fuck her into oblivion.

'I want you to bleed for me, my wife.' Cadian growled, pressing his firm erection against Scarlett's back. He felt her tense up as the waves of her own pleasure subsided. 'I want to taste it.'

Scarlett nodded, shivering against his fingers that worked gently into her opening. There would be no recov-ery, only pleasure. This was it, this was his moment. Cadi-an kicked her legs wider and pushed her gently forwards, her hands landing on the table on front of her. The skin on her back was perfect, unblemished in any way. She was porcelain. The dagger seemed darker in comparison as he gently let it glide down her spine while he continued his fingerings. A single rivulet of blood trickled down her back from the small line Cadian had made. He leaned in closer, slowly licking the blood away. Oh, how perfect she tasted, he truly could devour her. Truth be told, he could drink every ounce of her blood.

It was an ancient practice, blood sharing, frowned upon by all who knew of it. But he craved it. It was the dark magic that gave him the appetite, that much he knew. But Scarlett was his cure. Another moan escaped her lips as his fingers slowly brought her closer to another orgasm.

'No.' He growled. Slipping his fingers away and turning his wife to face him. 'You only come again when *I* allow it.'

Lifting her quickly, Cadian sat Scarlett on the table then lowered her backwards. Gliding the knife down her stomach and drawing another trickle of blood. Once more he licked it away, looking into his wife's wide eyes as he did.

She knows what I'm doing and it's turning her on.

Spurred on, Cadian ran the blade across her perfect skin once more, gathering up the blood on his tongue, but instead of swallowing, he dropped lower and ran his tongue up her slit. The moan that escaped her lips echoed throughout the house and she brought her pussy up to grind into his mouth. *This fucking perfect creature.*

Cadian was filled with her taste, her scent, it was turning him wild. While he knelt, he drew the dagger down his own arm, splattering blood across the floor as he brought her closer to the edge once more with his tongue. Just before she could finish again, he quickly stood and held his wrist to her mouth. The shock that crossed her face was gone in an instant as she tasted his crimson liquid for the first time. Soon her mouth was painted red, droplets fell from her chin onto her breasts turning her into a vampiric looking fiend.

It was getting to be too much. Cadian ripped the top of his own breeches and freed his hard cock from its cloth prison and swiftly sank into the soaking hole his wife displayed. It wasn't gentle, he didn't let her become accustomed to his size, he just filled her completely in one smooth thrust. She screamed, not in pain but almost like an animal as she licked the blood from his arm while he fucked her.

His free hand found her clit once more, covered in blood and her own juices. It became the target of his fingers, and she mewled as his touch. It was overwhelming when her walls tensed against him. She was already tight, but this was almost unbearable, he could feel her getting closer and Cadian was ready to fill her.

'Come for me. Right now, on my cock.' Cadian commanded and with a few more thrusts she was crying out in orgasmic pleasure. It wasn't long before Cadian felt himself nearing the edge. 'Oh fuck.' He growled as he pumped harder into her, ropes of hot cum exploding out of him. It was the most intense sex he'd had in centuries.

The perfect, ruined creature, on the end of his dick, covered in sweat and blood looked up at him.

Oh, the exquisite downfall of innocence.

The downfall of innocence

A Wedding of Convenience

The City Square of Ashton Glade was a beautifully decorated space. A large square garden filled with flowers and trees was the defining feature. It had benches along the paths and lush grassy areas that were perfect for a picnic. On a warm day like today, Finn would have expected the space to be filled with children playing and old ladies doing their crochet while sharing gossip, but it stood hauntingly quiet.

Finn followed the path through the park and arrived out the other side in front of the City Hall. The stone building that housed the political minds of the era. Hand chosen by the King to ensure the day to day running of the city was carried out in line with his wishes. Out front stood a huge wooden sign, plastered with flyers and bits of information. Things like reminders of birthdays for prominent members of society, or spectacular market sales that would guarantee a bargain or two. And most importantly, job postings for all over the city.

Finn scanned the board carefully, until he spotted what he was looking for. A business set up for furniture moving was hiring hands to do all the heavy lifting involved in setting up a certain royal wedding celebration. Finn grabbed the paper and marched deep into the heart of the Market District. Stopping only when he reached the store named on the flyer.

Confidently he walked into the shop and slapped the flyer from the job board onto the wooden counter 'I'd like to apply for this.' Finn smiled. 'When can I start?' The older man standing behind the counter looked up at the golden haired elf and frowned. 'You any good at lifting?'

Finn nodded. 'I've been a farm hand for decades. Lifting and carrying is all I'm good for.' He looked down at the paper. It was hard to talk with the humans, even those who pretended to tolerate the elves still preferred to hear them talking badly about themselves. It allowed humanity to keep feeling superior.

'Hmmm, yes well. It is what your kind were built for. All strength, no brains.' With a sigh the man handed Finn a slip of paper. 'You'll need this to show the guards. They'll allow you access. You need to use the third gate. No one else is allowing in visitors. No exceptions. I'm not responsible for what an upset guard might do to you if you piss them off.'

'I get it, third gate. Anything else?'

'Yes, you need to locate Mr. Belmont, he will point you in the direction of the furniture deliveries. You will unload the carriages and take the items to the grand hall. Do you think you can remember all that? Maybe I should write it down.' The old man started rooting for more paper, but Finn interrupted. 'It's alright. I'll remember, third gate, Mr. Belmont, unload carriages to great hall.'

The old man nodded again, 'Alright, the pay is...'

'Yeah, great thanks.' Finn called over his shoulder as he ran out the door. The old man looked around the empty room. 'Well, I'm not paying if he doesn't ask.' He said to no one but himself.

While the old man talked, Finn rushed the streets of Ashton Glade. Along the cobblestones, past the stalls and shops that made up the market district. He ran with determination past the city halls and through to the hills that led to the palace itself. Now was the time to put a stop to this nonsense. Not once did he falter, not even for one moment did Finn stop to take stock of the situation. All he knew was the King was making a mistake, and he was going to stop it.

He ran the ring road around the castle, his lungs now burning from the cardio and blood rushing through his ears, deafening him with the roaring sound of the ocean. As he reached the third gate, he held up the paper to the closest guard.

'You run here, elf?' The guard asked.

'No, I took a gentle stroll in the morning sunshine.' Finn gasped as he tried to catch his breath. 'The old man said I'd only get paid if I got here before the morning shift started.

The guard grinned cruelly. 'You made it, just about.' He stepped aside and Finn strutted past into the Palace proper. That was the first hurdle, now he had to find the King, or at least one of the elven advisors he'd heard so much about. Just as he was about to step into one of the many corridors that made up the castle, an older man placed a hand on his elbow and gripped tightly. 'You one of the movers?' He asked in a kindly old voice. Finn looked him over and nodded. 'Yeah, I'm...uh...looking for Mr. Belmont.'

'Well, you found me.' He chuckled. 'Come on, let's put you to work.'

'Actually, I was hoping I could...' Finn looked down at Mr. Belmont. Hoping he could what? Wander off alone and have a chat with the King? Yeah, that sounded likely. He took a beat to really look at his situation. Here stood

Finn, loner of a man who wanted nothing to do with anyone, standing in the middle of the palace, risking imprisonment to save the King from making a mistake. And for what?

For her.

Scarlett Rose had made her way into his head. And probably his heart. And while she may love someone else, he still couldn't let any harm come to her.

'Spit it out, son. Hoping you could...?' Mr. Belmont pulled Finn back out of his own head. 'I was hoping I could, use the bathroom?'

The old man smiled, 'Sure thing. Just head down the corridor, past the throne room and there's outhouses down that way for the workers.' Finn nodded. 'Thanks.'

As instructed, Finn followed the long corridor towards the throne room and peeked through the doorway. It was virtually empty. Certainly, no King in sight. So, off the well-travelled path once more. He thought to himself as he darted towards a stone stairwell that spiralled upwards. Even if he had to break into the King's own chambers he would, to bring the news of Scarlett's safety.

Gonna end up in prison. He thought to himself, and he moved silently along the upstairs corridors. Once upon a time, when Finn and his wife had been happy, he would hunt in the woods, moving effortlessly and silently through the bracken to hunt deer. An ability that was due to his elven nature. As he walked, he looked through door after door, mostly bedrooms and bathrooms, guest suites and store cupboards for the handmaidens. It was starting to look as though the King wasn't on this floor when he finally reached something that seemed suspicious.

A locked door.

The first of its kind on this long corridor.

One only locks a door when one has secrets to keep.

Finn smiled at the words his wife used to say. She never locked the doors to their home, she believed they had nothing to hide from the world. With a shake of his head, Finn pulled a small piece of metal from his pocket and gently slipped it into the lock. It took a few twists but soon the lock clicked, and Finn opened the door.

It led to a dark windowless room. There were chains on the wall, potion vials on the vanity and a large bed covered in red silks. In the centre of the bed sat a book, bound in leather, just begging to be opened. If you asked him, Finn couldn't tell you why he had opened the door, or why he picked up the book. He felt as though a hand was guiding him. The hands of the gods perhaps? But he'd turned his back on religion when she died.

Maybe it was her?

Whatever it was had led Finn to the discovery of Alessandra's own journal. He sat on the edge of the bed to read the most recent entry.

Today was a challenging day The situation at the palace remains tense as the King continues to isolate himself, leaving me with the burden of planning the entire wedding. Despite my hopes for his involvement, I have come to expect his emotional detachment. He just sits, crying over drawings of Scarlett. It's pathetic.

Not that it matters, By the time Cadian arrives, I will have ascended to the throne, Farandorn will be dead, and his new heir will be in my belly. A male of course. Scarlett will have no claim to the Throne and my era will begin.

It will be my greatest pleasure to kill the little bitch before Cadian does. I deserve the honour for listening to twenty five years of her incessant whining.

Finn slammed the book closed as his stomach lurched. There was no point. He shouldn't be here. The horror of realising he stood in the middle of a mage's private quarters seeped into every pore in his flesh. Without thought, he stuffed the book into his coat and fled the room. Running along corridors, down the stairs, past the throne room and straight into Mr. Belmont. 'I was just coming to look for you.' The old man smiled gently. 'You're white as a sheet, you alright?'

Finn shook his head. 'I think I'm going to be sick.'

'Oh well, better out than in is what my wife always says. Away with you then, can't have you getting ill and spreading it around the palace. Go get some rest, son.'

Finn couldn't even appreciate the kindness shown to him by the old human. He was too wrapped up in his own head. But one thing stood out to him, one thing he knew, one truth that could never be changed.

He was going to save Scarlett.

The Decline

'I never want to leave the bed.' Scarlett smiled snugging further under the thick duvet against Cadian's hard chest. His arm wrapped around her shoulder, pulling her in close. 'You never have to.' He whispered as he kissed the top of her head, burying his face into her curls. 'Mrs. Vordane.'

The actions from the night before were clear on her skin. Long red slices across he back that would heal slowly. But there wasn't any worry there, she had wanted it and she bore her new scars proudly. Or so it seemed.

Scarlett froze for a second before looking up at Cadian. 'Who said I'm going to be a Vordane? The Era is of the Rose. You should take my name.' She grinned.

'Oh? Am I to be nothing more than the plaything of a tyrant Queen?' Cadian flashed a grin.

'A tyrant, am I?' Scarlett laughed. 'I like to think of myself as benevolent. A generous, giving Queen.' She grinned as she climbed on top of his naked frame. 'And that my husband, King Vordane *Rose* will have the honoured seat by my side.'

Cadian grinned wickedly. 'As beautiful as your name is, uniting the races under a new era may be beneficial.'

'Alright.' Scarlett began to gently rock against Cadian's growing hardness. 'I assume Vordane is elvish?'

'It is.' Cadian sucked in a deep breath as he looked up at her, she seemed to know exactly how to turn him into liquid with her touch. *When did this happen?*

'What does it mean? In the common tongue?' She asked.

Cadian closed his eyes and smiled once more. 'Magic.' He whispered. 'To take my name would bring forth the Era of Magic.'

'The Era of Magic.' Scarlett repeated. Uniting the realms with *magic*. It was unheard of and yet to Scarlett, in that moment it seemed like the most perfect thing.

'I'll take your name. I will be Princess Scarlett Vordane.' She smiled as she continued to grind against her husband.

Cadian let out a deep breath as he looked up at her. 'Fuck.' He moaned gently. She was truly a vision to behold, her hair was growing ever darker in his presence, her skin even whiter. The mere idea that he was claiming her soul, corrupting her into his own image hardened his cock immensely and Scarlett ground down against him, the friction massaging her clit in the gentle morning sunlight. There was no deep burning passion, at this moment Scarlett was just openly using Cadian to masturbate. To bring herself to release against his manhood. An act she would have considered awfully inappropriate once upon a time. Now look at her, eyes closed, breathing heavily reaching one had to her own hard nipple and squeezing it.

That was enough for Cadian. If his wife was to have release, then so too would he. He reached down to her slit and slid a finger between them. Scarlett's eyes fluttered open, and she looked down at her husband. He pressed a finger between her folds and deep into her hole. A low moan escaped her lips as she lifted higher. As she did, Cadian made his move, positioning his cock at her entrance and allowing her to slowly lower herself onto the length, sighing as she stretched for his size.

The feel of her, wrapped around him sent shivers through Cadian's whole body. And as she rocked gently on his shaft, still grinding her clit against his pubic bone, her moans began to coming quicker, Cadian let out a growl of his own. It was so exquisitely slow, the way she languidly rolled her hips against him, coaxing an orgasm slowly from his depths was something he'd never felt.

His burning desire for release always overtook him and he would ruin any woman that lay beneath him if he truly let go. But this...this slow build, the way her thighs clenched against him as she got closer, the way she bit her lip, her hand as it pinched at her own nipples. He felt the heat build quickly now as her gentle rocking increased. She was getting close too. Her breath was hitching as she fucked him slowly.

But he came first. The burn in his cock finally exploded into her as she ground harder against him, she was going to cum, the noises emanating from the depths of her soul kept him hard, riding the wave of his orgasm until she jerked hard against his cock and cried out, her juices soaking him down to the hilt.

He looked at the woman that still sat astride him. Still gently rocking as the final shivers of her pleasure faded.

Her hair looked even darker.

After their morning tryst, Scarlett had gently drifted off to sleep in Cadian's arms. Looking down at her, he could see the energy swelling within her. It was time to see how well the corruption was spreading through humanity. With ease, Cadian freed himself from her and dressed in a black shirt with a leather waistcoat. He ran his fingers through his dark hair and left the room silently. The princess didn't even stir. Elves were good at silence when they needed to be.

The short walk to the village was brisk in the cool morning air. After the heat in the bedroom, Cadian relished in the freshness. Soon he was in the heart of the market. Or what passed for a market in such a small space. The four stalls stood quietly, manned by a few human traders. Confidently, Cadian marched up to the closest stall. The wooden surface was covered in raw meat. Some of it was wrapped in paper but a lot was simply laid out on wooden trays. Under normal circumstances this was an excellent place to buy fresh meat and was Cadian's usual supplier. But the man behind the stall did not look well and a strong, pungent odour filled Cadian's nostrils. As he looked closer at the meat, a lot of it had turned. Dark brown spots had grown on the raw animal flesh, and a few were home to small maggots.

Cadian smiled. 'Seem to be having some trouble with your produce, Alistair?' He asked the stall owner. Slowly, the man looked at the elf. Dark circles sat under his eyes and his lips looked dry and cracked. Exhaustion was clear on his face, but as he looked up and saw the elf, his tired eyes narrowed. 'What do you want, *elf*?'

The way he spat the final word actually took Cadian by surprise. Alistair had always been kind to the mage, he had no reason not to be. Cadian spent a lot of coin at the market and was well respected by the folk that lived here. It raised in interesting question for the mage. *Does the corruption make you despise elves, or does it simply reveal the prejudice that was already there?*

'I was hoping to buy some deer. I intend to cook for my dear wife this evening. But it seems your wares are no longer up to my standard.' Cadian smiled and tossed a copper at Alistair. 'For you troubles, *friend.*' He mocked as he turned to walk away.

Looking around it was clear the village was sluggish. People seemed not to care, would they just lie down and die? It didn't matter much to Cadian how it happened, as long as it did. The people here would be the first to die, given their proximity to the Princess. The corruption would spread from her, slowly across the continent. But not quickly enough for Cadian. The city would likely be feeling the beginnings of the magic. A swell of hatred and anger, but it would take longer for it to progress that far away.

It seems as though my Scarlett will be returning home. It only made sense, if she was in the heart of the city, thousands would die quickly, including the King and Scarlett would become Queen.

And Cadian would stand by her side as the King of Novastraad, Ruler of the Elves.

The Race to the Rose

In the open fields, just beyond the ruins of Fellglow rode Finn. A journey that should have taken him a day so far had only taken until just past the midday sun. Star was breathing heavily beneath him as they galloped along the road, but time was very much of the essence right now and Finn promised himself that Star would have a good rest once they reached Briar Heath, once Scarlett was safe with him.

The words he had read in Alessandra's diary still ran through his mind. Not just the last page, but all of it. Paragraph after paragraph, page after page detailing her hatred for humanity. That woman had been given a position of power, had been treated well among the Kings Court, had even been granted access to the Princess herself, and all the while she was planning to destroy them. Finn however, had been outcast, hated, and treated like dirt, and yet he had still fallen in love with a human woman. He let out an involuntary snort of derision. *Just one?* He asked himself, already knowing the uncomfortable truth. Scarlett was the second woman he had fallen for. And once again, she was human.

He will do for her what he couldn't do for Ellie. He would save her life.

And what of Cadian? The diary was descriptive in Alessandra's fear, and it was clear he had powers beyond any mortal. How would Finn even begin to fight that? He had no magic, no power, nothing except the resolve that Scarlett would live. All he could do now was pray it would be enough.

The only blessing for Finn in all of this was that the corruption she wrote about would leave him untouched. A small mercy for the elf, but an advantage that no human would have.

As hours passed and the moon rose high in the night sky, Finn stopped Star and dropped to the ground. Sleep would take him and the horse quickly, but by dawn he would once more be on the road.

Scarlett ran her fingers through her hair. After only two days of marriage, there was very little left of her red curls. Instead, Scarlett's hair was black, matching Cadian's own. In stark contrast, her skin looked even whiter. Dark blue veins had begun spreading across the snow white landscape of her body and somewhere deep inside, her soul was afraid. But it wasn't enough to outweigh her desire for her husband. Together they would return to the city and Scarlett would reunite with her father and introduce the people to their future King.

A smile spread across her red lips at the thought of it all. The way she had changed made her more like Cadian. A true match for him. Perhaps this was the true magic of love.

'Darling?' A deep voice echoed into the room seconds before Cadian himself walked through the door. Scarlett turned to see him enter, a momentary look of surprise spread across his handsome features before quickly morphing into nothing more than a smile. He has been doing it more and more. Every time he saw her it was a shock to him. Scarlett wondered if he knew what was happening to her, but the way he smiled always made her forget her worries. She was safe with him.

'Yes, husband of mine?' She grinned. He always got a twinkle in his eye when she called him that.

'Tomorrow the day is yours to spend as you wish. I have business in the village, and I won't return until late.' He crossed the room to her side as he spoke and snaked an arm around her waist, leaning close to her. 'Get some rest tonight, love.' He whispered into her neck as he placed a kiss.

'You're not staying with me?' Scarlett asked. She wasn't prepared for the wave of loss that washed over her at the thought of being with him.

'As I said, I have business in the village.'

'You're going there now?' Scarlett manoeuvred herself out of his arms and stepped back. 'You'll be gone all night as well?'

'Yes, so please stay in the house and avoid any wolves that might come calling.' Cadian closed the gap between them once more, whispering as he spoke. 'My heart is connected to yours. You are safe here.'

'Connected?' Scarlett asked. It made no sense to her. In fairness, magic was quite new to her as the court mage always practised in private, and even if she took into consideration the fact she and Cadian were soul mates, there was still no physical bond holding them together. Love was ethereal, ineffable. Not something that can be quantified in the physical world.

Cadian started peppering gentle kisses down her neck to her collarbone, eliciting a heavy sigh from Scarlett's lips. 'We are connected by our union.' He took a step back and grabbed Scarlett's hand, placing it on her chest over her heart. He took her other hand and held it to his own. 'The magic of that day will keep our hearts beating as one.'

It was incredible to her that she could feel her heart beating in perfect unison with Cadian's. Even as she considered the implications and her heart began to race, so did his. With a gasp she pulled her hands free and stepped back. 'What does this mean?'

'In truth, it means you and I cannot be parted by death. Your life will last as long as my own.'

Your life will last as long as my own. Scarlett sucked in a breath and held it. That meant one of two things. Either Cadian would perish at the end of Scarlett's human life, or she would live as long as the ancient elf that stood before her. Cadian didn't seem to be the sacrificial type, no one lives for a thousand years and then gives it all up for a human life.

'You mean...' Her voice trailed off as the realisation truly hit her.

'Yes, my love. You and I will rule the kingdom. For thousands of years the Era of Magic will reign.' He wrapped Scarlett in his arms and held her tightly. 'I love you, my princess. I couldn't bear the thought of you being gone from my world.'

So that was it then. Scarlett's life had been changed irreversibly. No longer truly human, and in no way an elf, she was something new. A human that would live for an eternity. Would that explain the physical changes? The hair, the veins? Scarlett's mind wandered back to the first time she had begun to notice the strands of black weaving through her copper curls. They had already been there on her wedding day. Whatever the cause, it wasn't her connection to Cadian.

'Princess?' Cadian's voice penetrated into Scarlett's mind as she had allowed it to wander. She focussed once more on the beauty of Cadian. 'Yes?'

'I'm taking my leave now.' He kissed her forehead gently, lingering for just a moment as he inhaled the scent of her. 'I love you, Scarlett.'

'I love you too.' She whispered back, watching as he turned and left the room.

Scarlett had moved her things into Cadian's bedroom the day after they married. After all, it was proper for them to share a bed now the God's had blessed their union. She paced the room aimlessly while she considered the ebony hair that now adorned her head. When had she noticed it? She thought back to her time in this house. She remembered looking in the mirror and seeing the first dark strands, but so much had happened here, which day had it been? Was it before or after Mateo?

She shuddered.

The memory of the dagger in her hand flashed back to her. She could feel the soft leather grip, the slight resistance as she drove it into his heart. It was the morning after that she first saw the change in herself. Is this was murder does to someone? It darkens your physical being as well as your heart? Or was it being so close to Cadian when it happened. He practically emanated magic from his very pores. One thing was certain, it was magic. And if Scarlett wanted answers, then she would have to delve into Cadian's library and find them herself.

Fight for your Life

The study was unchanging as far as Scarlett could see. The plush armchairs, the fireplace and most importantly, the walls that were lined with books. She didn't know if this was where Cadian kept his magical tomes, but she didn't have any other options. In the short time she had stayed here, she had already learned that this room was a sanctuary for her husband. As she crossed the room her fingertips gently ran across the table, he had taken her on. Small spots of blood still spotted the rug beneath her feet. The far wall looked like a good place to start, and Scarlett quickly approached the shelves, tilting her head as she started reading the titles of the books there.

The Unicorn and The Virgin by E Honeysuckle

Little Almia by Elise Tanner

The Runaways and Other Tales by Various

Scarlett sighed heavily as more and more books proved to be nothing more than fairy tales. Shelf after shelf of parables and stories with strong moral compasses. This was useless. With a frustrated grunt, Scarlett walked to the small drinks trolley in the corner and decanted a glass of amber liquid. Surely a mage would have magic books. The idea that an ancient elf, the most powerful mage in all the land, didn't have spell tomes was ridiculous to Scarlett and she refused to believe it. That knowledge was somewhere in this house and Scarlett intended to find it.

But that would mean taking her prying a step further and seeking out spaces where Cadian would keep secrets. Where he might hide his magical knowledge. The mere thought of betraying Cadian almost brought her to tears. He was her soul mate. He loved her so much he made her basically immortal. No matter how bad things seemed, he would take care of her. So why hadn't she asked him? Why hadn't she run into his arms and asked him what was happening to her?

She knew the answer to that, she just wasn't willing to admit it. But it was painfully obvious why she couldn't ask him, why she couldn't seek comfort in him. Why she felt a ball of fear growing in her stomach every time she looked in the mirror and saw a mere shadow of her former self. The change in her was so clear.

But Cadian didn't speak of it.

It was impossible to deny that she was different. And yet the man that loved her didn't say a word, didn't ask her about it or ease her fears. He acted as though there was nothing different at all. Was it guilt? Did he know this was his doing and now he was blaming himself? She didn't know and that scared her even more. The mere fact that she was now considering her husband's involvement in her physical decline tipped her over the edge. Scarlett felt the breath in her chest begin to burn, almost as if she couldn't get more air regardless of how hard she tried. Her eyes began to see little silver spots as her breath quickened. 'Cadian.' She gasped as she reached out a steadying hand to the shelves beside her.

If our hearts beat as one, then he must know something is wrong. Scarlett pressed her other hand against her chest, trying to feel her heart beat but her hyperventilating and dizzied mind meant thinking straight was not an option.

For the first time since she arrived in this place, she wished Finn was here.

The road was a straight run from here to Cadian's little village and as the last of the day's light dimmed, Finn slowed Star to a trot to give the beast a rest. They'd saved a day on the journey by resting only a few hours a night and pushing hard through the day. The journey had been far from uneventful, and Finn winced as his hand touched the bruise on his cheekbone.

Yesterday morning there had been a part of him that after two solid days of travel, had craved the coffee from the tavern he and Scarlett had spent their last morning together in. And he figured an hours rest would be good for both of them. He'd been eating fruit leather for every meal and needed his strength if he was to take on Cadian Vordane.

So Finn had slowed as he reached the small town, made his way to the heart of it and then tied Star to the horse post outside the tavern. Almost tasting the coffee and bread, Finn hurried inside and strode to the bar. He adopted his usual demeanour in a village of humans, shoulders slumped, head down and hood up. It was always better not to draw attention. The people here had been nice enough the last time, but old habits die hard.

'Good morning.' Finn smiled politely at the grumpy looking, pot-bellied barman who looked up and grunted in Finn's direction. 'Alright.' Finn mumbled before continuing. 'Could I get a coffee and a bread and cheese plate?' Finn looked away from the barman for barely a second while he reached down to his pouch for coin. Before his brain had the chance to catch up, the barkeep was reaching over the wooden bar and grabbing the front of Finn's cloak, entwining his fingers tightly into the fabric. 'What the-' Finn started but was quickly cut off by the fist that crunched into his face.

'Who the fuck said your kind were welcome here, elf?' The man growled as he brought his band back for another swing. Finn looked at the man who was now attacking him. It was hard to believe it was the same person that only a short while ago had been serving him coffee and laughing with him. Only, now he looked older, paler. Long thin veins of blue were spiderwebbing their way across his neck and face and his eyes were bloodshot.

'What happened to you?' Finn grunted but the man didn't answer. Instead, he swung his fist again. This wasn't Finn's first fight, and he pulled his own arm up to block the attack. 'I don't want to hurt you, I just want to leave.' Finn yanked his shirt out of the man's grasp and stepped back.

'You never should've come here.' The man's voice was low, and he never looked away from Finn as he walked around the counter and started to close the gap. Finn took a step back. He knew he was strong, he could easily out-match the old fella in a fight. But what would that end with? A dead human and an elf on the run? *Not worth it.*

Finn decided and instead her turned and stepped out of the bar.

Finn had seen an angry crowd of humans before. Humans that hated elves so much they wanted them to suffer. Humans that were so enraged by the mere fact that a human could possibly love an elf, that they were willing to destroy one of their own to make him suffer. The people here looked remarkably similar in demeanour to the group that had beaten Finn's own wife until the life had drained from her.

He balled his fists.

'I intend to walk away from here.' He shouted. 'I'm taking my horse and leaving.' It was the most difficult thing in the world not to start ripping these men apart. The blood was rushing through his ears and there was the thought in his mind that these men were no different to his wife's murderers. Killing them could be cathartic, therapeutic.

'No.' He said to himself as he took another step towards his horse. But as he looked over to Star, he saw the man standing there, holding a knife and scowling. 'You're both going to die here, you and your horse.'

Finn took a deep breath, then ran at the man with the knife, tackling him to the ground hard. The weapon bounced along the straw covered dirt floor and the man's face turned into an O of surprise as Finn's fist connected with it. He stayed down after that, Finn didn't consider whether the man's stillness was temporary or permanent, but at that point, he didn't much care. He scooped up the knife and cut through Star's rope, then turned to look at the men who were approaching quickly.

The fight was a blur to Finn. Fists and feet were everywhere, and he took absolutely no prisoners as he defended himself, but the defence started to take the shape of revenge when he started seeing the faces of the men who had killed his Ellie.

That's when Finn, for the first time in his life, became a danger to humanity.

A red mist began to cloud his mind and it was almost like he had disconnected from himself. Standing watching the violence from a distance. While he stood there, he felt a delicate hand intertwine with his own. A familiar hand, one that had held his own for many years. Until it was taken from him. Finn's face crumpled as he felt Ellie's touch and he turned to look at the perfect woman standing beside him, her long blond hair flowing down her back. She even wore the nightdress. Oh how he hated that nightdress. No matter the time of day, as soon as she was home Ellie insisted on comfort and immediately changed into her nightdress and slippers. Finn smiled through the tears and opened his mouth to speak, but not words came out.

'Oh Finn. What have you gotten yourself involved in?' Ellie's voice was exactly as he'd remembered it. He tried to answer but emotion had a choke hold on his voice. 'Listen to me, my love. You can still save her, but you need to let go of your anger.' Finn looked at her, how did she know about Scarlett?

'What?' He managed to croak out.

'She's really beautiful you know. And human. You certainly have a type.' Ellie laughed, the perfect laugh. It was windchimes dancing on a summer breeze. Finn stood silent once more.

'You *can* still save her. But not if you die here. Let go, Finn.' She paused and looked up into his wet eyes.

'Run.' She whispered.

The red mist cleared, and Finn was suddenly back in the midst of a violent struggle explosions of pain covered his body as his fists were swinging. *Run.* Finn disengaged from the fight, swiping away hands that tried to grab him as he ran. Within seconds he was beside Star and swiftly, he leapt on the fence beside the horse and jumped gently onto her back.

Finn and Star made their hasty escape from the village. Riding hard as the people left behind threw rocks and weapons at them.

And that's how he found himself bruised and riding gently towards the small hamlet. Towards Scarlett. He'd read the diary, he knew this was the corruption spreading. Alessandra had written about the humans that would all die as Scarlett fell to the darkness. Which is why a ball of dread had formed in his stomach. What would he find when he arrived at Briar Health Manor. Would she still be Scarlett? Or would she try to kill him like the villagers did. There was still hope though, the words Ellie had said rang through his mind,

You can still save her.

Fresh tears threatened to spill as he thought about Ellie again. He didn't understand what had happened, was it really her? Or had he imagined the whole thing. It would be easy to take comfort in the fact that she was happy and watching over him, but there was a part of Finn that didn't believe that the soul lived on after death, didn't believe in the gods, just simply thought that this life was all you got, so you had to make the most of it.

Only a few hours to go. He thought as he rode on into the night.

Secrets

His heart was pounding faster than it should for the gentle walk to the village and he knew what that meant. It was Scarlett, whatever she was doing, it was making her heart race. Considering she was home alone, Cadian wondered if she had taken the opportunity to romance herself. Visions of his dark beauty writhing under her own hands swam in his mind as he meandered. It was a mistake to allow his mind to wander on such topics while outwalking. He readjusted, tucking his now firm cock under the waist of his pants. Pinning it mercilessly into place with his belt. The desire to turn and run back to his home to ruin his wife was overwhelming, but Cadian had work to do. Alessandra was still hidden to his eyes, no magic so far had found her which had enraged Cadian. She was up to something, and she was going to ruin a centuries old plan because of her own fear.

Every elf should be willing to lay down their own life to see their people finally become whole again. The mere fact that Alessandra cared more about her own survival disgusted Cadian. Didn't she understand that his Era would be perfect? That the elves would rise up and claim this land in the name of their ancestors and the humans would be all but gone? Except one of course, his Scarlett. Perhaps he would let Alessandra live, but not a life worth having. Keeping her as a plaything for his court, constantly brutalised. A daily reminder of her insolence, her betrayal. He would make her beg for death and still would not oblige. A dark grin spread across his handsome face as he imagined Alessandra's torture.

Perfection.

The village stood dark at the end of the long dirt road, normally filled with the twinkling orange glow of candles and hearth fires. Instead, it looked abandoned. Cadian inhaled deeply. The corruption had taken this place. Only his elves would remain alive here, and they would help him to see the bitch Alessandra and uncover her secrets.

Deep breaths. Scarlett repeated the words as a mantra. *Deep breaths, deep breaths, deep breaths*...But no air would come. She found herself kneeling on the floor of the study, one hand pressed to her chest and the other on the floor for support. 'Cadian.' She whispered. He hadn't come back for her, which spoke volumes to the Princess. If she was going to get through this, she was going to have to be strong. She was going to have to do it alone. Her long black hair hung over her shoulders, a reminder of what was happening to her.

'I can do this.' She whimpered as she sucked in a deep breath and counted slowly to four. The wooden floor was slightly rough under her fingers. A single sharp piece jutted out and she ran her finger over it, focussing on the sharp scratching sensation. She let out the breath, counting once more to four, still focussing on how the woodgrain felt.

'I can do this.' She spoke through gritted teeth and sucked in another breath, pushing herself up and onto her knees. The room looked the same as always but there was something different. Scarlett rose slowly to her feet, still counting her breaths and steadying herself on the wooden desk. 'I can do this.' The voice came out bold, the thing that was changed was the princess herself.

Cadian's secrets were no longer safe from her. Scarlett would find the truth, she would learn what was happening to her and Cadian was going to help her change back, whether he liked it or not. *He is my husband. He vowed to be my protector.*

But where to begin? Where would Cadian keep his secrets? His books on magic? Where in this house would the answers be? Scarlett stood, perfectly still as she looked around the study. There were no rooms left unexplored by the curious Scarlett, unless he had secret doors which would be difficult to uncover, especially if they were sealed or hidden by magic.

But then, there was one room she'd only seen once. Her heart sank as she recalled the time she had been in there. The room that had turned her into a killer. A room Cadian would be certain she would not venture into again.

The basement.

Cadian reached the small town just as his heartbeat returned to normal. He smiled to himself as he passed by the darkened buildings, keeping his eyes open for his own kind. He expected more bodies to be in the streets, but perhaps the humans had crawled into their homes to die. As he reached the small market square, he rapped gently on the wooden door of a small, run down building.

'Who's there.' A nervous voice called out.

'Open the door, Arleya.' Cadian hissed at the wood.

'Master Cadian?' The door creaked open slightly and a pretty elven maiden peered out into the dark night. 'Quickly, come in my lord. It's not safe out there.' She stepped aside while she spoke, ushering Cadian inside. He politely obliged and stepped over the threshold. The door was quickly closed and locked behind him.

'What do you mean, not safe?' Cadian asked the elf. The corruption was to kill the humans, not his own people.

'Forgive me my lord, but the humans, they've lost their marbles. They attacked my mother on the street outside. Right in the market square. I managed to drag her in here but, she's in a bad way.'

The corruption was making them violent? Bringing out the underlying racism that lived in their vile hearts. No matter, the loss of a few elves would serve as proof that Cadian did the right thing. There will always be death in war.

'I need your crow.' Cadian looked down at Arleya. 'Bring it to me and then leave me in peace here to work.'

The elf maiden bowed. 'Yes, my lord.' Quickly she darted from the room and Cadian stood perfectly still as he waited for her return. It didn't take long before the maiden came back with a stone statue of a crow. She held it out to him, and he swiped it quickly from her hand. 'Now go. Sit with your mother and do not disturb me.'

'Of course.' Arleya bowed again and backed out of the room. Cadian closed his eyes and held the statue in his hands. It had been centuries since he had used this magic, but desperate times called for desperate measures. The stone began to feel warm in his hand. He ran his fingertips over the delicate features, channelling magic into it. A dark mist emanated from his grip, circling the stone and wrapping it in his magic.

Soon, two spots of light begin to glow on the statues face, it's eyes alight with magic, Cadian's own flew open, revealing a matching glowing light. While his body stands in the maiden's living room, Cadian's mind is far away, looking through the eyes of a crow as it soars over field and forest. It wasn't far from the city, a few hours in flight would get it there. Cadian's mind nudged the bird to change direction, to fly towards the King's city, Ashton Glade.

The Basement.

Scarlett shuddered at the thought of it. Her feet had taken her to the door in the kitchen and she stood silently before it. Scarlett wished she was braver. She wished that she could throw open the door, rush down the stairs and deal with whatever secrets she may uncover.

But Scarlett was scared.

Scared that Cadian wasn't the man she had fallen for, scared that he was the one doing this to her. But mostly, she was scared that he didn't truly love her. Because in her heart, she adored him. Craved him. Cadian was her soul mate and Scarlett wasn't ready to choose between love and fear.

But if you don't do this now, you'll never know the truth.

There wasn't a choice. Not knowing was gnawing away at her insides, there was no truth too vile. She had to know.

Bravely she flung open the basement door before her brain had the chance to stop her and marched down the stairs. *There's nothing to be afraid of Scarlett.* She told herself. There was nothing down here that could hurt her. She reached the bottom of the stairs and stepped into the basement fully.

And there stood Mateo.

A scream escaped Scarlett's lips before she could stop it. This wasn't possible, Mateo was dead by her own hand. His shirt still bore a dark patch where the blood had seeped out of his heart. His skin was paler than before, the golden glow replaced with a sickly green pallor and his brown eyes were milky white.

'By the gods...' Scarlett whispered as she took in the sight before her. 'You *are* dead and yet you walk.'

Mateo didn't respond, simply stood, unmoving, unblinking in the place he had perished. A sorry existence for anyone to suffer, a fate worse than death. But one wholly deserved by Mateo, and Scarlett found herself wishing that he was in pain.

'You did this to yourself, Mateo. You deserve this.' It was clear he didn't have the comprehension to understand. Scarlett stared at the standing corpse. How was this possible? She'd heard rumours of dark magic that could do this sort of thing, what was the word they used? Scarlett thought back to the horror novels Alessandra had snuck into her room on late summer evenings.

'Necromancy.' She whispered. Could it be that all this time Cadian had been capable of such evil magic? Scarlett shook her head. No. She wouldn't believe it. He had a hold on her heart, and she had his. They were soul mates, he wasn't evil. He couldn't be, she had married him, she was connected to him, he was the future King of Novastraad. *And he was a necromancer.*

If Cadian had created this monster that stood before her, and they were connected by magic, then perhaps...The thought trailed off as she took a step closer to Mateo. 'In the books, the mage always had control of his own creations. And if Cadian and I share a life span, if his lifeforce keeps my heart beating for eternity, then I am your creator too.'

She took another step closer. 'Show me where Cadian keeps his magic books.'

Mateo tilted his head and looked at the princess with dull, lifeless eyes. Slowly he turned and walked to the far right of the room, into the shadows. He stood facing the stone wall. As Scarlett approached, she frowned. 'This is a wall.'

Mateo didn't move, just continued to stare at the stone. Scarlett reached out a hand and ran a finger down the rough surface of the wall. As she did a small glimmer ran down one of the cracks in the stone. 'What?' Scarlett muttered. She reached out again, gliding her fingers along the wall, stepping back as more silver light began to emanate.

'Oh Cadian, you have so many secrets.'

Soon the wall was shining brightly as the stonework seemed to vanish and nervously, Scarlett stepped into the light.

The city of Ashton Glade stood proudly beneath the soaring wings of the crow. Cadian manoeuvred down, closer to the people as they walked, living their lives. Many were dressed in black with dark flags adorning their homes.

The city mourns. Cadian thought. *The king is dead.* He smiled at the revelation as the crow flew lower. He could hear the muted chatter of the citizens as they went about their day. It was glorious.

The crow gained altitude and flew towards the palace itself, banners of black hung along the walls reinforcing Cadian's belief in the plan. Perhaps Alessandra *had* earned her life back. The King's room sat at the top of the palace, with his royal balcony looking out over the city below. Cadian flew up and rested on the stone, looking into the room.

There he saw Alessandra sitting in nothing but her silk nightdress and King Farandorn sadly putting on his overcoats. *What the fuck is happening here?* Cadian felt anger swelling inside him. He brought the crow closer, listening to the conversation between the two.

'My King, we have less than a week until the wedding, I wish to announce your new heir on that day. The tonics can only do so much, we still need to...come together.' Alessandra's voice was deep and low. And Farandorn turned to look at her. 'What does it matter if you are with child now or in a year?'

Cadian could answer that. As soon as she carried his heir, she would put the King to the blade and seat herself as Queen. The rage inside Cadian began to rise. The mourning of the city. It wasn't for the King. Talk of a new heir, and the King's sadness meant only one thing. The city believed the princess was dead.

'You vile bitch!' Cadian screeched but it came out as nothing more than a crow cawing. Alessandra glanced over then did a double take. She knew, she was powerful in her own right. Her eyes widened as she leapt to her feet flicking her arm at the bird. Cadian's vision exploded into purple light, and he found himself back in the small living space of Arleya's home. With a roar Cadian grabbed the wooden coffee table and hurled it against the wall. It exploded into shards and scattered it's pieces across the floor.

'I will kill her!' He grabbed the bookcase and pulled it away from the wall, toppling tomes and ornaments as he did. Nothing was safe from his destructive rampage. He could hear whimpering with every crash, knowing the maiden was terrified only spurred him on. He needed to return to the city with Scarlett. They needed to go tonight. With one final growl, Cadian kicked the wooden door from its hinges and stormed into the night.

The Bond of Desolation

Darkness enveloped Scarlett as she stepped through the barrier of silver light, and she blinked hard as her eyes adjusted to it. She could make out the shape of a table and a chair, something against the wall perhaps? A jolt of fear stabbed her insides as the thought crossed her mind that Mateo may not be the only corpse down here. Scarlett felt timidly along the wall until her fingers met with a glass box hanging from the stone. A lantern? Gingerly she felt around until she found a small latch on the side. Pulling it gently, she opened the front of the lantern and slipped a hand inside. It was like the ones out front of Cadian's house. They have little knobs inside to turn a gas on and off and a small flint you can spark to light it. It wasn't easy to do in the dark but eventually the lantern flickered into being and an orange glow filled the room.

She had been right about the desk and chair. There they sat, wooden and unmoving. The table holding books, quill and ink, a small mortar and pestle and some scattered dried herbs. Beside them against the wall was a large wooden cabinet, with an ornate keyhole. It pulled Scarlett's attention, and she crossed the room with her hand out, ready to open it.

But what if it's bad?

Scarlett faltered, her hand dropping slightly. What if it *was* bad? What then? Would she leave him? The man that had given her the love she has always craved? A love so true he had linked her life to his own. It was impossible to believe he would do anything to hurt her.

So open the cupboard.

Scarlett steadied herself, nodding slightly to no one but herself. 'Alright.' She whispered. 'Let's see what secrets you have, my love.' Slowly she reached out, wrapping her fingers around the small brass handle and turning it. Gently she pulled the door, but there was no movement. A frown crossed Scarlett's pretty features. 'Damn.' She cursed, glancing at the ornate keyhole. Cadian was keeping this cupboard past a walking corpse, through a secret door and behind a lock. Scarlett had had enough.

Whirling around she allowed her eyes to dance across the small room. What could she use? Cadian would be keeping the key on his person, so no use trying to find it in the house. What were her other options? Pick the lock?

You need certain skills for that, and at the very least, some tools. Smashing the door off its hinges? It was violent, and she would have no chance to claim ignorance if she made such a gesture. But he couldn't harm her now they were connected. If he killed her, he would be ending his own life.

Scarlett had power over the necromancer.

The chair sitting beside the table was heavy looking and sturdy and she wasn't even sure if she could lift it, let alone hurl it at a cupboard. But if she didn't, she would never know what was happening to her, or why. There was no one coming to her rescue, no Finn to swoop in and scare away the monsters, no handmaidens to do the hard work for her. Scarlett was alone. With a cry, of anguish perhaps? Or more likely rage, Scarlett picked up the back of the chair and swung it in an arc, through the air. It crashed into the cupboard, splintering the door and Scarlett released it from her grasp. Shards of wood clattered to the ground as the door broke apart.

Carefully, she pulled open the cracked wood, looking into the space behind and sighed heavily. She was expecting potions or magical artefacts. But the cabinet held only books. Ancient tomes that lined the shelves. As she pulled a book from its home, Scarlett Rose sighed heavily then seated herself on the floor among the splinters.

The night air was cool as Cadian stepped out into the street from Arleya's house. He had left destruction in his wake and well deserved. Scarlett's claim to the throne would be nullified if the King had a male heir. One to continue the King's own era, and if Alessandra was carrying the child, gender was guaranteed. Rage crept up once more and Cadian took a deep breath. He needed to keep it together, long enough to pack Scarlett's things and return her to the city. If Alessandra was with child by the time they arrived, then Cadian would ensure both would perish.

Cadian was going to be King. No matter the cost.

As he marched past the small buildings towards his own manor house, he suddenly felt an explosion of pain in the back of his head. Something warm seeped through his hair and down his neck. Without thinking Cadian clutched the back of his head, pulling his had away to find it soaked with crimson. A deep growl escaped his throat as he turned to face his attacker. Further back down the way he had come, three men stood. Two were holding rocks, while the one in the centre was grinning in a dismal way. It was unsettling.

Cadian took a step towards them as the other two raised their arms to throw.

'Your lives just became forfeit.' Cadian spat though gritted teeth as the men threw their rocks. Cadian dashed closer, dodging the airborne stones and reached the man in the centre. He gripped the human tightly around the throat and pressed his fingers deep into the flesh. The man choked out blood as Cadian's fingers became a fist, closing around the man's throat and ripping it out.

One of the others leapt into action jumping at Cadian and raining fists down onto the still bleeding wound on the back of his head. The elf let out a cry and shook hard, trying to dislodge the human as the other one stepped in to fight. With a flick of his wrist, Cadian shot a black energy from his fingertips into the approaching man's face. Once the darkness cleared all that was left was the skull. The flesh had been eaten away by Cadian's magic.

As he tried to get the man off his back, more humans approached from behind buildings and alleyways. Every human in the village had turned up for this fight looking tired, pale and dishevelled. They were almost walking corpses at this stage, barely clinging onto life. This is what Cadian wanted, an end to humanity. But not at the cost of his own life. With a roar, Cadian finally flipped the man over his shoulder onto the floor and hit him with the same darkness, only this time, he hit the chest. Leaving behind a cavernous hole where the human heart should be.

Then the crowd descended.

Pain erupted from all over and fists and feet connected with Cadian's body. He threw magic at his attackers, not knowing if it was hitting them, but with every spell, his power depleted. Already weakened from the magic with the crows, Cadian tried to push through the bodies surrounding him, but they were packed in tightly. Darkness danced on the edge of his vision. If he allowed it to take him, he would never awaken. And if he died...

Scarlett.

An inhuman screech exploded from Cadian as he thought about Scarlett. If he dies, she dies with him.

'No!' He dug deep, there wasn't much left inside, he needed rest to allow his magic to grow once more inside him. But he wouldn't let her die.

A flash of dark green energy pulsed from Cadian as he roared, and the crowd fell stunned to the ground. He had bought himself mere seconds to escape. But it would have to be enough. He tried to run, his shaking legs arguing with every short step. But as he tried to run, weak and depleted he was once more grabbed by strong hands and yanked off his feet. Confusion arose as the dark elf realised, he had been dragged upwards, onto the back of a beast. As

Cadian tried to peer at his saviour, he managed to make out some dark green leather before he was taken by the night.

The Bond of Desolation:

Verum amoris est atrox vinculum
In tenebris nos, corpus et animam coniunge;
Adducite nos in corruptionem
Malum per humanitatem

The Bond of Desolation is a powerful corruption spell designed to connect a human princess to her people, enabling the dark mage to corrupt her with his twisted love. This spell establishes a metaphysical link between the princess and humanity, making her the vessel through which the dark mage can spread his malevolent influence and bring about the downfall of all humanity.

When cast upon a beloved princess, the spell taps into the deep emotional bonds she shares with her people, exploiting their trust, loyalty, and love for her. It harnesses these connections to forge an unbreakable tie, which, when corrupted by the dark mage's influence, will bring a slow and painful death to all humans.

The Bond of Desolation requires a profound understanding of dark magic and an adept control over manipulation and corruption spells. Its execution demands utmost caution, as any mistake or imbalance during the casting can result in catastrophic consequences for both the dark mage and his intended victims.

The corruption is underway when the princess shows signs of physical changes. Darkening of the hair, thinning of the skin and an unquenchable thirst for the mage himself.

'Oh Gods.' Scarlett muttered as she read the book. Her heart was racing as she began to understand. It felt as though it was about to burst out of her chest. This spell, it described her. The way he loved her so quickly, her body changing and him not saying a word. Scarlett blinked back tears. All of this was to destroy humanity. Destroy her people, the people she loved. Terrified, she continued to read Cadian's words.

Oh, the anticipation! The mere thought of tricking the princess into loving me, becoming the vessel through which my corruption shall spread, brings joy to my ancient heart. Her innocence, vulnerability, and capacity to love will be my tools, the very foundations upon which I shall build my dark empire.

In the deepest recesses of my mind, I concoct elaborate schemes, intricate webs of deceit, and manipulation that will ensnare her heart, leading her down a path of obsession and blind devotion. She will see only me, for I shall position myself as her saviour, her confidant, and the sole source of light in her life.

The delight that stirs within me stems not only from my insatiable lust for power but from the inherent pleasure I will derive from watching her descent into corruption. The very fabric of humanity shall unravel as she becomes the conduit for my desires. Her love for me will be the catalyst that triggers the downfall of men and gives rise to my people. Elves shall rule this land and I will stand before them as their King.

A wave of nausea washed over Scarlett as she read the words from her lover's own hand. It was true she had given herself over to him so completely, but it was an illusion. He wasn't her soul mate. He was the most powerful practitioner of dark magic the world has ever known.

And Scarlett Rose was his wife.

Tears flowed heavily then as she started to tear pages from the spine. Scarlett wanted the book to be gone, destroyed. She wanted the corruption to fade with it, but even as she tore at the parchment, her long black hair continued to hang over her shoulders.

I love her.

The words caught her eye as she wept. A torn page lay on the stone floor and as Scarlett reached for it, she began to read Cadian's words once more.

Scarlett's love for me has evolved into a force that I struggle to comprehend. I find myself caught in a game of my own making, as my heart betrays my desires and begins to yearn for her in return. I often watch as she gazes upon me, her eyes radiating pure adoration, and a part of me craves that love, my very soul begs for it like a lost spirit seeking redemption. The closer we grow, the deeper my internal turmoil becomes. I fear that the darkness within me is being tainted by a glimmer of light, and I cannot allow that to happen. Love, even in its most twisted form, has no place in the heart of a dark mage. It weakens resolve, clouds judgment, and endangers the very foundations upon which my power rests. But even now as she lies asleep in my bedchamber, all I can imagine is the hole in my heart when she is ripped from me, either by corruption or mortality. I cannot lose her to death. My only hope is to make her my wife and love her for eternity.

It was sick. It was twisted. Scarlett shuddered as bile rose up her throat, threatening to besmirch the pages she held in her hands. She couldn't love him not now. Not knowing the truth.

'SCARLETT!' The voice echoed through the house and for a moment Scarlett froze. If Cadian returned and found her like this, with his books destroyed by her hands.... 'Scarlett, where are you?' The voice called out again, dancing through the corridors to her own ears. But it was not the voice of her husband calling to her. It was a voice that filled her with a warmth she hadn't felt in a long time.

'Finn.'

With great effort, Scarlett made her way out of the chamber and into the basement, where the silent Mateo still stood, she wondered for a moment if he still remembered the night in the tavern. If he understood why he must endure this torture for eternity. She still hoped it was painful.

As she dragged her slender form, she realised just how exhausted she had become. Her body felt heavy, as though her limbs were someone else's and were weighing her down.

'Scarlett?' Finn's voice was closer now, and Scarlett forced herself to take step after step.

'I'm here.' It was nothing more than a weak croak. How had she gotten so tired? She had come down here filled with vigour and now she was completely drained.

'Oh Gods.' The voice was at the top of the stairs. Heavy footsteps hurtled towards her as her legs finally gave out from under her. Strong arms wrapped around her as she fell, saving her from the stone floor. 'Scarlett? Is that you?' Finn's voice was filled with doubt as he lowered himself to the floor, holding Scarlett on his knee.

'Do you see me, Finn? Do you see what's wrong with me?' Scarlett muttered as he held her.

'You...your hair...' Finn trailed off as Scarlett burst into tears. She was overwhelmed with relief at the confirmation she wasn't insane. Cadian *had* done this to her. And then fallen in love with her, and she loved him in return. It wasn't fair. She wanted Finn to scoop her up into his arms, run away into the night with her and return her to the palace. But she knew the uncomfortable truth.

She couldn't leave Cadian.

As she wept, Finn held her close, stroking her black hair. But soon he faltered. His entire body stiffened and slowly he rose to his feet, still holding Scarlett in his arms. 'We have to get out of here now.' He whispered to her as he backed towards the stairs.

'What's wrong?' Scarlett whimpered.

Finn didn't answer. Instead, Scarlett founder herself being tossed over his shoulder as he bounced back up the stairs, slamming the door behind him. He placed Scarlett gently onto the large wooden table in the centre of the kitchen and started looking around. Within seconds he had large butcher knives in each hand.

'Finn stop, what are you doing?' Fear started prickling along Scarlett's spine as she watched him. Was he going to attack Cadian? 'Finn! Talk to me.'

'Scarlett, Mateo was in the basement. He was dead. But he was standing.' Finn's voice was low, that of a hunter and Scarlett's mouth fell open. How could she explain this to someone like Finn. He was pure and this was a darkness that she needed to protect him from.

'I'm going back down there. I need to put an end to it.' Finn turned to the door.

'Finn wait!' Scarlett called out, her voice still gentle. 'Mateo has been down there for days. He is under Cadian's control. Which means he is under my control.'

'What?' A look of disgust crossed Finn's handsome features and Scarlett felt a pang.

'It's a long story Finn and I promise I'll tell you, but there's more important things to deal with.' Scarlett tried to push herself towards the edge of the table. 'I need to find Cadian.'

That seemed to by the final straw for sweet, pure Finnadan.

'Why him? Huh? Look at you, Scarlett! Loving Cadian is killing you! I can feel your bones when I hold you, your hair looks like it's falling out! He has ruined you, and all you can say is you *need* him? I CAME HERE TO SAVE YOU!' Finn exploded and threw the knives into the kitchen sink. 'I nearly died on my way here, Red. Because his corruption is spreading and soon, it'll be in Ashton Glade. Violence, murder...people tearing each other apart with their bare hands. Humanity is destroying itself!'

'I know.' Scarlett muttered.

'What?' Finn asked. 'You know and yet you stay?'

'I only just found out, Finn. I found Cadian's books. I found the spell he used, his diary, all of it. I don't know how to process it, but right now, I need to see my husband.'

'Your...husband?' Finn took a step back. 'You married him?'

Scarlett nodded. 'On Aur'Iya.' She dropped her legs over the edge of the table. 'Please help me down.'

With a sigh, Finn was by her side, easing her lower until her feet touched the ground, but he didn't let her go. 'You got married on Aur'Iya?' Finn shook his head, I didn't know people still did that.' He spoke sadly as he helped Scarlett take a few tentative steps.

'You know what it means?' She asked surprised and Finn nodded. 'It's an old tradition. To link together the lives of two elves, so that they may share their life force. When one is hurt, the other helps them to...' Finn stopped walking and looked at Scarlett. 'When did this weakness come over you, Red?'

Scarlett thought about it. She'd been sat in that room a while, reading Cadian's notes. It wasn't until she tried to run to Finn that she realised. 'I don't know, a few hours? Maybe less? Why what's going on?'

'Cadian is draining your life to save his own.' Finn growled as he lifted Scarlett and carried her out of the room to Cadian.

The Truth

'Cadian?' Scarlett whispered as Finn lowered her onto the floor of the study beside her unconscious lover. He didn't look like himself. Blood had splattered on his shirt and his lip was split open. Puffy bruises had already formed across his face. Someone had attached him viciously.

'Careful, Red.' Finn warned as she placed a hand on Cadian's chest. 'He's not doing this on purpose. He's not even aware of what's happening.' Scarlett's face took on a look of concern. but why? She knew what he was, she knew what he had wanted from her all along. This man was trying to destroy humanity using Scarlett as the trigger and yet she still sat by his side. Why?

Because I love him.

It was ridiculous, she was dying right by his side, and forgiveness was on the tip of her tongue. In the basement she had been so destroyed by betrayal, but in his presence, she couldn't hold onto the anger.

'We need to wake him up. Maybe he can stop what's happening.' Finn's voice brought Scarlett out of her heady thoughts, and she nodded as she looked at Cadian's bruised face. 'Cadian, my love. Wake up. Please.' Scarlett begged, but there was no reaction. She turned to Finn. 'What happened to him?'

'He was being attacked in the town. The human folk were all over him. They would have torn him to pieces if I hadn't turned up when I did.' Finn shifted uncomfortably from foot to foot. It's what happened to me on my way here.

Scarlett looked up at Finn's face. Sure enough the faint remnants of a bruise were still visible around his eye. 'It's the corruption.' Scarlett murmured. 'It's my fault. I let him under my skin and now humanity is falling apart.' A tear slipped down Scarlett's cheek. It was true. Her love for Cadian was destroying the kingdom.

'It's not your fault, love.' The voice was croaky and weak, but it was Cadian. Scarlett looked down at him. Even now when he called her love, her stomach filled with butterflies. He looked sheepish as he pushed himself up onto his elbows and groaned. He looked towards Scarlett and his face changed, concern took over and in an instant, he was on his knees holding Scarlett in his arms. 'Oh, my girl, I'm so sorry.'

'Can you help her?' Finn's voice was commanding. Scarlett hadn't heard that voice come out of him since the night he saved her from Mateo. Cadian nodded gently as he stroked Scarlett's dark hair. 'I can.'

Scarlett felt Cadian's warm hand press gently on her chest. 'You didn't know it, love. But you were giving your life for me. I'm sorry, that shouldn't have happened. Our connection was designed to keep you alive throughout what comes next. But I didn't foresee my own life being in danger. Forgive me, Scarlett. I need you to live.' Cadian leaned down and gently pressed his lips to Scarlett's own. Warmth spread through her as they kissed, and Scarlett allowed herself to relax into his embrace.

Soon her legs stopped feeling like jelly, her arms were fully under her control, and she wrapped them around Cadian's neck. Just as she pulled him closer to her, he broke the kiss, looking deeply into her eyes. 'We have company, love.'

Finn.

A blush spread across Scarlett's face and neck as she pushed herself tentatively to her feet. Finn still didn't look happy. 'Are you alright? Your hair is still...and your skin...? I can see your veins.'

Scarlett traced a finger along her neck, she knew what she must look like still, and Finn had every right to be afraid for her. She stepped closer to her friend, her back to Cadian. 'It's the corruption.' Scarlett answered matter-of-factly. 'This is the result of Cadian's efforts to murder my people.'

'How much to do you know?' Came a calm, smooth voice from behind her.

'All of it, Cadian. I know all of it.' Scarlett still faced Finn while she spoke. She had stronger resolve when she wasn't looking into Cadian's dark eyes. Finn would have to be her strength here.

'Then you must have many questions.' Scarlett could hear the smirk on Cadian's face. She listened as his footsteps echoed along the tiled kitchen floor. Then came the clang of a pot and the sound of cups being placed on the countertop. 'Both of you sit down while I brew coffee.' Cadian ordered. 'Then we open the floor to questions.'

It was an awkward affair, the three of them sitting around the kitchen table. There were secrets among them, that much was obvious but now was the time to air it out. It was uneasy though. Cadian knew he couldn't kill Finn without incurring the eternal wrath of Scarlett. Finn couldn't kill Cadian without losing her as well and Scarlett was hoping they could get through this without violence.

'Who would like to begin?' Cadian's low voice wrapped around Scarlett's mind, and she took a sip of her coffee followed by, 'I will.' She put the cup down gently and looked at Cadian. 'Do you really love me?'

'That's what you're asking?' Finn's voice burst out. 'After all he has done, that's the burning question on your mind?'

'It is yes. Because I already know Cadian's not my soul mate. And I already know I was chosen for this the moment I was born. I even know that he's not just a dark mage, but a necromancer.' Scarlett looked at Cadian as a moment of realisation crossed his features. 'You went into the basement.' Cadian smirked. 'Naughty girl.'

'You think this is a joke?' Scarlett asked. It was becoming increasingly more difficult to keep her temper in check. 'For my entire life, I have been nothing more to you than a catalyst for corruption. Your heart is evil, and I'm connected to it. Why? Why not just let me die out with humanity, since you despise us so much?'

Cadian sighed heavily, looking down at the table. 'That was my intention, Scarlett. To let you die with your people once we were married. And as the new King, I would lead my people into a better world. But...I didn't expect you to be so...you.' He looked up into her eyes and Scarlett felt her insides dance again. 'I may be evil, but I do have a heart, princess. It belongs to you.'

'I'm afraid your marital problems may have to wait.' Finn interrupted.

'And wouldn't our *marital problems* just make your life easier. I do wonder what brought you all the way here, to play saviour to a woman you barely know.' Cadian growled in Finn's direction.

'I came here because Alessandra burned Fellglow to the ground. No one survived.' Finn blurted, a pinkish hue spreading across his cheeks. Scarlett's mouth dropped open. 'What? No...' All those people she had seen in the tavern, and Oromore. Tears stung her eyes. 'Why would she do that?' Scarlett whispered.

'Because then she could convince your father that you had been killed in the fire. The whole city believes you're dead. They mourn you, Scarlett.' Finn explained, his voice easing until it soothed her fraying nerves. 'Alessandra intends to marry your father and give him an heir.' As he spoke, Finn took a book out of his pouch and dropped it onto the table. 'Alessandra's diary. She's been working with Cadian for centuries, waiting for the perfect moment to strike.'

Scarlett sat in silence staring at the book, the threat of tears was getting stronger. *Do not let him see you cry,* Scarlett told herself. 'We must return to Ashton Glade. Rid my father of his *court mage and* end the corruption.' She looked at Cadian.

'I cannot do that, Princess.' Cadian muttered.

'You must. This cannot continue, Cadian. You cannot kill the humans of this world.' Scarlett pleaded with her husband, but he wouldn't even look at her.

'Let me rephrase. I will not do that. Humans and elves cannot live side by side, and I will not see my people treated as second class citizens for another eternity. I will not sacrifice my people to save your own.'

Scarlett looked down at the table. All thoughts of bravery dissolved away as the tears now fell. Cadian refused to save her people, refused to stop the corruption. 'Then what now?' Scarlett raised her voice. 'You believe I will have you as my King if you slaughter my people?'

'Scarlett...' Cadian's voice was soft, but it came out as a warning.

'What? What exactly will you do?' Scarlett rose to her feet. 'You cannot kill me, Cadian. You cannot force me to change my mind. Any time you hurt me, your life will be drained as mine was! You have no power over me!'

Silence fell in the room and the three of them stayed motionless for an eternity in Scarlett's mind. Until Cadian suddenly gripped the edge of the table and flung it across the room. It shattered into a thousand splinters as he stepped forwards towards Scarlett. Finn moved closer to her side but found himself being flung away by a flick of Cadian's hand, landing hard on the stone floor.

Cadian was so close to Scarlett, their faces were almost touching. 'Our souls are bonded, princess.' Cadian growled. 'You cannot leave me.'

'What?' Scarlett whimpered.

'You think I am not your soul mate?' Cadian laughed, it was a bitter sound. 'Soul mates only exist through magic. And magic has bonded our hearts. I *am* yours.' His words hung in the air as Scarlett struggled to comprehend them. After everything, the lies and the curse, she would never be free of Cadian.

With a quiet voice, Scarlett whispered. 'I hate you, Cadian Vordane.'

'Eternity is a long time, love. You'll forgive me eventually.' Cadian's beautiful face was devoid of all emotion bar a sinister half smile. She wanted to run. Flee the room and never return. Escape from the love of her life.

'Scarlett.' Finn groaned as he rose to his feet. 'Get away from him.'

She took a step backwards. 'I never realised you could be such a monster.'

Cadian grinned. 'That's because you never knew me at all. Pack your things, we leave for Ashton Glade in the morning.'

'You still want to go?' Scarlett asked? 'But why if not to stop Alessandra?'

'I intend to be King. Alessandra cannot be permitted to birth a male heir. Now pack your things.' Cadian growled.

She stood there, unmoving while Cadian left the kitchen. She felt a strong arm around her shoulders, Finn's arm. It was all too much for her and Scarlett wept openly onto the green leather armour. There was only one way to stop all of this now. Destroy the mage, destroy the magic. Cadian was too powerful for Scarlett to kill, but she knew one way, the one way he couldn't defend against.

Scarlett would end her own life.

The Beginning of the End

The cold night had lightened into a dull grey morning. The birds had begun their morning choir as the dawn had broken and Scarlett awoke gently in her bed. She had slept in her old room, the first one Cadian had presented her with. It didn't seem right to share a bed with him now, knowing all she did. Finn had slept in the room beside hers. Although slept was probably a strong word to describe the night he had had. Scarlett imagined no rest came for her saviour, not if he was keeping watch over her. Testing the theory, Scarlett gently knocked on the adjoining wall between their rooms. Within seconds he knocked back and Scarlett let out a breath.

The outfit of the day was a grey dress and a travelling cloak. She pinned her dark hair away from her face and looked in the mirror. If this was how she looked forever, then she would always look like a stranger to herself. This wasn't Scarlett, this was Cadian's version of her.

As she pondered, there was an almost imperceptible knock on the door. Cautiously she crossed the room and opened the door a crack, peering out into the hallway. Finn's sheepish face smiled back. 'Hey, Red.'

A sad smile crossed her face as she motioned to her hair. 'I'm not sure you can call me that anymore.' Scarlett stepped aside and let Finn into the room, closing the door gently behind him. As she turned, she watched Finn as he stared out of the window at the dull morning.

'We're probably not getting any sun today. It's going to be a bit cold, but dry.'

'So, not like our first outing then.' She thought back to the storm that had soaked them both to the skin on their first day travelling together. She had been an entirely different person back then and it was barely two weeks since. The side of Finn's face was all she could see as he looked out the window but the slight smile as she spoke of the storm let her know he held that day as fondly as she did. The smile didn't last long though, it faded quickly as Finn looked away from the window and down to the ground. 'I wasn't sure...' He mumbled 'I thought maybe you would have done something stupid last night.'

Scarlett felt her heart drop to her feet.

'He would've known.' She whispered and heard Finn gasp in response. *Say something, comfort him.* But there weren't any words coming to mind.

'So that *is* your plan then? To kill him by killing yourself?' Finn finally turned and looked at her. His eyes were glistening, and his lips formed a tight line as Scarlett nodded.

'You can't.'

'Finn, I'm sorry. But my people are *dying*. Do you understand that? Giving up my life will save thousands of others.' She needed him to understand, to respect her choice. And while she would never ask him to help her, she needed to know he wouldn't stop her.

'Red, please...' Finn pleaded.

'Don't call me that.' Scarlett turned away from the blonde elf. She wasn't *Red* now. The naïve princess he had known was gone for good. This woman was stronger now, braver now and was willing to give her life for her people.

Scarlett Rose was a Queen.

The awkwardness of that morning encounter stayed with Scarlett as her and Finn walked down to the kitchen. It had been her intention to make breakfast and pack some food for the trip but as they reached the bottom of the stairs, the aroma of freshly brewed coffee invaded her nostrils. Cadian was awake. She couldn't help but wonder if he knew as well. If her plan was truly that obvious to everyone it would be more difficult that she had hoped. But not impossible. This wouldn't be a slow death type of situation. It needed to be instant, something he couldn't use magic to fix, something that wouldn't have the time to drain his life. Just instant death.

As she walked into the kitchen, followed by Finn, she saw Cadian by the kitchen counter wiping up crumbs. 'The bread is almost baked, we should use the last of the butter considering we may not be returning for a while.'

Scarlett wanted to scream as how calm he was being. He had quite literally cursed her and was behaving as though it were perfectly normal. She gritted her teeth.

'Now Scarlett, I know things are a little tense this morning,' Cadian continued, 'But don't worry. Once I've resolved the problems in the city, we will have the time to focus on our marriage.' He poured a cup of coffee, crossed the kitchen and offered it to Scarlett. 'Perhaps we could look at counselling?' Cadian smiled smugly and Scarlett took the cup and hurled it across the room.

'We don't have a marriage. We have an abomination' She spat as she sat purposefully at the kitchen table.

'Seems as though my wife awoke on the wrong side of the bed today.' Cadian was already pouring a second cup and placing it on the counter in front of her. 'Now, love. I know you're upset. But you're a smart woman. You know you must eat.'

Scarlett clenched her jaw and was ready to fling the second cup until a small voice stopped her. 'He's right.'

Finn. The betrayer.

'What?' Scarlett turned on him. 'You agree with *him?*'

'It's not an easy ride Re-' Finn stopped himself as Cadian raised an eyebrow. 'Scarlett. You need energy for it.'

'I have already packed rations for the road and last night I got the carriage out of storage.' Cadian smiled as he took the bread from the oven and brought it to the table with a bowl of butter and a breadknife. Scarlett pondered thrusting the blade into her heart at that moment. But Cadian was too close. Even if she did successfully pierce her heart, it wouldn't be instant enough. His magic would save her.

'Wait, carriage?' Finn asked.

'Yes. You have a horse, it can pull the carriage.' Cadian sliced off the bread, buttered the piece and placed it in front of Scarlett. 'Eat.' He commanded and Scarlett found herself putting the bread in her mouth and chewing. It was actually delicious which made her even madder.

'Star's never pulled a carriage before.' Finn warned. 'I'm not even sure if she can.'

Cadian's face was unchanging. 'She had better learn quickly then. I don't intend to ride on the back of a horse.'

'You'd be walking.' Scarlett murmured. It was enough to cause Cadian to falter for a moment before he continued. 'You'll drive the carriage, and I will ride in comfort with my wife.' He took a bite of his own piece of bread and washed it down with the coffee.

'Listen, I know you're a fancy guy but...the carriage is gonna add a day to the journey at least.' Finn buttered his own slice as they talked.

'And me walking the entire way will add on at least three, will it not?' Cadian smiled and Scarlett recognised it. It was his smile of pride. The smile he had when he won something. It was the way he smiled when she gave her body to him. He was right. The carriage would be the fastest way to get back to her home, to her father. She looked to Finn who was gritting his teeth. He was worried about Star, that much was clear, but they really had no other options.

'I'll go and get the carriage set up, *my lord.*' Finn spat as he turned and walked out of the room, leaving Cadian alone with Scarlett. She tried to decide if she was afraid of him or not. There was nothing he could do to her that was worse than what she was planning to do to herself. So, why was she anxious? She stared at her husband while he ate, watching him take every careful bite, his lips were slick with the butter, and she watched him clean them with his tongue. Vivid memories of that tongue and the things it could do to her flew through her mind, sparking something deep in her core. That's why she was afraid of him. The way her body betrayed her around him was clear. Even now, after everything the thought of pushing him onto the table and climbing on top of him, spearing herself on his cock and riding him to climax was right at the front of her mind. Scarlett felt her wetness in her undergarments and flushed, quickly picking up the cup and drinking the scalding coffee.

The worst part was how he smiled at that moment. Almost as if he could see the images her mind was conjuring. It was something she had wondered about him since she met him. Could he hear her thoughts? Did he know that even now he was on her mind? Scarlett shuffled uncomfortably in her chair.

'Are you alright, love?' Cadian asked, not looking at her.

'Call me Scarlett. You lost the right to call me love when you cursed me.' She shot back.

'I cursed you before I'd ever met you.' He purred back, as if it were a seductive comment.

'Then you never had the right.' Scarlett shot back as she ate another piece of the bread. At this point she just wanted to keep herself busy.

'I'm sorry.' The voice was suddenly less confident, the cockiness was gone, and it was just bare. The apology. Pure and simple. No long speech about their fated love and their eternity together. Just the simplest apology in existence. Scarlett kept her face still.

'I'll go and help the farmhand with the carriage.' Cadian spoke softly, and with one more sip of coffee, left the room.

Scarlett finally relaxed. Her nails had left little half-moon slits in her palm.

The carriage stood proudly in front of the manor house on the gravel driveway. It was varnished in black and polished to a high shine with gold accents. It actually looked quite beautiful being pulled by the pure black beauty, Star. In stark contrast was the blonde haired Finn, finishing up fastening the straps around his horse with a stern look on his face. Scarlett watched as he moved to the front of his horse and gently stroked the side of Star's face, whispering something as he did. They definitely had a connection and Scarlett hoped Star wouldn't be too upset about the journey.

As she watched, the door to the carriage opened and Cadian stepped out, not seeming to notice Scarlett he was turning to look at Finn. 'The bags are stored. Once the princess is ready, we shall depart.'

'I'm ready now.' Scarlett announced as she walked closer. Both men turned to look at her and she felt remarkably exposed by their stares. Scarlett looked past them to the driving seat of the carriage. It was large enough for two. If she could be alone in the carriage, by the time Cadian realised something was wrong it would be too late to save her.

'The two of you can drive together. I wish to be alone.' Scarlett made her way to the carriage door but found her path swiftly blocked by Finn. 'Actually, I think you should sit with me, up front.'

Scarlett's eyes widened as did Cadian's. It was clear to her why Finn was doing this, he knew her plan, and clearly, he had no intention of allowing her to do it. Her heart pounded as the necromancer stepped forward, 'If my wife is to sit anywhere, it will be by my side.' Cadian growled.

'I will make my own decisions, thank you.' It was taking all of Scarlett's energy just to try and remain calm in the face of such an insane situation. 'Finn, I will ride with you today.' Scarlett started to make her way towards the carriage when she heard Cadian mutter under his breath, 'Afraid of what you'll allow yourself to do if we're alone together, pet?'

That was the last straw for Scarlett. After the lies, the curses and the pain he had put her through, Cadian's acknowledgment of her physical reaction to him humiliated her. As she turned to give him a piece of her mind, Finn stepped forward and swiftly punched Cadian in the face. Hard. The dark mage stumbled to the gravel with a grunt as Finn stood breathing hard, his fists still clenched. *Oh God.* Cadian's wrath could be devastating, Scarlett had seen firsthand what happened to people that pissed him off. Mateo is testament to that. But she couldn't allow anything to happen to her protector. Quickly, she stepped in front of Finn as a barrier between the two men as Cadian rose slowly to his feet, gently massaging his jaw. He looked to Finn. 'You saved my life last night. And for that I am grateful. It's the reason you still breathe now.' He moved closer. 'Do not attempt such a thing again, or I will mutilate you until you beg for death.'

Scarlett stood, wide eyed as Cadian stepped past them, entered into the carriage and slammed the door behind him. Scarlett could breathe again. Her heart was pounding, and she couldn't tell if was her fear of Cadian's rage that caused it. In silence, Finn and Scarlett moved to the front of the carriage, he held out his hand to help her up to the seat then climbed up after her.

No words were shared as they began their journey.

For My People

Scarlett sat in the carriage. Her face was set in a sulk as Cadian glared at her. She refused to speak, wouldn't even look at him. But she could feel his gaze boring into her. It was their second day on the road and the night before had not gone according to Scarlett's plans. It has seemed simple to her, as a group they had decided not to stay in any of the towns, in order to avoid the wrath of the corrupted. Instead, they would sleep rough, no time for camps being set up or broken down.

Scarlett had laid in the grass unmoving until she was certain Finn and Cadian were sleeping. Their breathing became deep and regular. Once she was sure, Scarlett quietly rose from the ground and started making her way into the woods. As she walked, she considered how she could possibly end her own life quickly. She had brought no weapons with her. There was the possibility of a hanging but getting rope from the carriage would certainly wake up her two guardians. What other options were there? As she thought, she stepped in a puddle. It was pitch dark and as she kicked her foot around, Scarlett realised it wasn't a puddle, but a pond. Potentially drowning? Not instant but if she stayed quiet then she wouldn't be easy to find.

This could work.

Was this really happening? Was Scarlett about to do this? The fear started creeping in and she thought about her father. Perhaps it was her survival instinct because for a brief moment she considered running back to camp, desperate to see her own father. But she knew she couldn't. Her survival, Cadian's survival meant death for all of humanity, including her father.

Scarlett would not let that happen.

'Well then.' She whispered. 'I suppose this is it.' Standing on the edge of the water, her eyes filling with tears, Scarlett looked up to the skies. 'Mother, I know we never got to meet. But I hope you're here with me. I don't want to be alone.' She whispered. 'I'm scared.'

As a tear fell, she quickly wiped it away, shaking her head. *No,* she thought. *I am saving my people, I will not weep.* Scarlett walked into the cold water, gasping at the low temperature. Slowly she made her way to the middle, her heart pounding. *Stop.* She told herself. If she panicked, he would feel it. He would know. Taking long and deliberate breaths Scarlett reached the centre of the pond.

It wasn't a big space, nor was it deep. It made its way to her waist. It would take all of her determination not to rise to her feet as she fought for oxygen. Images of herself thrashing in the water flashed through Scarlett's head and she shook them away. With one final deep breath Scarlett closed her eyes and lowered herself into the murky water.

For my people.

For my people.

The thought echoed through Scarlett's mind as darkness swirled around her. There was a frightening calm for a few moments as Scarlett became accustomed to the water. Her lungs started to burn, and she knew that any moment now she would need to breathe. Instinctively, her body started to make its way to the surface. *No!* That was not the plan. Scarlett dug her hands into the knotted plant life at the bottom of the pond and gripped tightly. *A few more seconds...*

It would have been easier for her to just breathe in, to take that control of the situation and fill her lungs with water. But her body wouldn't allow it. It was fighting her decision every step of the way. She felt her heart pounding against her chest as she gritted her teeth. *Any moment now...*

That's when the arms wrapped around her, pulling her quickly upwards and out of the cold liquid. As soon as the night air tickled Scarlett's face, she gasped for air, tears rolling down her face at her bitter failure. She was unceremoniously hoisted from the water and within seconds found herself being gently placed on the soft ground a few feet away. As she wiped the water from her eyes, she realised she was in Cadian's arms.

It was too dark for her to make out his features, but she recognised the familiar feel of his embrace and she hated that it soothed her.

'Scarlett...' His voice was shaking. *He knew how close he came to death, s*he thought.

'My love.' She felt his hold tighten around her as he rocked slightly. 'Why...I thought you...' He was choking on his words as tears ripped through him. 'Why did you do this?'

Scarlett closed her eyes. 'To kill us both.' She whispered.

'What?' The rocking stopped and Cadian released her slightly in order to look down at her face. She couldn't see in the darkness like an elf so kept her own eyes closed.

'I did it for my people.' She muttered as exhaustion took her consciousness away.

The morning after had been awkward and silent. Cadian hadn't spoken a word to Scarlett, which in truth had been a relief. Finn must've realised something had happened but had the good sense not to mention it while they chewed on their rations. As they were leaving, Scarlett made her way to the front of the carriage, to sit on the drivers bench with Finn but Cadian grabbed her arm, holding her in place. 'I don't think so, Princess.'

Scarlett looked up at him. 'Excuse me?'

'Now I know your intentions, I will not be letting you out of my sight. I will not allow harm to come to you. Do you understand?'

'What's the matter Cadian. You afraid?' Scarlett smiled slightly, it was satisfying to know the world's most powerful mage was on the back foot.

'I fear nothing except being parted from you! Don't you understand that yet?' His grip tightened slightly before he released her completely. 'No matter what you do here Scarlett, the only thing I am truly terrified of, is an eternity without you in it. We don't know what awaits us in death. But the thought that I may not be able to reach you breaks me in ways I cannot describe.' He shook his head as he tried to calm his breathing. 'Get in the carriage.' He commanded.

Scarlett faltered for a moment under his dark gaze, was it worth being defiant right now? Or would that tip him over the edge.

'What's going on?' Finn asked as Scarlet made her choice and opened the carriage door.

'My wife tried to kill herself.' Cadian growled as Scarlett climbed into the carriage and he followed. Closing the door on Finn.

Scarlett stared at the carpeted floor as they travelled. Cadian sat across from her, looking out of the window. Hours had passed in silence as they got ever closer to the city. Every now and again, Cadian would take a breath, as if he were to say something then change his mind. Each time Scarlett steeled herself for the conversation and each time there was nothing but silence. It was infuriating.

It was around the fifth or sixth time that Scarlett finally snapped. 'If there's something you want to say Cadian, just spit it out.'

His jaw clenched in response. 'Fine. Is there any part of you that still loves me?'

'What?' Scarlett's mouth dropped open. She had expected an argument about her attempt on her own life, not this.

'I want to know if my wife still loves me.' There it was. That was the burning question on his mind. Not power, not corruption, simply love.

'I don't know.' Scarlett was honest. 'Everything was so whirlwind between us. I don't know what was real and what was your manipulation. You had been preparing to make me fall in love for centuries, and I was so desperate for affection that I really didn't stand a chance.' Scarlett shook her head. 'But I don't know if it was love, or lust.'

There was a flicker of a smile on his face as she spoke. 'The one thing you cannot deny is how your body craves me.'

Scarlett bit her lip and looked out of the window.

'There's no need to be coy. We both know how exquisite we are together. I couldn't fake that. Neither of us could.'

She still didn't respond. But mostly because he was right. Even now, knowing what he was and what he had done, there was a part of her that burned for him. That wished he would drag her onto the floor of the carriage and fuck her into ruins. She felt her skin flush at the memories.

Seconds later he was in front of her, his mouth next to her ear. Scarlett's breath caught in her throat at his speed.

'I can tell what's on your mind. You're remembering the first time my tongue plunged into your depths. The first time I tasted you.' Cadian let out an almost imperceptible moan. 'Oh, my Scarlett, your taste is unlike anything I've experienced in a thousand years. You are the nectar of the gods themselves.' Cadian gently dotted a kiss on Scarlett's neck. Even just his words could make her wet for him. Scarlett was being betrayed by her own body and for a moment Alessandra's words rang through her mind, *sleeping with him, it ruins a woman. You will spend the rest of your life craving him.* She was right, Scarlett inhaled sharply. 'Cadian...' She whispered. 'I can't...'

'Oh yes you can, my love. You're still my wife.' More kisses down to her collarbone. 'You belong to me, and I want you to remember that I am your weakness, as you are mine.'

'Stop...' She whispered as Cadian ran his fingers through the raven black tendrils of her hair, pulling her mouth closer to his.

'Behave.' He cautioned as she tried to pull away from his grasp. 'This is what you desire.'

It didn't take much, and Scarlett caved to his will, allowing him to capture her lips. If she wanted to, she could still stop this. It was the lie she told herself as his tongue slid beyond her lips, immediately assaulting her own. The kiss was urgent, his passion for her was undeniable and slowly she melted into it. It was her own personal shame that Scarlett was putty in Cadian's elegant hands.

The moan that escaped her lips betrayed her and she felt him smile against her mouth. Oh, how he drank it in like an elixir. As he deepened the kiss, Scarlett found herself being pushed backwards into the carriage seat, his body pressed against hers, practically moulding into one. Raking her hands up his back tracing the back of his neck she dug her nails in. Eliciting a hiss from him. If he was doing this to her, she was going to hurt him. Cadian broke the kiss.

'I want to feel how ready for me you are, how drenched your sweet cunt gets every time I touch you.'

Even his words could flood her. She stiffened as she tried to resist, tried to stop her body from soaking through her underwear. But failed as his icy fingers vanished up her dress. Cadian lowered himself down and a squeal left her as he ripped the fabric away from her pussy and she heard him inhale deeply. There he would find her core, throbbing, dripping for him.

'My darling, your body betrays you.' A devilish chuckle erupted from Cadian as he lowered himself further, getting ever closer to her. Urgently delving between her folds. His tongue flattened, licking a harsh stripe from hole to hole.

'Cadian, please.' She mewled.

'Are you begging me to stop...or carry on?' He whispered against her moist cunt.

An answer was not forthcoming, she didn't want to say it aloud but, in this moment, she wanted to come right on his face. So instead of words she pressed herself against his mouth as he swirled his tongue against her clit. Oh, he felt perfect as the knot of heat tightened within her.

'Such a needy little cunt, aren't we?' He growled against her clit, the throbbing nerve centre of her body, as it pulsed against the tip of his tongue. Sweet juices leaked out and he drank them down taking it in like oxygen. The knot grew tighter still.

Without warning, Scarlett felt two fingers delving in, drawing back, and then sliding back in with a curl at the end, Pulling at her. Thrusting again he forced his fingers deep inside with fervour.

'You bastard.' She whispered, and her voice hitched on a lewd growl as his fingers found a sensitive area inside her, something he hadn't found before.

'Perhaps.' He breathed against her juicy flesh. 'Perhaps I am a bastard, and all of the other names you will call me, but I am the only bastard that can make you come undone, the only one who can make you writhe and squirm.' He pursed his lips to suck harshly on her clit, drawing another moan from her. 'The only one, whose name you will scream as you coat my tongue with your intoxicating flavour.'

Her walls twitched around his long fingers and Scarlett could feel herself losing control. Being finger fucked in the back of the carriage was a new level for her and while Cadian alternated strokes and pressures her hips bucked forward against his face. Grinding hard as waves of pleasure exploded within her.

She wanted to lie here, but knew she needed to clear her mind of him. She wanted to push him away, to tell him she was done with him. But he hadn't moved from between her legs and was still sliding a finger into her.

'Cadian stop, I'm done.' She panted, coming down from the rapid orgasm. The fingers moved faster as his lips grazed her sensitive clit. 'Oh no love, you've got another one in you. You forget how well I know you...'

Cadian plunged his tongue into her delicious opening once more, his fingers still grazing the rough spot as he worked. The heat built quickly, and Scarlett felt herself panting and grinding against his face as her own fingers made their way to her clit. She teased herself and her squeals came faster. The noises were erratic as he fingers fucked her furiously.

A sharp gasp was pulled from her, from the depths of her lungs. The innocence of her slipped as a warm sticky gush of her juices squirted out. It was like nothing she had ever felt. Immediately she wanted to feel it again, but the wave had crested, leaving her spent. Cadian brushed his fingers over her sensitive core, grinning like the devil at his work.

'Such a good girl, coming on my face like a whore. Remember whose tongue made you do that, who made you defy your body and reach the gods.' An angry sob slipped out of her mouth as he smiled. 'Mine.' He growled.

As Cadian gently pulled down her dress to cover her, he looked up at the princess. Scarlett felt sick. How could she be so weak to him. It was clear he needed to be stopped, and yet she couldn't say no to him. He had ruined her again.

'Just remember, Scarlett. The plan was always for you to die.' Cadian smiled as he wiped his mouth with a handkerchief and settled back into his seat across from her. 'For centuries the human princess was always intended to be disposable. And yet here you are, the woman with the power to have me on my knees. Connected to me in the deepest way. I didn't mean for it to happen like this, but you intoxicated me. For a thousand years I've been alone, I fucked of course, but it was for pleasure. Nothing more. So, imagine my surprise when I fell in love with you. The mortal.'

Scarlett couldn't look at him. Moments ago, she was writhing under his touch. The touch of a killer. This was evil, it was dark, and she couldn't bear to be a part of it. But she knew in that moment that she would crave him, the pleasure he could bestow upon her for the rest of her days.

'Tell me how to fix us and I will.' Cadian's voice was low, and Scarlett finally looked at him. His face had gone from playful to deadly serious. *Give it up.* She thought. If he walked away from all of this, if he saved her then maybe...

'Stop the corruption. Put an end to your centuries old plan, Cadian. Do that for me and I'll know that you do love me. That I am the most important thing to you. Otherwise, it's all just words to save your own life.'

'Scarlett, please.'

'No. This is the line, Cadian.' Her mind was made up. There would be no compromise. Either he saves her people, or she would find a way to kill them both and save the Kingdom herself.

'The choice is yours.' She whispered as she watched Cadian's jaw tense up. She knew what his answer would be, and maybe that was why he didn't say it. He couldn't walk away from this, and she wouldn't let it continue.

One of them would have to lose.

The Rose and the Thorn

For the remainder of the journey back to the city of Ashton Glade, Scarlett sat in uncomfortable silence with Finn. If he had heard what had transpired in the carriage with Cadian and herself, he was too much of a gentleman to mention it but they both knew she was avoiding alone time with the dark mage. When they slept, Cadian had her arm chained to the wheel of the carriage. 'To ensure we both wake up in the morning.' He assured her as he clicked the cold iron around her wrist.

'Why do you even have these?' She asked but his response was to simply smile. 'Forgive me love, and you'll find out.'

Scarlett opted not to ask any more questions of Cadian. In fact, through the rest of the journey she didn't speak with him at all. Instead, she spent her time sitting quietly watching Star trot. And as the time passed, Scarlett began to enjoy it. The roads were quiet, and the birds sang songs for them along the way. Just as she had settled into a happy place, the remains of Fellglow appeared in the distance. 'Oh, Finn. She muttered and placed her hand gently on his own. He was holding the reins and Scarlett could feel his grip tighten.

'Don't worry Scarlett, we don't need to go into what's left. The road will run past it.' Finn tried to sound okay, but his voice was strained. Scarlett knew what Fellglow must've meant to him. After all, it's where he had lived with his wife. All his memories, keepsakes, anything that tied him to her was gone. It was heart breaking and yet he wouldn't show it. *Perhaps he already mourned the loss?* Scarlett pondered. After all, he had found out about it over a week ago. It struck her then that she didn't really *know* Finn. Obviously, he was kind hearted, a protector of innocence and generally a good man. But the facts about his life escaped her. They didn't sit and talk about his past, or his wife. Scarlett realised quickly that she didn't even know the name of the woman he had loved. Was she so wrapped up in her obsession with Cadian that she hadn't even thought to ask?

Scarlett scolded herself silently. For a brief moment she planned on asking him when all of this was over, but the reality was, when all this was over, Scarlett would be dead.

Either way, Scarlett's hand remained firmly of Finns while they rode.

Heading past Fellglow meant Ashton Glade was mere hours away and Scarlett's heart soared at the knowledge she would soon be home with her father. No matter how bad things were, she would still get to hold him in her arms.

As they neared the city, Finn wrapped his green woollen cloak around his shoulders and raised the hood over his head, covering his ears. Two Gatemen stepped forward as they approached the city wall, holding up their hands.

'City ain't open to visitors today. What's the nature of your business?' One of the men asked, looking at Finn. The other man started at Scarlett, his mouth agape. 'Your hair...it's changed...' He muttered.

'I'm bringing the lady home to her family.' Finn responded, motioning towards Scarlett. If he had learned anything the last time he was here, it's that the guards don't much like his kind.

The other man glanced over at Scarlett then did a double take. 'That's impossible.'

'You're meant to be dead!' The other chimed in.

'I assure you, I am very much alive and I wish to return home. Why is the city closed?' Scarlett demanded to know. The city didn't just close its gates without a big reason.

'The Royal Wedding, your majesty. Your father's wedding.'

Scarlett's heart sank. 'That's today?'

Both guards nodded.

'Well then, move aside. I must congratulate my father in person.' She forced a smile as the men moved away and opened the gate.

The city had changed drastically for Scarlett. Black flags adorned the front of many houses and hung from poles in the market place. It was in stark contrast to the colourful bunting that has been hung for celebratory purposes, but the inhabitants of Ashton Glade didn't look ready for a joyful day. Their hearts were still weighed down by the loss of their princess. The very woman that now rode through the centre of the city on the front of a black gilded carriage. No one was looking up, but Scarlett could see them, the dark circles, the pale veins...

The corruption was here.

'Finn...' She whispered.

'I see them, Red.' He whispered back. 'Maybe you should get into the carriage.' He suggested but Scarlett shook her head.

'The way I see it, they're more likely to kill an elf than their princess. Maybe I should take us the rest of the way?'

Finn let out a short laugh. 'You think you can drive this thing through a city of people?' He asked and Scarlet looked down at her hands. He was right, of course. A few days sitting beside someone as they navigated empty roads was not akin to driving the thing herself. 'Fine. Just, keep your hood up and your head down.'

Scarlett did the same, trying to make herself as small as possible, allowing her black hair to hang over her face. Most people wouldn't think for a second that the dark haired woman, sitting on the driving bench of a carriage was a Royal and she remained unnoticed until they reached the palace walls. The guards there were armed and stood in front of the carriage.

'No access, turn around.' One of them commanded as Scarlett rolled her eyes.

'I don't wish to be late.' Her voice came out commanding. 'Move aside and allow me to see my father.'

'And who exactly is your father?' One of the guards asked as he sniffed back some phlegm.

'King Farandorn Rose.'

The guards head snapped upwards to really look at Scarlett. She may be paler, and her hair was certainly changed but her face was unmistakable when you stared directly at it. She watched as the guards eyes widened and began to well with tears. 'My lady...your highness, I mean...We thought we lost you.' A tear streaked its way down the guards face and Scarlett felt a wave of emotion. Without thinking she was climbing down from the carriage and wrapping her arms around the guard. 'I'm so sorry you all had to feel this. I promise, I'm here to fix everything.'

'Can't fix everything.' One of the other guards muttered and Scarlett released the man from her embrace and turned to look at his colleague. 'What do you mean?'

'Fucking elves.' He spat on the ground as he spoke. 'They've been filling this city for decades and now the king plans to marry one. People won't stand for it.'

Scarlett's brow furrowed before she noticed the dark veins on his neck. 'I'm going to fix this. I promise.'

'Only way is to kill them all.' He growled and Scarlett shook her head. Silently she climbed back onto the carriage and Finn got them moving again.

As they pulled into the courtyard, King Farandorn Rose stood waiting at the top of the palace steps. The exact spot he was in the last time Scarlett saw him. Finn stopped Star and Scarlett leapt back down and ran across the driveway towards her father. There was confusion on his face that quickly turned to recognition, then relief as Scarlett ran into him and he wrapped her in his arms. 'My baby.' He wept as he held her. 'My beautiful girl.'

'I'm alright, I'm alright.' She reassured him as he held her.

'Alessandra told me...she said you died in Fellglow.'

Scarlett pulled back slightly. 'Alessandra is a liar and a bitch.' Scarlett's voice had turned venomous as her father's moth dropped open.

'Is that so?' The sly voice came from behind the king and Alessandra stepped out from the doorway. 'I'm so pleased to see you still live, Princess. But what has happened to your hair?' She reached out to Scarlett who stepped backwards. 'Get away from me.'

'Tell me, how did you escape Cadian?' Alessandra asked, looking almost amused.

'What? He was to be her husband?' Farandorn asked but both women ignored him.

'What makes you think I wouldn't bring him here?' Scarlett asked, a smile now spreading across her face. 'After all, the two of you are old friends and I'm sure you have a great deal to talk about.'

Alessandra's eyes widened. 'He's here?' She hissed and Scarlett nodded as the carriage at the bottom of the stairs opened. Cadian stepped out beautiful and dark, even now Scarlett felt her heart beat faster for him and silently chided herself. *Get a grip.*

'I have to go.' Alessandra's voice was shaking, and she turned to run but in an instant Cadian was beside her. 'Oh no, pet. Stay. We have a lot to discuss.'

Scarlett noticed Cadian was gripping Alessandra's arm and the fear in her eyes was clear. The king stood frozen, watching the encounter beside his daughter.

'I'm pregnant!' Alessandra yelled, but it sounded more like pleading.

'What?' Scarlett gasped and looked to her father who was now staring at the ground. 'You're having a baby? With *her*?'

'ENOUGH!' Farandorn yelled and every person in the courtyard froze, including Finn who was simply unbuckling Star from the carriage. 'I am the King of this land, and you are behaving as children. I wish to speak to my daughter and her fiancé alone.'

Cadian grinned at Alessandra and her eyes widened. The King turned and walked away while Scarlett took Cadian's arm and pulled him gently away from the court mage.

'Now, would either of you care you explain to your King, what in the hell is going on?' Farandorn paced in his office behind his large red velvet seat. On the other side of the table sat Scarlett and Cadian, both silent.

This office wasn't new to Scarlett. She had spent many years in here while her father worked. She would sit on the floor, with colouring pencils and parchment spread around her. It was a place of fond memories with him. But he didn't look fond now.

'I'm sorry, father.' Scarlett looked down at the desk and picked at a splinter.

'What has happened to you, child?'

How could she tell him all the ways the world was going to end for them. How could she tell him that humanity's downfall was her fault. That by falling in love, she had brought about violent deaths for all humans, including her father.

But she didn't need to explain, she didn't need to break it down for the King. Cadian was kind enough to step in. '*I* happened.'

'What?' The king's face became a picture of confusion.

'Alessandra sent Scarlett to me, so that I could make her love me. And in doing so, I could spread my hatred for your kind through the lands. Your people will die, Farandorn. And when they do, I will sit on your throne as the new King of the Elves.' Cadian's expression never changed. Scarlett watched him speak and he was calm, almost as if he was telling someone about making renovations in a guest room.

'You will never be King!' Farandorn slammed his hands on the desk as he yelled. 'I would die before I let you marry my daughter.'

Scarlett felt her heart sink all the way to her feet. 'Father...' She whispered. She had to tell him, he needed to know that she had already made the mistake.

'I married your daughter days ago.' Cadian grinned and Scarlett sank into her seat as her father's face crumpled. 'And to be honest, I thought you would give your new son-in-law a much better reception than this.'

Farandorn looked to Scarlett desperately. 'Tell me this isn't true, Scarlett.'

She couldn't meet his eye. Couldn't speak the words. Now her father would see how this was all her fault. How her desire for love had made her the perfect victim for the elves. 'I'm sorry, father.' She whimpered.

The King turned his gaze slowly to Cadian. 'There are guards outside this door. I intend to have you arrested. You will be beheaded for your treason against the crown and your crimes against humans.' He was speaking through gritted teeth. Scarlett had never seen her father this angry.

'I wouldn't do that if I were you.' The smug smile had never left Cadian's face. 'After all, if you kill me...' His voice trailed off as he looked at Scarlett. She knew what was coming and finished the sentence for him. 'I die too.'

'How?' Farandorn sputtered. 'What have you done to her?'

'I connected our hearts. Your daughter is my soul mate. Her life and my own are connected. My intention was to keep her with me for all of my life.' For the first time since the entered the room, Cadian's demeanour changed. Gone was the smug, over confident necromancer and in his place sat Cadian, the man she had fallen in love with. 'You see, the plan was always to make her love me but, I never expected to love her in return. I cannot imagine living if Scarlett isn't in this world.'

That was the last straw. She couldn't listen to this anymore, her head was spinning so fast she thought she was fall off the world. Scarlett stood quickly and turned to leave the room. 'If you really loved me, you would end this,

Cadian. But you won't.' She sighed deeply. 'I will be in my room, and I don't wish to be disturbed.'

'Take Finn with you.' Cadian commanded but Scarlett shook her head. 'I wish to be alone.

In a flash, Cadian was by her side. 'I said take him with you.' Cadian hissed. 'I will not risk you ending both of our lives while I deal with this *mess.'*

'You don't get to tell me what to do, Cadian.' Scarlett stood tall against him, but Cadian leaned in close to her ear. 'Take Finn or *I* will come with you, and we can repeat what happened in the carriage my love.'

Scarlett froze, flashes of memories ran through her mind. The heat pooled quickly. *Damn you, Cadian.* He knew how her body would betray her mind for him.

'I do love the idea of ruining you in your own bedroom.' He purred and Scarlett took a step back, her breath had quickened. 'I'll take Finn, just please, leave me alone.' It was a plea from the depths of her soul and Cadian grinned.

'Your wish is my command, darling.'

The mirror shattered as Scarlett threw her chair into it. What had once been her childhood vanity was now covered in shattered glass. The perfume bottles she had used over the years were destroyed beyond all repairs. There Scarlett stood, out of breath, in the tattered remains of her childhood home. She had done an excellent job in her destruction, and nothing had escaped unscathed, except Finn. He watched silently as all of the princess' anger and hurt came pouring out.

And now she was finished.

I need to kill Cadian. Was the thought that ran through her mind as she looked around the room, her eyes landing on Finn.

Finn the protector, the saviour.

'Finn.' She wanted to say his name, it made her heart swell. 'The elf that saved my life.'

He looked at the ground. Not speaking while Scarlett rested herself on the edge of the bed, her back now to Finn. 'If you had let me die, all of humanity would be safe from the Era of *Magic*' She spat the last word. Scarlett knew it was unfair to him, but the thought had been circling in her mind. If Mateo had killed her, none of this would be happening.

'And knowing that, I would still make the same choice, Red. I'd choose your life over every other human in the world.' He spoke quietly as Scarlett smiled bitterly. 'Wait, what do you mean the Era of Magic?'

Scarlett shook her head, 'It's what Vordane translates to in the common tongue.'

'That's not...it doesn't mean magic.' Finn paused, a look of grief now spreading across his handsome features.

'Then what does it mean, Finn?'

'Vordane translates to darkness.' His voice was barely more than a whisper as Scarlett let out a choked sob followed by a bitter laugh.

'I've ruined all of us. I've brought for the Era of Darkness upon my people.'

Silence fell between them as Scarlett pondered her marriage. How could she have done this, all of this. And yet Finn managed to marry a human and all was lovely. Untill she died that is.

'Finn?'

'Yeah, Red?'

'Would you tell me about your wife?'

the elf sighed heavily and walked to the bed, sitting himself beside the princess. 'Her name was Elanor. She was human and she was beautiful. I don't know if I ever told you but, you remind me of her. You're headstrong, beautiful and you care so much for others. Maybe too much.'

'What happened to her?' Scarlett asked gently.

'Not all humans are like you, Red. Some of them are vicious and filled with a bitter hatred towards my kind. Ellie, she was killed by humans. They took her from the road as she walked, abused her and beat her to death. Because she married an elf.' Finn's voice was thick with emotion as he spoke, and Scarlett sat in a stunned silence. No matter how bad she had thought it could be, the truth was so much worse.

'Finn, I'm so sorry.' It made sense to her now. Why he would be happy to let the human world die to save her. The uncomfortable truth is that, Finn really had no reason to protect her people. 'If Cadian wins, you don't lose.' She whispered. As she did, she could see Finn nodding out the corner of her eye. 'That had crossed my mind, Red. But the truth of it is, I couldn't live with myself knowing your heart was breaking for humanity, and I did nothing to help you. After all, that's how you see me, right?'

'What?' Scarlett turned her head to gaze at Finn while he talked.

'Ever since Fellglow, you've seen my as your saviour. And, I've tried to live up to that, Red. Truly I have. But I let you down.'

Scarlett shook her head. 'No...'

'No, I did. Because for a moment there, I was willing to let thousands of people die, just to keep you in my life.

But I can't be selfish with you, Scarlett. Loving you means letting you make your own decisions.'

Scarlett watched a tear roll down Finn's cheek. The dawning realisation of what he just said to a second to sink in. *Loving me?*

'You...love me?'

'How could I not? The God's rarely make perfection, I'm just glad I got to see their work in my lifetime.' Finn rose to his feet, his back to Scarlett. 'If you're going to end this, then I'll hold the fort. Slow him down if I need to. Whatever it takes to save your soul.'

Finn was going to help her. *Finn was going to help her.*

Because he loves her.

A sob escaped Scarlett's lips. 'Finn...' She stood and took a step closer to him. Reaching up, she felt the leather of his armour under her hand. She circled around him, stopping when she stood in front of his chest, her hand still connected to him. 'Look at me.' Scarlett spoke gently, she was almost afraid of how close they were to each other. Slowly, Finn dropped his gaze to meet her own and it felt like they stood there for hours, just looking at each other. For Scarlett it was almost the first time she had really seen him. The first time she had allowed herself to. All the time she'd known him, her heart had been clouded by Cadian.

But not now. Now she could truly see him.

'Finn...' She whispered again, but before she could utter another word, his lips crashed into her own. It was hungry, it was passion. It was a kiss he has been waiting for since the moment he saw her. She could feel it.

Finn's hand wrapped around her waist while the other gently gripped the back of her neck, his fingers twirling into her hair. Scarlett sank into it. If this were to be her last memory of life, it couldn't be more perfect.

Long Live the King

'Your insidious scheming knows no bounds, Alessandra.' Cadian growled as the door to her chambers closed quietly behind him. This was a moment he had been picturing since he lost sight of his old protégé. 'Tell me, are you afraid?'

The two elves stood in the large room, facing off against each other, silhouetted against the golden glow of the large, ornate fireplace. There was a flicker of joy in Cadian's old soul as Alessandra instinctively took a step back. 'The guards will have you executed if you lay one hand on me, Cadian.'

Oh, how wrong she was. After all this time, the bitch still believed she held power in this realm. 'The guards will do nothing of the sort to their *King.*' He let the last word hang for a moment in the air between them. Alessandra's eyes widened. 'But you're not...'

'Alessandra, my sweet, Farandorn has kindly filled the court with *our* kind. If given the choice between the half breed that grows inside your belly, or the pure blood of an elf that actually remembers our Isles, I am certain they will make the right choice.'

She stepped back again, and Cadian's smile grew wider. 'I wanted to make this slow. I wanted it to be excruciating for you.' Cadian began to close the gap and the dark elf hit the wall as she tried to back away.

'Please, Cadian...even you wouldn't be so cruel as to kill me while I'm with child.'

Begging. He usually enjoyed it when people begged for his mercy, it meant he could extend their agony and masquerade it as a kindness. But not this time. 'All the years I spent with you, Alessandra, all the long days of teachings. I gave you my knowledge, and my magic. And yet you stand before me now, knowing me as you do, and you beg me to spare you for your unborn child. Do you truly think your pregnancy would save you from me?

'Cadi-' A flash of deep purple left the fingertips of the dark mage and hit the woman, surrounding her in darkness. In the end, all that remained of Alessandra, High Court Mage to King Farandorn Rose, was her bones.

The copper tub stood in front of Scarlett's fireplace, filled with warm water and a rose scented oil. As the water settled, Scarlett started into it. Unmoving. This was it now, the final moments. For a second, she hated how dramatic this all felt, but why shouldn't it? This was quite literally the end for Scarlett. Her life was forfeit in the grand scheme.

Finally, she pulled her gaze away from the tub and instead allowed herself to steal a glance of Finn. His back was to her as he faced the door. He was here to guard her, but she couldn't make him watch. The only regret Scarlett held now, was not running away with him before she ever met Cadian. The kiss they had shared fuelled her, it set her alight in a way she hadn't felt before. It was only after kissing Finn that she realised, she lusted after Cadian. His touch was electric to her. But Finn made her feel like her eyes were finally open. Like she could see the whole world and all the joy in it.

She wished for one night with him. One night to explore the contours of his muscular frame, to experience him inside her. Just one night to bring ecstasy to them both.

If she asked it of him, he would. But she knew it couldn't happen. This was her duty.

For my people.

The dagger she had chosen was her mothers. It was used for ceremonial purposes, but Finn was a craftsman as heart, he'd sharpened it up for her, enough to penetrate skin. Scarlett had chosen the bath to spare the maids the trouble of cleaning her blood from the hardwood floor. This situation would not be a burden to the people she cared about.

Once more her eyes fell to the water.

When you're ready, princess.

Cadian stared down at the bones of his former lover and student. Alessandra had had so much potential, together they could have brought about the new era. With Scarlett by his side and Alessandra as his mage, they would have been unstoppable. But she had to be stupid. 'What a waste.'

As he looked at the remains, the door opened swiftly behind him. Cadian turned to come face to face with King

Farandorn. With a flick of his hand, Cadian's magic sent the door slamming shut behind the King.

'What is the meaning of this?' Farandorn stood tall. 'Why are you in my chambers?'

Cadian looked back down at the bones. 'I was killing your wife and unborn son.'

'What?' Horror spread across Farandorn's face as he followed Cadian's gaze. 'How...why would you do this?'

'A male heir would have been a threat to my claim to the throne.' Cadian grinned.

'You have no claim, bastard!' The King cried out. Cadian was actually impressed. The King was smarter than he looked, hadn't even attempted to open the door. Instead, he was holding his ground, right in front of Cadian.

'When you're dead Scarlett will be Queen and I will rule beside her as King. The only thing is, your Majesty, I believe I made a mistake in connecting Scarlett's life to my own.' This wasn't fun for Cadian, admitting his own mistakes ruins the joy of taking lives.

'It seems she is committed to taking her own life, and in doing so will ensure my own demise.'

Farandorn's face fell and that did spark a small amount of happiness for Cadian. 'I know you don't want to see Scarlett dead and luckily for you, I do have a way to break the connection. You see the magic of Aur'Iya is powered by familial bonds. The stronger the connection between the lovers and their families, the stronger *their* bond will be. Scarlett's love for you has strengthened the magic.' Cadian sighed. 'Unfortunately for you, the only way for me to destroy the bond between me and your daughter, is to kill you.'

'You can't be serious. She would never forgive you.'

'We're far beyond forgiveness now, *my liege.*'

Cadian thrust his arm forward into the chest of the King, wrapped his fingers around the still beating heart, and with force, pulled it free. As Farandorn's lifeless body fell, the elf turned away to look at the heart. *You know what comes next.*

This was the part he had not been fondly anticipating. The utter desecration of the heart. With a deep breath and a shudder, Cadian opened his mouth and took the first bite of blood soaked flesh.

'I'm ready.' Scarlett whispered. After staring into the water, building her courage, Scarlett finally took her final steps and climbed, fully clothed, into the copper bath. The water was barely warm at this point but that hardly mattered now. Scarlett glanced over to Finn and smiled slightly. It would be nice to have him be the last person she ever saw in this life.

He deserves so much better than this.

Scarlett began to lower into the water, holding the dagger tightly.

For my people

'Scarlett my love, I have some news for you.'

She froze. Cadian's voice echoed through the room as he rapped on the door. 'I think you'll be pleased. I just saved your life.'

'What?' Scarlett manoeuvred onto her knees and stared at the door.

'Do you want me to open it?' Finn whispered to her.

'Of course, she does.' Came Cadian's voice. 'I've broken the connection between us. Ending your life now accomplishes nothing.'

Scarlett's heart sank. 'I took too long.' The dagger sank into the water as she let it go. The tapping on the door quickly became a pounding. 'Open the door, Scarlett. I have more good news.'

'Red?' Finn asked.

'Open the door, Finn.' Scarlett spoke softly and Finn quickly obliged.

Cadian stepped into the room and Scarlett swallowed a scream. Fresh red blood covered Cadian's mouth, hands and clothes. He walked into the room, calm and smiling. Finn backed away quickly, coming to stand beside Scarlett, her protector.

The necromancer walked slowly across the room as Finn lifted Scarlett out of the water to stand bravely against the approaching storm. Until, in no time at all, Cadian was standing before his wife. He took her hands in his own, smearing blood onto her pale skin. 'Oh Scarlett, you are my angel. My beacon in the darkness. My redemption.'

His hands released hers and slowly trailed up her arms and wrapped around her as he pulled her close to his chest. Scarlett was unmoving. Terrified of what would happen if she dared to speak against the blood covered monster before her.

'I have done something terrible, in order to assure our survival my love. But remember, I did it for you. I had to break the connection, I couldn't let you die.'

'What have you done, Cadian? Just tell me, who's blood is this?'

With a heavy sigh Cadian's lips met Scarlett's ear, leaving sticky redness behind as he whispered.

'The King is dead. Long live the Queen.'

'What?' Scarlett felt like her soul had left her behind and attempted to follow her father. As her knees buckled Cadian held onto her. 'Don't worry my love. Everything will be alright now.'

Scarlett turned to Finn in desperation as Cadian lifted her off her feet and lay her down on the bed. 'Wait here. Finn will stand guard while I tell the news to the court. When I return, we will be crowned King and Queen of Novastraad.'

As soon as they were alone, Finn wrapped Scarlett in his own arms while the floodgates opened, and she began to scream.

'I'm sorry. But we have to get moving.' Finn's voice was flat as he spoke into her hair.

'What?' Why would he make her move? After all of this, doesn't she deserve to mourn? To grieve her father. 'I don't want to be crowned, Finn. I don't want to be his queen. Please, don't make me go.'

'I don't intend to. I'm getting you the fuck out of this palace before it's too late. Can you run?'

Could she? She didn't know. Scarlett slowly stood up and took a few steps before nodding. Her legs felt like jelly and her heart was beating so fast, she thought she might die.

Finn took her hand in his own. 'I'll be right beside you, Red.'

They ran, Finn and Red. Through the halls of the castle. Past the guards, who had turned their aggression on each other. Those that were elven were slaughtering their human colleagues.

They ran though the roses in the gardens, past the corpses of Mr. and Mrs. Belmont, who's blood had stained the gravel path the same colour as the flowers.

They ran into the courtyard, where Star awaited them, whinnying as swords clanged, metal against metal.

Finn and Scarlett fled Ashton Glade on the back of a horse into the forests of the wilds while Cadian sat upon his throne. Human bodies piled around him and his elven court bowing to him on their knees.

Long live the king...

Long live the King...

More to come

Scarlett's journey will continue in The Era of Darkness...

Sensitive Topics

Below is a list of the topics you may find disturbing within this book. If you are struggling with anything relating to these topics then please, contact your local support groups for more help.

Do not struggle alone my angel.

Racism

Violence and murder

Sexual assault

Suicide

Made in United States
Troutdale, OR
11/29/2023